HONOR & OBEY

A Submissive's Revenge

Alan Horn

TITLE

Copyright © 2017 by Aerophyte

Book and Cover design by Aerophyte

ISBN: 9781521195505

First Edition: May 2017

10 9 8 7 6 5 4 3 2 1

Honor & Obey

PROLOGUE 1
Chapter 1 13
Chapter 2 52
Chapter 3 70
Chapter 4 93
Chapter 5 109
Chapter 6 124
Chapter 7 152
Chapter 8 180
Chapter 9 203
Chapter 10 210
Chapter 11 223
Chapter 12 237
Chapter 13 260
Chapter 14 278
Chapter 15 323
Chapter 16 339
Chapter 17 364
Chapter 18 377

iv

PROLOGUE

I was jammed in the tiny metal box with a dozen other office workers. The elevator stopped at the forty fifth floor and I stepped out into elegant emptiness. The foyer was paneled in rich teak and mahogany. The receptionist was a perfectly coiffed, tastefully dressed black woman about my age. I strode confidently to her and said, "Good morning," I have an appointment with Ms. Glover at nine. My name is Cynthia Lukens."

She looked at her desk, looked back at me and said, "I'll let her know you're here, please have a seat," and she waved at some plush chairs behind me.

I sat and looked around. Expensive furnishings. Well-dressed people on errands. No doors visible from here. An expensive wool carpet in striking colors. I could work here.

Thirty minutes later I had a job. My first real job. I even had a key to a company apartment I could use until I found a place of my own. Ms. Glover said the company owned several they used for visiting employees from other cities of sometimes customers here for meetings. I knew rents were exorbitant in the city so I had to find a place with roommates. I didn't know anyone here and would have to find some friendly strangers. I suspected there were lots of single women fresh from school in my situation. I planned to scour the papers and internet as soon as I found this apartment.

The apartment building was close to the office and had a doorman. I told him I was going to stay in 412 for a while and showed him my key. He smiled warmly and opened the front door for me. The apartment was luxurious. It was professionally decorated and spotless. I put my bag in the larger of the two bedrooms and looked around. It had two bathrooms and a laundry room and large closets with lots of storage. There was a locked door that my key didn't open. The master bedroom had his and hers walk-in closets. I identified the women's closet because it already had a number of female garments in various sizes. I found several in my size: a tiny black cocktail dress, a red topless evening gown, a yellow sundress, a beige suit and several brightly colored blouses. I opened a cupboard in the closet and found Goth accessories. Black leather collar , cuffs, and anklets. A leather halter top with cut outs for nipples. Black leather mini-skirt.

Shocked would too harsh a word. I was halfway between intrigued and embarrassed. I had played bondage games with a lover in school. He had a collection of items like this, but much lower quality. He'd tie me up for sex and I loved it. Once he took me to a BDSM club. After an hour and several beers he convinced me to do a scene with him where he tied me to a cross and used a flogger on my bare ass. It didn't really hurt but I got to act as if it was excruciating. Lots of men and women watched my performance and applauded. I mostly watched others playing. It was a turn on. My favorite memory was whipping a girls ass. Her Dom had strung her up in a large room and warmed her up with his hand. Then he invited several girls in the audience to take turns with a whip. The girl kicked her feet and twisted and moaned. She kept saying, "Harder, Harder." I was the fourth one to use the whip on her. The sounds she made were so erotic. It was like the whip was giving her an orgasm. I think she really did have an orgasm when I was hitting her. I stopped and her Dom said, "Keep going. She loves it." I wasn't the last girl, and I think she orgasmed four or five times. She might just have been a good actress, but she sure enjoyed it.

I've dreamed of being the damsel in distress for as long as I can remember. I always wanted to be the helpless victim when we played "Cowboys and Indians", or "Pirates", or "Cops and robbers." I always saw myself as the helpless prize of the alpha male who would bend me to his will. I thought of them as harmless adolescent fantasies. After I started playing bondage games with men and sex my dreams grew more vivid. Details were burned into my conscious mind and I started to daydream about men using my bound body for raw animal sex. After wearing the leather cuffs or a visit to the BDSM clubs I would have the most vivid dreams. There were variations but after my first BDSM club they were always very similar.

My recurring dream started with me walking behind a Roman General's chariot into Rome. I wore only an animal skin around my loins. My hands were tied together in front of me and the rope was tied to the back of his chariot. He was big and heavily muscled, a warrior that fought in front of his men. I was the daughter of the Gaul chief he had slain in personal combat. I was the prize he held before the citizens of Rome. The throng jeered me and I hated Rome. I wanted to get my barbarian hands around all of their throats, but I was helpless.

He led me up the hill into a villa. His villa. He took me inside and handed me to his servants, "Clean her. Put her in the chains of a wild slave. Bring her to my quarters."

They took me to the baths, chained me by the neck in the bath, untied my hands and stripped me. Four naked women, all lovely, joined me and bathed me with water. They scraped my skin clean with brass strigils, then rubbed fragrant oils in my skin. The men returned and took me to his smith who fitted me with chains suitable to control the barbarian.

He riveted heavy metal bands on my wrists and ankles. An iron collar riveted on my neck with a four foot length of chain attached. Heavy locks fastened my hands behind me and locked a short chain between my ankles. I was helpless in twenty pounds of iron. A man led me to the General's quarters. I snarled like a wild animal and fought the leash all the way. I hated the General. He had killed my father in front of me.

His man handed the end of my leash to the General. He took it in one hand. I tried to back away, but it was like trying to move a tree. He smiled and said, "Cynthia, daughter of Divico, I have conquered your nation and taken you. By right of conquest, you are now my slave. Now I will conquer you."

I screamed defiance at my captor, "Never, you Roman dog. I will die before I submit to you." I meant it. I would find a way to kill myself. I would not give this General a son to kill more of my people.

He spread-eagled me on his couch. Loosely at first then he slowly tightened the ropes holding my limbs. He was patient and ignored my epithets. As he tightened the ropes holding my legs, I felt my nether lips spread apart, opening me for his use. My arms and legs were stretched tight, the chain from my collar draped off the end. He had put a cushion under my bottom so my loins were higher. I tore at my bonds but I had been fastened by a warrior. I couldn't move. I was secured helplessly.

He stripped himself and perched beside me, his fingers playing with my oiled breasts, and is eyes glowing with lust. I fell silent as I felt his fingers play with my sensitive nipples. The traitorous nipples swelled to rock hard nubs under his tender ministrations. He said, "Your first climax as a collared slave should be memorable. A milestone on your journey to total slavery."

I opened my mouth to reject his notion, to swear vengeance for my father, but before I could speak he held a finger to my lips. "A slave girl that speaks without permission is gagged and punished. I will not hesitate to teach you this lesson. You would do well to heed my words, slave girl."

I gulped and shut my mouth and clenched my teeth. His stern expression both excited and frightened me. This was not a man to test. I was certain he meant every word and I did not want to learn how slaves were punished in Rome.

He reached between my taut legs and ran his fingers around my spread lips. I felt my belly respond to his touch. His fingers caressed me, stroked my damp and glistening sex. My belly was on fire. I writhed in my bonds, frantic to escape the torment he was stoking in me. I clenched my teeth tighter as I fought not to scream and beg him to make me come.

I couldn't win this battle and I was not sure I wanted to. My pride made me try, but my need was rapidly overcoming my pride. Losing the battle I would concede my soul to the fiery passion his bondage and touch had ignited in her. I couldn't stand it and screamed my defeat, pleading with him, calling him master, I begged him to make me come. His busy fingers continued their work and flung me into a mighty orgasm. I screamed my pleasure to the world and bucked against my bonds.

I was still spasming in the throes of the orgasm when I felt his hands at my mouth. He pried it open and shoved a leather ball into it. He tied a thong around my head and his fingers resumed their delightful frictioning of my sex. I couldn't stand it. My eyes sprang wide as he pushed me to the edge again. I struggled frantically to free myself, my hands twisting and clawing at my bonds. I must stop this tumultuous growing in my body, but I had been bound by a warrior and all my struggling loosed nothing.

I stared up at my tormentor, my new master, realizing he was in total control. I was his toy and he was going to play with me.

He smiled grimly down at me and said, "You are my slave now and you will submit totally to me."

I whimpered through my gag and convulsed as he thrust his fingers deep into me and a second unbearably wonderful orgasm slammed through me.

I opened my eyes as I felt his weight descend on me and his stiff member replaced his fingers. It was even better. He fit me so perfectly. His thrusts were driving me to the edge of that bottomless chasm of joy again. I stared into his eyes and heard, "I am your Master and you are my slave. You will obey me, won't you?"

I stared at him, entranced. I couldn't speak, so I nodded my head. I was his. And I would obey. I was broken to heel.

Waking up was a shock. I was always laying in a puddle of my own juices. I had orgasmed in my dream and in reality, too. I lay there, wondering how a dream could be so real. I wanted it to be real. I had never felt so deeply in reality. My dream defined femininity for me. In the real world I was somehow less, and I regretted it.

I picked up several of the items and fondled them. It was making me excited so I decided to play a little. First, I made sure the door was locked and all the shades were closed. I was a size 6 in everything but my bust. I had shot through bras in high school. I had size 10 breasts before I stopped swelling up. I had to give up soccer because I got top heavy and wasn't as agile any more. It seemed these things were designed for amply bosomed girls. Surprise. I stripped and started trying on the bondage gear. I had several choices. After a few minutes I had leather cuffs on my wrists and ankles and a leather collar. I tried the halter and it didn't do anything for me. I had a nice firm rack and the halter just covered it. I tried a black bustier with red trim. That was better. It cinched my already trim waist and pushed up my breasts, making them look even bigger and perkier. Last I put on the tiny black skirt. It just barely covered my pussy. I pirouetted in front of the mirror.

Shoes. I needed shoes. I looked and found some black five inch, "Fuck me" pumps with ankle straps that fit.

I quickly put these on and strutted in front of the mirror again. I loved what they did for my legs. I was hot, and just looking at myself made me excited. I looked like some of the girls in the BDSM club. I faced the mirror and crossed my arms behind me. I arched my back and stuck my boobs out as far as I could. I was getting aroused just seeing myself. I needed something else. I was ashamed of my behavior but I couldn't stop. I loved the feeling of wanton exhibitionism. I wanted someone to see me and lust for me. I wanted an audience. It had to be a man. A woman would be envious and maybe lustful. A man would take me and master me before he loved me. I wanted it all.

Hunt clubs originated in England and spread to the U.S. Only the wealthy can afford membership in the exclusive clubs. Foxes are not their only prey, in some clubs young women are the preferred prey. Young, agile, greedy and excited this prey feels the excitement of the hunt as much as the hunters. The captured prey and her hunters celebrate her capture with sexual abandon. The hunters proudly display their naked capture to an envious audience. Their prey enjoys her time as the center of attention. She proudly displays her sweaty, perfectly toned body, flaunting her bonds, knowing she will enjoy her hunter's attentions all night long.

Chapter 1

New Hire

A ghastly face looked back at me in the mirror. It was pale and bedraggled. My eyes were bloodshot, day old makeup was smeared, and my tears had left mascara tracks down my cheeks. My head throbbed with pain. I had killed that cheap bottle of whisky yesterday and I looked like it. My t-shirt was stained with food, I think. My life was as bad a mess as I felt.

I took a moment to feel sorry for myself then I set out to recover. I took a long, hot shower. As I washed I dreamed of ways I could kill my brother slowly. Interesting scenarios involving blow torches and knives filled my vision. I wouldn't really, but he deserved something bad. When I lost my job and went groveling to him for a little help, he had laughed, called me a filthy whore, and hung up. My only brother. He was doing quite well as a divorce lawyer and he only lived a mile away. Asshole. We were never close. He was ten years older than me. I was an "Accident."

I had taken an "Assistant to.." position straight out of college. I wasn't too picky. I was an average student and tired of school and there weren't many jobs for girls with psychology BA's. They offered me good money and a company apartment with an affordable rent. After a week I learned the apartment was a love nest four executives used for trysts. I was expected to keep the place clean and vanish when one of them needed it. I decided I wanted in on the action as a way to cement my use of the apartment. When one was coming over, he'd call or text me. So I started wearing the bondage gear and hanging around until the guy showed up.

The first couple of times I apologized, threw on a long coat and cleared out. It wasn't long before they started calling me for dates. It was clear to them I liked the bondage scene so we usually started the evening with me wearing the bondage things and playing their slave girl. Then we'd go out to dinner and a show or maybe dancing. We began to go to BDSM clubs and play there often. After an hour or so we would go back to the apartment after dinner and I'd be bound to the bed or just tied up while they played with me. I liked the feeling of helplessness. I also liked a mild spanking to warm me up before the main event. I'd have a "Date" with one of them four or five nights a week. I was well fucked and my job was OK. It didn't pay much and I spent my money on clothes and makeup. I wasn't saving anything, but I lived well. I considered just being a high priced call girl. I decided against it after reading about some girls being killed by their johns. This was fun and safer. I got several raises and liked always having a handsome man taking me places and giving me presents.

I know I was expected to find "Mr. Right," get married, have a family, etc. I wasn't ready for that. I would never be this young or pretty again. I wanted to have fun and I liked all of my "Boyfriends." They were all a few years older than me, vigorous in bed, active in sports and they took me on all sorts of adventure outings. They were friends as well as coworkers and we'd often stay in. Two or three of them and me. I got to try out all sorts of new positions. One of the books they had in the apartment when I moved in was The Kama Sutra. We never figured out how to get into some of the positions. but those we did manage were fun, kinky, and pleasurable.

They were all "Take charge" types and I liked that. They never asked me what I wanted to do, they just said, "Come on," and I went. It usually turned out their ideas were more interesting, surprising, or fun than my half formed ideas, anyway. Some evenings when I was alone I thought about doing something on my own, but I never did. I was in a rut, but it was a nice rut. I had "Dates" four or five nights a week and I went to the gym most other nights. I was effectively alone in the big city and not too adventurous. I just preferred to have a hunk with me, maybe because they were young, fearless, and aggressive. Just the opposite of my timid approach to life. I knew I was a follower ever since I was a child. Maybe that's why I was a so-so student. I was not interested in being best, or even in front. I certainly didn't want to outshine a boy. I was most comfortable being eye candy, hanging on his arm. I just didn't feel right taking the initiative. I went with the flow.

It turned out that Allen, one of the executives I was "Dating," was married. Maybe more were too. They never gave me their home phone numbers. Things blew up one day. Allen's wife had a PI follow him and apparently he got pictures of me with him. A week later I had to move and my job was gone. None of the guys I had "Dated" returned my calls. I was too depressed to do anything for a couple of days. I bought a bottle of whisky and tried to drink my troubles away. Didn't work. I had a week to move, no place to go, and exactly $1,374.67 in the bank.

I needed to do something soon. I dried off and considered my options. I thought I could be a stripper. I posed in front of my mirror. I looked good. I had a firm, athletic body. I had played soccer in high school and had only quit when my chest developed. At first I wanted to keep playing, but my breasts got too big. My mother had been "Well developed" and I followed her plan. So I had switched to running two to three miles a day, a healthy diet and regular trips to the gym. It showed. I'll save stripping for last. I knew most of them were hooked on drugs and burned out as fast as their bodies.

I looked through the newspaper. Nothing. I got online and looked at Craig's list. They had a lot of categories, but the only thing I thought I was qualified for was the Admin/ Office category. I opened it up and scanned it. Most were pretty low pay. Certainly insufficient for an apartment in the city. A personal assistant job caught my eye.

ROLC seeks a highly motivated, inventive, amiable, flexible and multi-talented Personal Assistant to our Founder and the executive team. Successful candidates bring smarts, creativity, a hard work ethic and a willingness to "make it happen." In short, this job is about doing whatever it takes from high-level creative problem solving to grabbing coffee to support our founder and free him up to captain the ship and navigate our growing business success with minimal   distractions.

Some key attributes and skills for this position include:

• *Ability to anticipate and support ever-changing needs of the executive team*

• *Our founder is an energetic go-getter. A successful candidate who values these qualities and demonstrates them in their own work is important.*

• *Eager team player*

• *Ability to maintain the confidentiality of information and decisions*

• *Exceptional planning, time management, and organizational skills*

• *A sense of humor. We work smart and hard but we also know fun, laughter and camaraderie are crucial in a successful business. We genuinely want our employees to find happiness in their work. This is a strong value for us.*

• Must be unattached and free to travel.

Superior pay with full benefits, including 401K, medical, dental, room and board. This is not for everyone. You will work 24/7 for a year with option to renew. You will forego any personal life save with your principal.

I read the ad over and over. It was perfect and daunting. 24/7, room and board, "Superior pay." I could bank all my pay for a year. I didn't care if the Founder and all his executive team wanted my benefits, either. I was used to that and I hoped ROLC would want me to renew.

This ad looked interesting so I emailed my resume and some photos of myself to the address in the ad. My only real claim to fame was my eidetic memory. I could recall anything I saw or heard perfectly. Thirty minutes later I got an answer asking me to come to an interview tomorrow. It said a car would be at my address at 8 am and it could last all day. I felt a shiver run down my spine. Tomorrow morning. I replied I would be ready.

I knew what a position with benefits meant. It used to be the norm for women getting a job. It was less obvious now, but it still existed, just like with Ralph, my current "Boss." I hoped "The Principal" was better in bed than Ralph. 24/7 for a year kept running through my mind. Every minute of every day for a year.   No personal life save with my principal. This was like being married. I couldn't imagine what my job would be like, but it couldn't be worse than with Ralph. "Room and Board" it said. I could save all of my pay. I liked that a lot. My hand-to-mouth existence precluded any savings and it was pretty scary being broke without a job. I wanted savings.

It was afternoon and I didn't have anyone to talk to. All my acquaintances were from work. I didn't know anyone else. No family except Steven and I never wanted to see him again. He was my brother, but we were never close. He was ten when I was born and he had always been terrible to me. He was a hot-shot lawyer in the city somewhere but I didn't have his address or phone number. Hell, he might be dead or relocated by now.

I could go to a bar. There were several in walking distance, but I didn't want a hook up . I picked out an outfit for my interview and made sure I had clean underwear and shaved my legs. I had some new pantyhose, but thought they were too stuffy. Its why they're still new. I went to the gym and worked out for a couple of hours. I worked up a good sweat. I showered and came home. I watched the news and then turned in. I lay there for a while, wondering about my life. I was lonely, I realized. Well maybe that's for the best if I got the job. It sounded like it wouldn't be boring.

I had this dream. It was essentially the same each time I had it. The setting changed but the same things happened. I was an Amazon, or a princess, or a queen, or someone important. I was captured and paraded through the streets of a big city. I was usually naked and always chained or tied to my captor's horse, or carriage, or chariot. There were cheering throngs lining the streets. I had lost. I was a prize. I was being shamed and humbled for my captor's benefit. I was usually displayed in a public square. Sometimes I was put in a cage. Sometimes just chained to a post. People threw rotten fruit at me. When my punishment was over my captor kept me as his slave. I was beautiful and he kept me with him always. I began by hating him. He made me dependent on him for everything. In the end I loved him and he loved me. I was still his slave, but he now protected me. I was so happy. I had it this night and it fit my interview. I was hired and the jet-setting executive took me all over the world with him. He was cloaked and hooded and naked underneath. I was his slave girl and never wanted to be parted from him. When we ate he fed me because my hands were chained, even in restaurants. I woke sweating at three am. I drank some water and got back in bed. I was terrified but couldn't tell if it was fear of getting or losing the job.

I woke again at 5 from force of habit. I was always a morning person. I found it useful both for school and work. I had a "Bump" that told me where I was and the time. I never got lost, even in the warrens of old Boston where I grew up. So I was ready at 8 when the car - a new Mercedes 500 limo pulled up. It was a shiny silver and the driver looked like he competed in body builder competitions, dressed in a well-tailored suit.

He parked and came around to where I stood and asked, "Ms. Lukens?"

I said, "Yes, I'm Cynthia Lukens."

He opened the door and helped me into the plush leather interior. He got back in the driver's seat and said, "There is orange juice and coffee in the bar. Help yourself. Breakfast will be ready when we arrive."

"Thank you," I said. I had butterflies in my stomach so I didn't get anything.

The drive took us north out of the city and into rolling farm country with mountains in the distance. The idyllic, pastoral scenery clashed with my expectations. Somehow I had expected a penthouse on Park Avenue. After we had been driving a half hour my stomach rumbled so I helped myself to both coffee with cream and OJ. After I finished my drinks, the car slowed and turned into a driveway. A massive gate rolled aside and we drove through. It took another five minutes before I saw the house. It was bigger than the library at school. Three stories and probably a basement, it loomed over us as we drove through an entrance into a courtyard and parked. The driver opened my door and helped me out. A butler, I guess greeted me by name and escorted me inside. He took me through a tall hallway to a dining room.

There was a woman my age waiting for me. She was a little older than me and looked like a model. She wore what I called office attire. White blouse with tall buttoned collar, dark skirt, and medium heels. She wore gold bracelets on both wrists. They were a little too bulky for my taste, but nice looking, in a retro-chic way. Well, there's no accounting for taste. She wore tall ankle boots with medium heels. There was a buffet along the wall I had entered through. Covered platters with eggs done three ways, bacon, sausage (two kinds), hash browns, biscuits, gravy, grits, bananas, strawberries, oatmeal, and more. Enough to feed thirty people. The woman introduced themselves as Julie Gore. She said she was in Human Relations and would do the interview after breakfast. So we got plates and food. I just got a little scrambled eggs, a scoop of hash browns, and a scoop of strawberries.

As we ate she asked me about my interests and books I read. Innocuous things. She said to just leave the dishes and staff would take care of them. She took me outside and into a well tended garden. We strolled a few minutes and talked about plants. As we headed back in I happened to glance into the dining room. I saw two girls collecting the dishes and stuff off our table. I just caught a glimpse, but it looked like they were naked. It must have been the reflection for when I looked again I couldn't see them.

She took me into an office and we sat at a round oak table with matching chairs. This was certainly a step above the utilitarian furniture in Ralph's office. Julie led the conversation and it was not what I expected. She opened a folder and said, "I won't ask you any questions. We have already done our homework and you qualify. You have the job." She slid a single sheet of paper to me. "Read this, please."

I read:

> Position: Personal Assistant. Salary
> "$20,000/month. Longevity bonus $200,000
> after one year. Position is continuous (24
> hours per day, 7 days per week, 365 days
> per year). There is no time off. You must
> wear the required uniform. You will
> provide sexual services as directed by your
> superiors. Corporal punishment will
> imposed at the discretion of your superiors.
> You may be recorded at any time. Nothing
> recorded here will be made public. You may
> leave at any time. You forfeit the longevity
> bonus if you leave before the year is up.
> One year of employment is guaranteed.

I read it again. Holy shit. This is a BDSM club or someone's been watching my dreams. This can't be real. There's a catch, I just know it. But, what if its real. Is the boss here creepy? I said, "I have some questions."

Julie said, "I thought you would."

"What does 'Corporal Punishment' mean?"

"You can be whipped or caned or strapped or spanked at the discretion of your superiors."

"You mean you will do those things to me if I mess up?"

"No," Julie said, "your superiors will do those things to you when they want to. You will not be injured, only given a little pain. You won't believe me now, but most times you will like it." She opened a drawer, took out a pair of handcuffs and tossed them on the table in front of me. She continued. "The simple explanation is that we are hiring your body and you will be, in actuality , a slave girl. You will be kept helpless and naked most of the time. You will do assigned work, be trained on behavior and given new skills. We will manage your food and exercise to keep you very fit. You will only be spanked or whipped if you disobey or ask for it. Given your history, imagine you will be staff in a BDSM club and everyone can use you for work or sex. You will love it. We do."

I asked, "You will pay me almost a half million dollars to do this for a year, and I can leave whenever I want?"

Julie said, "Right. Remember you only get the big bonus if you stay a year. Still, $20,000 a month isn't bad pay for a PA."

25

My mind kept repeating "A half million, a h..." I went back to the offer wording. "Too right." I said. "What is the required uniform. What you're wearing?"

"NO," Julie said, "Come over here and look out the window." We were on the second floor on this side of the building. I went over and looked out. I saw a bunch of young women in a big fenced yard. Some were pretty close and I could see them clearly. They were naked except for large gloves and black boots with steeply angled soles. All of them had black collars and springy tails , apparently coming from their bottom holes. Most were crawling on hands and knees. A couple were running surprisingly well on their hands and feet. I don't think they could stand on those weird soles. They seemed happy and were playing with each other, just like puppies. It looked like all of them were wagging their tails.

I said, "Pet play?"

Julie smiled and said, "Yes, all of the first year girls are puppy girls for their exercise period. They also help garden and maintain the woods. Every month or so we host a hunt. Hunters from all over the region come here for the hunt."

"I don't suppose they hunt foxes?"

"Only the two legged kind. All the girls love the excitement of the hunt. The hunters get to use the captured prey for their pleasure. The prey enjoy it too."

So you want to hire me to be a sex slave and prey for a hunt?"

"Exactly," She said.

We sat back down and I stared at the handcuffs.

"Have you worn them before," she asked?

"No, I've played bondage games with leather cuffs. These look scary."

She opened the drawer and took out the handcuff key. She laid it beside the cuffs. "Put them on. Think about everything I've told you. If you want to leave, use the key and go home. If you want to stay for a while, leave them on."

I picked up the cuffs and played with the action. "What the hell? I closed one on my left wrist and squeezed it snug. I couldn't get out of this without the key. I quickly put the other one on before I changed my mind.

She said, "Now squeeze them tighter, until they feel tight, not snug."

I closed them two more notches and they were tight.

"Tell me what you feel now, not how tight they are."

"I feel like I've just sold myself into slavery. Maybe even a little relieved."

"Have you decided to accept our offer?"

"I'm not sure. I'm tempted but scared."

"OK. Use the key and remove them."

It wasn't easy but I finally managed. I had put them on so my fingers couldn't reach the keyhole. I managed by using my teeth to hold the key.

Julie said, "We're going to see Sylvia. Take the cuffs. Leave the key and your bag."

I followed her out of the room and into another room. Another young woman about my age, also gorgeous was kneeling in the middle of the room. She was dressed like Julie.

Julie said, "Sylvia, stand and strip."

"Yes, Mistress, "Sylvia said, standing up. She unbuttoned her blouse, pulled it out of her skirt, and dropped it on the table. She wore no bra so she was naked from the waist up. She wore a gold metal collar on her neck and those gold bracelets on her wrists. A disc with the number twenty one hung on a ring in front of her collar. I watched in astonishment as she dropped her skirt to the floor, picked it up and put it with her blouse. She wore no panties so she was naked. Her loins were shaved clean. I hadn't noticed it before, but she wore more gold bands on her ankles.

"Now turn around for Cynthia."

Sylvia pirouetted for me to show she was entirely naked. She had large, erect breasts with rock hard nipples. She must be part exhibitionist to get turned on by stripping. I probably would too. She was so nonchalant about her nudity. I wish I could be as uninhibited as she was. I was proud of my body but not so much my soul. It was like I was playing a part. It was one that didn't fit me. I wanted to be like Sylvia. She was beautiful physically and mentally. She didn't care what I thought. She was happy being herself.

Julie said, "Relax and talk to Cynthia. I'll leave you alone. Cynthia, if you want the job take off your clothes except your shoes. put on the cuffs and come back to my office with Sylvia." She left and closed the door.

29

I looked at Sylvia and said, "This is the most bizarre job interview I can imagine. How many girls take this job?"

Sylvia smiled and said, "All of them. No girl we've offered it to has refused it. We are very selective in who we choose to interview. We only invite pretty young women who are somewhat submissive, have tried bondage play, and are not in a relationship. Think about it. It is safe, erotic, fun, exciting, relieves you of all responsibility and it secures your future. I signed up a year ago for the same deal and just re-upped for a lifetime of happiness because I found a man I want to be my Master. I love it. I admit I'm a bondage junkie. I love feeling totally out of control. Look at my jewelry. This isn't all. Usually My ankles are chained together." She walked to me and held out a hand. "Inspect my bracelet, Cynthia."

It looked like a plain wide, thick bracelet. I looked at it more closely and saw a pattern, like an engraved "U" on the inside. I touched it and the curved part sprang out to form a staple.

She said, "All the bands have those. They're for fastening us."

I realized I wanted to be like her. She was a wonderful role model. I wonder if I have the courage to follow my dreams like her? "Sylvia," I asked, "are you a Personal Assistant too?"

"Yes, I'm the current PA. I do hope you accept the position. You'll replace me as soon as you finish training. I'm ready to just tend to my Master."

I thought about all I had heard. I said, Sylvia, I have some more questions for Julie, Would you take me there?"

"Sure, follow me." She nonchalantly walked to the door and opened it for me. I gripped the handcuffs and followed her.

"Julia, what are you?"

She stood up and said, "I'm a slave too." She stripped off her clothes and showed me her collar and cuffs. Her number was five. She also had rings piercing her nipples and two rings in each lip of her shaved labia. "I've been here almost six years."

"Ladies, you say you're slaves. It looks like you can just walk out and leave."

Julie said, "We could. We can go through the gate like this. But we wouldn't like it outside. We've adopted the lifestyle and we like it here. Our lives are richer than before. And the benefits are wonderful."

"What do you mean?"

Sylvia replied, "Sex, honey. More sex and better sex than I even dreamed of before I came here. I think Julie and I are best described as 'Wanton sluts' rather than 'Sex Slaves.'"

"Well, who are my 'Superiors' who can whip me?"

Julie said, "Everyone, since you're new. But you'll see. Its better than you think. After a while its always better. I like them to start by whipping or spanking my bottom. It heats me up really quick."

"OK," I said, would you review this year thing again?"

Sylvia replied, "You can leave when you want. No questions asked. You have to sign a nondisclosure agreement that you won't say anything about this place or the people. If you leave, you get paid all the money you've earned. If you stay a year and then leave, you'll get the year's pay and the bonus. That's almost half a million. The first year you will be an employee. If you want to stay longer, you have to volunteer to be a slave to a master. Only slaves have these metal collars. Yours will be leather."

"What if I want to stay after that?"

Julie said, "The money is to convince you to stay a year. If you want to stay after that, you're already way into the lifestyle, and you can be a slave like Sylvia and me. You can leave after that, but you won't want to. You'll have money in the bank and an unbeatable retirement plan. You'll wake up every day excited, full of joy and anxious to get up. You'll be valued and appreciated like never before. Like us, you'll be hooked on the sex, freedom from worry, and comfortable separation from the outside world."

"I've always read and been told that slavery is terrible."

Sylvia said, "It can be, depends on who owns you."

"So, who owns you and does he want to try me out?"

Julie this time, "My Master is Brian Cosgrove, he's security chief here. I love him and he's a great lover. For the first year you'll belong to Robert Faris Olander, one of the richest, most unknown, and best people this planet has produced. And he is the best lover you will ever meet. You'll be his PA and then you'll find a master. Mr. Olander has never taken a slave. You might be the lucky one."

Four hundred and forty thousand dollars for a year of my life. Let me see...Yes. My greed had overcome my common sense. I was going to let them take my clothes, hit me when they wanted, and be locked away from the world for a year just for money? Hell, yes. That much money would let me live in luxury for the rest of my life in the Caribbean. I shouldn't be hasty though. "OK, I said. "I will need some time to think about this. Can I call you?"

"Julie said, "No. You know you will never get a better, more exciting offer. We all know you've already decided to stay. You're just scared to commit. Take off your clothes and put your cuffs on. Keep your shoes. Then we'll take you to see your new master. Remember you can leave whenever you want, no questions asked. No one wants an unhappy girl around."

She was right. I had decided. I hated being that transparent, but everything she said was true. It wasn't because of the money, though that was nice. It was thrilling to give up my freedom to a man who was a good lover. If what these girls had told me was half true, it was my dream and I wouldn't need the money or the year. I was ready for this adventure. I slowly, dreamily removed my clothes. When I had dropped the last filmy scrap I was blushing with shame, but filled with a strange new excitement. I was entering a society that valued women for their submission and beauty.

It must be the same for all girls. I wrapped my arms across my chest, one hand over each breast then tried to bend down far enough to get my elbows to cover my other girl parts. You can't, but you try. I'm sure I looked silly. There was no way I could cover everything that mattered. I saw Sylvia and Julie watching me with expressions of both pity and understanding. Even the attempt was beyond embarrassing, standing between two beauties so nonchalantly naked.

Sylvia said, "Its OK, Cynthia. Every girl here does that silly dance the first time they realize they won't ever wear clothes again. You've been covered all your life. Hidden from the world's view. Now you're wide open and letting everyone see all your secrets. You should be proud. You have a magnificent body. Stand tall and smile."

She was right. I could be proud of my body. I straightened up and stood proud, as naked as Julie and Sylvia. Sylvia took the cuffs, I held out my hands, and she closed them on my wrists until they were snug. I held them in front of my face and twisted my hands around, There was no way I was getting my hands apart without the key. Julie showed me the collar. It was a wide, thick band of black leather with a lock built in and the number twenty nine embossed on a steel plate under a heavy ring. She fit the collar on my neck and, careful not to pinch my skin, closed it until the lock snapped shut. It too was a perfect fit, resting halfway up my neck and touching me gently all around.

"How come it fits me so well?"

Julie said, "We have done a lot of research on you since last night. I feel confident in saying we know everything worth knowing about you. We know every one of your measurements. From the books you read and the essays you wrote in school, we know you have a sense of adventure, Yet you are submissive, wanting others to guide you. That's one reason we were confident this is perfect for you."

It was startling to know I was so predictable, yet comforting that these people's conclusions were so correct. I could hardly wait to meet my new Master. I guess I have been waiting to meet him all my life.

Julie knelt and locked cuffs around my ankles. These looked like the handcuffs but had a longer chain connecting them. I could walk, but my stride was constrained and I couldn't kick. I wouldn't anyway. She said, "Let's go see Master Robert. Just follow our lead, do what we do."

They led me out of the room and to an elevator. Sylvia held onto my upper arm. They took me down. I was surprised the Master was on a lower level. I said, "He's in the basement?"

Julie said, "No, we're meeting him in the Pub."

"There's a Pub in the basement?"

Sylvia said, "Everyone calls it the Pub, but its really a private club for staff and guests. We're staff. Its kinky but fun. We all like it when its our turn to work there. You'll see."

The doors opened onto a large foyer with a mural showing Barbarian warriors looking over a string of naked slave girls in coffle. A city burned behind them. My dream captured in paint. This is the right place. Two young women, almost naked, stood by the far door. They wore black, fuck me heels and a tiny white French Maid's apron that hid nothing. They had collars and cuffs like Julie's. There was a gold chain joining their ankles, but their most conspicuous ornament were the large gold rings hanging from their septum's. They glittered and shone in the light. Beside them was a large, serious looking security man.

We walked up to them. I tried to hide behind Sylvia, but she wasn't good cover. Julie said, "Hi Margie, Susan, Andy. You know Sylvia and this is Cynthia. Brand new and not used to nudity yet.

The Master is waiting for us."

They all smiled and one of the girls said, "Welcome, Cynthia. I'm Margie. Will you all follow me, please?" The other girl opened the door and we followed Margie inside.

It looked like an Irish Pub. Not too dark, with a long bar on the far wall and a dozen round tables with two chairs and two overstuffed cushions, a dance floor, and small stage. There were four men at the bar. Two of them had women standing and talking to them. They were all smiling and looked happy. There were two big screen TVs glowing with a soccer match on different walls. The sound was turned way down. Several tables were occupied with men and women. The table in the far corner was occupied by a single man. We followed Margie to his table. I hadn't registered it when we walked in, but as we were walking to the table I saw that every woman in here was naked. Three of them wore handcuffs but no collars. The rest were like Julia, Sylvia, and I. Margie pulled another cushion to the table and slid a chair away as we got there. Julie said, "Cynthia, use this cushion." She pointed to the one in the middle. She and Sylvia knelt on the other two. I saw them spread their knees very wide, cross their hands behind them, and stick out their breasts. The man, my new Master, I suppose, sat there and smiled at my confusion.

He said in a deep, resonant voice, "Cynthia, slaves are not allowed to use furniture. The cushions are to protect your knees. Kneel on the cushion, please." God, he was magnificent, like a lion surveying his domain. His voice gave me shivers and I felt moisture seeping into my pussy. "Calm down girl," I thought, "He's only your employer. So far."

I did as he said and knelt between Sylvia and Julie. I spread my knees. I noticed Margie was standing rigidly beside us. Her posture looked like Julie and Sylvia, only standing. Her back was arched and she crossed her hands behind her.

He spoke to Margie, "Margie, thank you. Would you ask Brian and Henry to join us please?"

"Yes, Master." She hurried off.

I studied Master Robert's face. The light was dim and much of that came from behind him. He had a strong, lean face. I saw a hint of smile lines. He saw his eyes scan my body. He was intent on me. I drew myself up tall and thrust my breasts out even farther. I was proud of my body and I wanted him to appreciate it too. I felt the heat rising in me. When I had walked into Pub I felt exposed. I wasn't used to going naked into public places. Now, under his gaze, I was becoming aroused. I felt moisture seeping into my pussy. Was this just because I was naked? Did the chains and my helplessness enter into it? Or was it just that my body was getting ready to be fucked by this man who held the power over me, my Master?

Margie returned in a minute with a tray and glasses of water for each of us. All except Master's had straws. Thoughtful. She said, "Master, I contacted them and they are on their way."

"Thank you, Margie."

"Master, would you like anything else?"

He shook his head and she hurried away.

He said, "So you decided to stay for a while. You understand you'll be in training for a while before you are my full time PA?"

"Yes. Master. Julie told me that."

"Why did you agree to enter what is obviously a slave training program?"

I thought about that. Why did I want this? I suspected I have wanted to belong to a man, a real man, all my life. I couldn't tell him I was hunting a mate. "The pay is incredible and I'm desperate. Also because I can quit if it doesn't work out."

He studied my face for a long time. The silence stretched out interminably. His bright blue eyes were piercing. I could feel them burrowing into my soul. I was afraid he knew I was lying. I blurted out, "I'm sorry. I was afraid to say. Its my dream. I'm afraid this is what I've wanted all my life. You're him. My Master."

He looked solemn. He said, "Cynthia, I'm the master of all the girls here, but I'm not the personal master of any of them. I'm not your personal master. I may be when you can make an informed submission and I accept. You are beautiful and I may accept your submission when you can prove you are a natural slave. I want no pretenses. You must love your slavery and take true joy in subjugation."

I believed him. I wanted him to take me now. I would work to hone my skills and make him proud to own me. I would. I wanted my dream to live, to be in it all day, every day. Now, I had to be logical. Force my intellect to overcome my lust, for now.

"Yes, Master. Can I ask some questions?"

He smiled and replied, "Yes, go ahead."

I wanted to ask if he would take me here in front of these people or could we have some privacy? What I said was, "What is this place and your business. It looks like you are using your money to make a harem."

He laughed, "No, None of these girls belong to me. All of those who've chosen to adopt the bondage lifestyle have other owners. While you're my PA I'll expect you to behave as my property. But you can quit whenever you want. Brian Cosgrove will be here in a moment. He's my head of Security and he owns Julie. Before a girl can choose to be a slave, she has to have a man accept her as his property. Sylvia is owned by Raphael, another of my managers. This place is my HQ. I have a number of enterprises in eleven countries. I know a lot about you, so you should know something about me. I got an engineering degree and joined the Marines. After the military I started designing medical devices and did well. it turned out I had a knack for turning failing companies around. What you personally need to know is that I like to be in control."

I asked, "Is that why are all the women here are naked and in chains?"

"The easy answer is because they want to be and I like them that way. You know they can leave anytime they want and be financially independent. The real answer is that over nearly all of human history, women had to be dependent on men for everything. Nature tailored them to be physically attractive and emotionally submissive so men would want to protect and keep them. Our current society is trying to change that evolution. Many women are clinically depressed and a lot more fit poorly in society. The evidence suggests to me that many women will be happier if they can express their submissive nature. Most men find a helpless woman sexy as hell. Many women like that feeling of helplessness. How do you feel right now? Be honest. I already know how Julie and Sylvia feel."

I hated to admit it, but he was right. I felt very exposed and helpless. Yet I wasn't scared. I also felt sexy and alluring, much like when I was wearing a revealing dress in public. I liked being desired by men. It felt right and I felt tingly, alive, and ready for sex. I said, "OK, I do feel good being helpless, exposed, and safe."

He continued, "You're beautiful and extremely sexy. I like my women very available and very submissive. Since I have the resources to enjoy my preferences I set this place up as you see it. Every woman here is, using society's biased vernacular, a wanton slut. They enjoy sex with anyone they want, as often as they can."

"But, Master, aren't you wasting a lot of money on this bondage estate that would be more profitably spent on expanding your businesses and keeping a couple of willing slaves? I'm not questioning your judgment, of course, Master, but I don't understand your goals."

"I didn't take offense, Cynthia, you just don't have all the facts yet. I started this in the way you suggest. It soon turned out that this estate setup allowed me to hire the very best people away from good jobs at companies that valued them. Of course I pay talent top dollar, but giving them sexual freedom and happiness was worth more than money. I free them from some of the less sensible restrictions society imposes. I've got setups like this in every country where I have a business. Almost twenty percent of my top employees are women that agreed to become sex slaves. You met Julie. She is head or Human Relations for all my companies because she is good at it. I treasure women's abilities and I let them use them and be happy at the same time. They gave up some freedom in return for feeling good and shucking their therapists. Of course the lifestyle isn't for everyone and as you saw, everything is consensual."

"The other major factor in keeping good talent is that they are participants in a sort of secret society apart from the outside. There are several estates like mine in a loose confederation. We are private clubs and we interact through organized hunts. Each estate has a team of hunters that travel to other estates to hunt . There is status in being the best, but the main reward is the betting. Being a member of the best team can be worth from a hundred thousand to a million dollars a year. So the hunters are serious about doing well in the hunts."

"What do you hunt?

"Girls, of course."

"What do the girls get from being hunted?"

"The thrill of the chase, lots of sex, and the chance to catch the eye of a hunter. The girls here are invested in the bondage lifestyle. Most of them want to be the slave of a virile, wealthy man who will value them and take care of them. In the hunts she sees and is seen by many men who are potential masters."

Two men walked up to the table and one scrounged a chair from another table he passed. Master introduced the younger, bigger man as Brian, his Security Chief and the other as Henry Oldman, his Vice President for US operations. Brian took the chair close to Julie and she put her head in his lap. He said that as his PA, I would be working with them on a regular basis and I would constantly communicate with his other managers.

He said to them, Cynthia is my new PA. She'll get her puppy training done now and be on the job in month or so. I wanted you to meet her. If you have questions or instructions for her, now is a good time." Both shook their head no and said they were pleased to meet me. Standard civilized greetings, but discordant to a naked woman. They excused themselves. Brian stroked Julie's head as he got up. I watched Julie. She looked up at him in pure bliss. I heard a faint sound from her parted lips. Part lust, part promise, part joy. Intense envy, jealousy, and desire flooded through me. I wanted to be like her. She was Aphrodite incarnate. Unashamedly naked and ringed in public. Caressed by her Master and glowing in her submission. She was so damned happy when he stroked her head. I wanted that feeling. I wanted to wear Master Robert's rings and show them off to everyone as he rubbed my head. Julie belonged to her Master. She reveled in her openness and was proud to be his girl. I knew this was what I wanted, why I had that same dream. Was Robert my Master? I felt like he already was.

Brian said, "I'll see you later."

Master Robert looked at Julie and said, "You and Sylvia take Cynthia around and show her the house and gardens then bring her to my quarters in two hours."

I was devastated. My loins were aching with need. I wanted him to take me now. My pussy was sopping wet and I was afraid I would gush all over the floor when I stood up. I kept a smile on my face, but I'm sure it looked strained.

They both said, "Yes. Master."

The three of us stood up and I felt wetness trickle down my legs. I felt the heat rise in my face. My Master was watching me as I stood. I could feel his eye tracks on my messy loins. He said, "Pleasure delayed is pleasure increased. Only two hours, Cynthia."

I didn't know what to call him. He wasn't my Master, yet. I didn't want to call him by name. I decided I'd just say "Sir." I opened my mouth and said, "Yes, Master." It just popped out. The ache in my belly got worse. He had seen my need and he wanted me to stew in own juices for two hours, damn him. I could see he would be a perceptive lover. I wouldn't be able to manipulate him. He had just made himself irresistible.

Julie led the way. I followed her and then Sylvia. We went through the building. It was part office, part hotel, part bondage dungeon, and part kennels. Two kinds, one for dogs, one for girls. The girl kennels had several rooms. I saw an office, and infirmary, a tack room, an institutional bathroom, and the kennels themselves. The girls were locked in them at night unless someone was using them. Then they were chained in the guests room.

We went outside and got a look at the grounds. There were a couple of large courtyards. The girl's yard was called the pound. It was maybe a half acre of grass and shade trees enclosed by an eight foot concrete wall. There were several gates, all locked. The ornamental garden was twice as big and neatly organized and immaculately maintained. The farm looked like it was ten acres. Julie said they grew all their fruits and vegetables and the girls worked in it often. The woods were a mix of wild forest and park. Lots of trails ran through them and a couple of gravel roads used by the foresters and security. Julie said, "The entire estate is enclosed by a tall wall. The wall and the woods are filled with sensors. If you come to a white line on the ground, don't cross it, even if you're hiding in a hunt. The space between the white line and the outer wall is forbidden to women. You'll be punished if you go over the line."

I asked, "You mean the sensors will report me and the master will have someone beat me?"

"No, no," Julie replied, "Your collar will shock you if you cross the line. If you ignore it and go further, the shocks get stronger until it knocks you unconscious. Security will come get you and then you'll be punished, unless you decide to leave, instead. I know several girls that tested the system. They decided to stay and accept their punishment rather than leave."

I heard bells faint in the distance. We watched people walk out of the woods. It looked like a work crew. Two men carrying power tools led the line, Four carts followed, each pulled by two girls in a harness. The girls were naked and their hands were fastened behind them. They had a leather harness over their shoulders and around their waist that were fastened to the cart's tongue. Each girl had a bridle around their head and a bit in their mouth. A man sat on a seat at the front of the cart using reins to steer the girls. Behind the last cart, another man led a string of a dozen girls. The girls were naked save for boots and gloves. They were fastened together by a chain between their collars. Each girl had a bell on their collar. At this distance they looked clean.

Chapter 2

Employer

They each took an arm and gently guided me down a hallway, around a corner, and up to a closed door. Julie knocked and the deep, resonant voice of my Master said, "Enter."

They led me into a study, from the looks of it. Dark wood trim, matching the desk. There was a thick rug in front of the desk. There were chairs for guests, but these were at the sides of the desk. The rug was for kneeling girls. I guess I was now a member of that class. My employer, my Master, sat at the desk facing the door. The two girls knelt and I followed them down. I watched them spread their knees wide and arch their backs to present their breasts well. They held their heads erect. I followed suit and looked at the man. He had a leonine head with chiseled features, and I could see him much better than in the dark Pub. He had both frown and smile lines. He looked like he had made hard decisions and had also laughed a lot. Before he said a word I knew I was in love with him.

He looked at me with his startling blue eyes. He looked right through me and I saw love and respect. He was the sort of man you wanted to protect you and love you. I wanted him in me so bad I had to suck in my spit to keep from drooling. He looked so damned competent. My craving for him was strong. I felt pulled to him.

I heard a faint noise and a dog walked in front of me. It looked curious and friendly. I saw he was male. He sat down in front of me. I wanted to pet him, but I knew I shouldn't move.

Robert watched my meeting and smiled. He stood up and came around the desk like a great cat ready to take his prey. I wanted to be taken so bad. I couldn't look away from his face. I tracked him around the desk, my eyes locked onto his. He said, "Jeb, Leave it." And the dog went back behind me.

Robert, stepped closer. Was he my Master? He stood in front of me, so close. He said, "Hello, Cynthia." I didn't know what he wanted, but I know what I wanted. I lowered my head to the floor between us and I licked his shoes. They tasted of carnauba and leather. I ran my tongue down the outside of a shoe then down the inside. I did the same for his other shoe. Then I raised back up and looked him in the eye and said, "I am Cynthia, your slave, Master. I will obey your command, I will make your pleasure my goal in life. I am yours. Please take me."

No. I didn't do any of that. I just knew how easy it would be to slide into submission. This house these ..slaves.., beside me, this incredibly powerful man before me. I could do this, but I needed to be sure I wanted this for all time. Getting out of this pool would be much harder than falling in. I just knelt and thrust my breasts out, showing my assets, as they were, but I didn't say anything for a long moment. Then I said, "Hello, Sir.

He said, "Stand up, Cynthia."

I stood and looked up at him. He was a good foot taller than me and much bigger. He lifted my cuffed hands, unlocked one cuff, turned me around, and locked my hands behind me. He wrapped his arms around me, pulled me close, and kissed me. A strong, deep, kiss. I felt his tongue force its way into my mouth. I relaxed my jaw and let his tongue feel my mouth. I kept my tongue in my mouth as a sign of my submission to him. He was a great kisser. I knew I was getting his full attention. Whatever he had been examining on his desk was not being thought about. One hand left my back and stroked down over my rump and around into my loins. His strong fingers rubbed on my nether lips and I felt my body moisten my pussy and thrust my loins against his. I wanted him in me so bad. But I was silenced by his mouth and made helpless by his chains. I must await his pleasure and that thought made me so much closer to an orgasm. Julie was right on, I was such a submissive.

Finally he released the kiss and with his lips only inches from mine said, "Julie, Sylvia, thanks for bringing Cynthia. You can go now. I'd like to see you here at nine tomorrow."

I heard them both say, "Yes, Master." I couldn't tear my gaze away from his. I heard them leave and close the door.

He said, softly, "Cynthia, you are lovely and I want you. But you're very new. I won't accept your submission until you've been here a year. For now you are my employee. You can leave anytime you feel like it. Clear?"

"Yes, Master."

"Cynthia, I'm not your Master. Call me "Sir, please."

"Yes, Sir," I breathed. It wasn't true. I knew he was my master already, but I also knew an order when I heard one. My lust had grown in his presence. My pussy was sopping and my love juices were trickling down my legs. I rubbed my hard nipples against his chest and heard a moan seep from my open mouth as my belly spasmed.

He scanned my face as his finger rubbed my swollen labia. He asked, "You're ready to come, aren't you?"

I gasped, "Yes, Oh yes."

He put his hands around my waist and lifted me like I was a doll. He turned around and set my ass on the edge of his desk and lay me on my back. He lifted my legs and pressed my thighs up over me. My ankle chain tinkled as he moved me around. I felt my bracelets under me and arched my back around them. With one hand he held my ankle chain over me and his other hand explored my pussy. One finger probed my inner lips and I felt my arousal soar. When his second finger probed me, I exploded in a shuddering orgasm. I screamed my surprise and joy. This was enormous, fantastic. It was the best orgasm I could recall. Everything prior faded into insignificance. Everyone from now on would be judged against this. This was my "Gold Standard."

When I recovered I saw everything was as I recalled. I was still laying on his desk and his hand was still holding my ankle chain over my head. He said, "That was a great orgasm. I enjoyed watching you. Hold still. I'm going to slide you a few inches further onto the desk."

I said, "Yes, Sir. You can do anything you want with me." I meant it too. He had made me feel better than I had ever felt before. I trusted him completely, already. I was likely naive, but I didn't have any concerns at all. I was helpless and content to have him taking care of me.

He slid me up on the desk and moved my feet onto the edge. He rolled me on my side and did something with my wrists and ankles. When he rolled me back down, my feet were held snug into my ass. He had fastened my ankles to my wrists. I was hogtied, most delightfully. I asked, "Now that you have me where you want me, what ever will you do to me, sir?"

He smiled down at me and said, "You are an oversexed young woman and have made a mess on my desk. I should leave you here to clean it up." As he spoke one hand was fondling my breast and rolling my rock hard nipple between his finger and thumb. His other hand was rubbing my labia lips.

I moaned and gasped, "Please don't do that. I'm a bad girl. You need to teach me not to leave messes. Punish me with your sex. Teach me not to make a mess. Take me. I'm ready. I need you in me."

He said, "OK. I suppose you're right." He rolled me over on my belly and rubbed my ass cheeks.

Oh no. He wasn't going to take me yet. God. I was so hot. I was in terrible need. I squawked, Please take me, Sir."

I felt his hand strike my left cheek. I yelped.

He said, You have been a bad girl. I need to teach you not to make a mess." His fingers stroked my swollen pussy and the heat from my stinging ass flowed directly into my belly. Another blow on my right cheek and I was hotter. I moaned, close to coming again. He rolled me back onto my back and said, "Are you properly chastised now, Cynthia?"

I said, "Not yet, Sir. I still need to be taught the rewards as well as the punishment." I smiled up at him. "I think now I'm ready to be taken."

I watched as he walked to my ass and took his cock out of his pants. God, he was big. He was erect and ready for me too. He put his member at my pussy and I closed my eyes. I wanted to feel everything. He stroked my pussy lips with the tip of his member and it drove me crazy with need. I begged him, "Please sir, take me now. I need you in me". My cunt was spasming hopelessly.

Finally, he thrust into me, far too slowly. I needed him to ream my cunt hard. He teased me by going slow at first. It was wonderful. It was terrible. I needed him to pump me up. I moaned. I couldn't say any words. Speech had been drowned out by my need. Finally he sped up and my arousal flamed higher until I came again with a scream of pleasure. I think I fainted with my joy. When I became aware of things again, He was still in me and shrinking. He had come too. Thank God. I hoped it was as good for as my world class orgasm. No wonder a job with benefits was so popular.

He pulled out and wiped his member with a tissue. He rolled me onto my side again and freed my ankles from my wrists. He cuffed my wrists behind me an left my ankles free. He stood me up and I almost fell on my shaky legs. He picked me up like a child and carried me out of the office and into a bedroom. He carried me into the bath and set me on the toilet. He said, "Use it if you need it. I'm be right back."

I did need it. I peed and waited for him. He came back, naked and said, "We both need a shower. Come on."

I stood up and he led me into a huge shower. No doors, just curved walls and an acre of tile. There were six shower heads so a person could have water flowing onto them from all sides at once. Water conservation was set back ten years when he turned them all on. I couldn't use my hands so he scrubbed both of us with green Bulgari Green Tea shower gel. I cuddled to him as much as I could while he lathered and rinsed me. He washed my hair and applied conditioner (Bulgari White Tea, of course). He paid special attention to my girl parts and when he turned off the water, I was ready for more loving. I could see he was too. But he had more self control than me. Despite my pleas and flirtatious behavior and my frantic rubbing (God, I behaved like a bitch in heat), he got us both dry and shoved my gasping body in bed. He picked up a chain from the floor and locked it to my collar.

He said, "Its long enough to reach the toilet." Then he got in bed beside me.

We made love three more times that night. and my internal alarm didn't go off. He woke me at 8, took the chain off my collar, unlocked my wrists, and took me into the bathroom. He shaved and dressed while I showered again. It was more fun last night. He took me to the dining room and we ate breakfast. He told me a brief description of his childhood and his companies. He said my first few months would be training to be good in the hunt and how to behave around here, the last six months would be helping him manage his companies. When the year was up I would have to decide on what status I wanted.

I said, "I'm ready to decide now, Sir." And I was.

He replied, " You're flush with lust right now. I want your decision to be an unbiased, informed one. I will not accept your answer before the year is up."

"Yes, Sir. What does training for the hunt and behavior entail. I'm in good shape now."

"There are some skills you will need. Julie and Sylvia will be your trainers for these tasks. You'll find your training ... different."

He took me back to the office to meet the girls. I looked at his desk and the floor, expecting to see some soiling. Nothing. Everything was clean and fresh. Julie and Sylvia entered the open door and knelt. Sir said, "Cynthia, examine Julie and Sylvia's position. Their knees are spread wide, backs arched, breasts out, head up, eyes down, arms crossed behind them. Kneel and assume the same posture."

I knelt beside Julie and tried to copy her. Sir said, "Knees wider. ..Good."

He said, "Julie, get Cynthia dressed and take her to John's office. She has the employment papers to sign. Then start her on pack training. Go."

Julie stood up and said, "Yes, Master. Come along girls." Sylvia and I stood and followed her out of the room. They led me back to the room where I had left my clothes and Julie had me put them back on. She combed my hair and then we went to another office. I wore the collar and leg irons but my hands were free and I was dressed. They ushered me into another office where "John," a young man in a suit was sitting at a desk with a stack of papers on it. Julie introduced us and said she and Sylvia would wait outside for me. They left and closed the door.

John said, "We have some paperwork to do. First is the non-disclosure agreement. It means you can't discuss anything you see or hear while you are here. Sign and date it, please. " When I finished signing he took the forms and started a new stack. He said, "when we finish here I will copy these for you. Please note there are cameras around the estate and you may be recorded at any time. This is a release allowing us to use them privately and for training. You can veto any public release but if you do agree to distribution, you will receive ten percent of net proceeds received, if any. OK, good. Next is your employment contract. Please read this over, then face the camera and read this paragraph. This is to show you agree to obey every command of your superiors and trainers and to accept corporal punishment at their discretion, provided you are not injured ..."

"Now," he said, "these are your employment contracts. read and sign each page." This went on for some time.

The paperwork was finally done and copies made. John said he would get rid of my apartment, store my goods, sell my car, etc. He opened the door and handed me back to Julie.

Julie took me back to her room and I stripped again. All three of us were again naked and Julie took us into the kennel part of the big house. We entered what looked like a Doctor's examination room. There was a man at a desk and a woman a few years older than me, fully dressed, just walking through a doorway. The man looked up and said, "Hello Julie, Sylvia. Is this beautiful girl Cynthia?"

Julie and Sylvia knelt and Julie said, "Yes, Master, Mistress."

The man said, to me, "Kneel beside Julie, Cynthia. Proper protocol is for you to kneel whenever you come into the presence of a master or mistress. Put your forehead on the floor and raise your tail in the air." I knew what was coming, but I obeyed. I yelped when I felt a stripe of pain cross my ass cheeks, but I didn't move.

Mr. Alistair continued. "You are in punishment position. Its good you didn't move or you would have earned more stripes for disobedience. Now kneel properly."

I adjusted my position .

He said, "We need to measure you now. Sit on this table, please."

I stood and sat on the end of a cold stainless steel table. The woman said, I am Ms. Johansen. You must address me as 'Mistress.' She removed my irons, measured my wrists and ankles and found leather cuffs in my size. She wrapped each one around my limb and squeezed the ends together until the lock clicked shut with a snap. She laid me back on the table and pulled my arms down beside the table. She clipped my cuffs down to the sides while Mr. Alistair lifted my feet up and set them in the exam stirrups. Not only that, he strapped them in place. Ms. Johansen put two leather straps across my body. One just below my breasts and one across my waist. She pulled them tight. I couldn't move at all now.

Mr. Alistair adjusted the stirrups so my feet were spread very wide and my tendons stood out taut in my legs. Ms. Johansen pulled a hose with a slender nozzle on the end of the table between my legs. She turned on the water and adjusted the temperature until she was satisfied. The end of the table under me was slanted with a drain at the end. She turned off the water, put on some exam gloves and greased my anus. She said, "I'm going to wash you out now. It won't hurt and if you relax it will feel better."

I couldn't do anything so I tried to relax. I felt her finger rubbing lubricant on and in me. The she inserted the nozzle and started the water. It was warm and felt soothing. I could see it running out of me and down the drain. When it ran clear she shut it off and removed the nozzle. I said, "Thank you Ms. Johansen. That felt weird but good."

She tched and picked up a riding crop. She struck my raised legs at the juncture with my ass. It hurt worse than last time. She said, sympathetically, "You did not have permission to speak. Ask first next time, Cynthia."

I said, "Yes, Mistress. I'm sorry."

She took the hose away and he brought a tool like a tapering rubber shaft maybe a foot long to me. He said, I'm going to measure you now. He carefully inserted the rod, narrow end first into my clean anus. He slowly shoved it in further and further, rotating the shaft. At last it reached the end of my cavity and he said, "Excellent. You can easily take a number six plug and you're deep enough for the longest male."

I was a little alarmed   I asked, "Do we get used there a lot?"

He said, simply, "You bet. You're well designed for use there and you'll get nothing but pleasure from your use."

"But," I protested, "I don't want to be used there."

He turned to Julie and said, come here and discuss your experiences with Cynthia while we're getting her ready for her responsiveness measurement."

Julie stood up and walked over. She said, "Yes, Master."

Then she said to me, "Cynthia, have you tried it?"

"No, but.."

She cut me off, "Most girls who come here have only read about it and think its 'Dirty' in some way. Once they have tried it every one of them like it. We all have to be convinced, but once we learn we can orgasm from any of our holes, we all love it. We learn so many ways to orgasm, its like we were blind before."

"I'm one of those girls that only read about it. Why do men like to use us there when our pussy is so well designed to receive them?"

"Simple, Our ass holes are tighter and warmer than our pussies. Physical sensation. Plus, they can spank our asses and grab our tits if they want. And most of them that have used me there, want to. Its OK by me. Those things feel wonderful if the guy isn't a total ass. Master doesn't let bad guys near us, anyway. You'll always feel loved and appreciated here."

She continued, "Now Mr. Alistair is going to force an orgasm from you and see what it takes to do that. We all are measured once a month to see how we are progressing. A lot of the training here is to make us more responsive, orgasm more easily. We all like that a lot. I usually get three or four orgasms a day and I get fidgety if I miss one. You'll see."

Ms. Johansen put sticky electrodes on me with wires running to a box on the side of the table. These were like the ones that they stick on you in a hospital to measure heart activity. She used a speculum to spread my labia lips apart. She put electrodes on my nipples, my labia lips, and my clit. She put some on my inner lips using light clamps. She shoved a small metal probe in my anus and clipped a wire to it.

Mr. Alistair picked up a stopwatch and flipped a switch on the box. The electrodes started sending small electrical shocks in to my body. The shock were rhythmical and seemed to run in order to my clit. Nipples, labia, pussy, clit, over and over. It was working. I was getting aroused. I realized I was panting and the pulses were coming quicker now.

I was embarrassed by this disembodied lover. It was unreal. It was working. I was getting closer until an orgasm burst through me. I screamed in pleasure. I wanted this machine. It was a lot better than a vibrator.

He stopped the timer and said, "One minute thirty one seconds. Very good time indeed. You're a hot girl, Cynthia.

FYI, most girls cut their time by a third in a month and by half in two months. And, no you can't have the machine. We have better ways."

They removed the electrodes and got me off the table, thank God. But they weren't done with me. They took me into a tack room, I'd have to call it. There was all manner or straps, and harnesses, bits, bridles, muzzles, gaga, whips, canes, and everything else one might want to use to bind and harness a girl. Mr. Alistair said, "Julie, Sylvia, put her puppy tack on her and Sylvia, take her and show her the ropes. Julie, come see me when they are out. We'll come into the yard in a half hour and examine her responses."

Chapter 3

Pet

Julie and Sylvia each took a hand and slid a glove on it. The gloves were elbow length made of black rubber. They had a metal reinforced slit the ring of my cuff stuck through then a small lock held it in place. The palms were of thick rubber and unbendable. I lost all flexibility and ability to grasp anything. Next they put kneepads and light boots on me. I wouldn't be able to stand in the boots. The sole was at an acute angle to the toes and the hells were far too tall to stand on. I had to crawl now. No walking. Julie showed me a long flexible rod, bent several times with a plume on one end and a butt plug on the other. She said, "This is your tail. Be sure and wag it whenever trainer or master is around." She inserted it into my still well greased asshole. It went in with a plop. "Now try it," she said.

I wagged my hips and I felt it respond and wag above and behind me. "Truly embarrassing," I thought.

They led me into another room. I looked at it in surprise . The far wall was filled with kennels, all numbered. The walls were concrete and the kennels were too, except for the doors. They were six feet deep, four feet high, and four feet wide. The doors were barred and hinged at the top. Now they were all open and standing straight out. There was a walkway level with the floor. Julie said, "That's yours," pointing at one in the second tier with 'CYNTHIA,' kennel number twenty nine, on a sign above the door. She continued, Behind us are lockers for you to keep toiletries, bedding and your tack when you're not using it."

I turned and saw one of the lockers had my name above it too. I asked, "What is this? What am I going to be doing?"

Julie said, "You're here to learn to be a puppy girl. You will be one of the girl pack. We all are, look." She pointed out her name and Sylvia's names on lockers.

I had read about pet play and some of the girls reasons they liked it. I thought, "For a half million, I'll try it."

Julie said, "Wait a moment. I'll put Sylvia's tack on her and she'll go into the yard with you."

I knelt an leaned on my stiff arms as Sylvia was transformed into a puppy girl too. When she was done she crawled to me and said, "Let's go, Cynthia. Follow me." She moved faster than I thought anyone could crawl on hands and knees to a half door in the wall next to the kennels. They were split down the middle and apparently spring loaded for she pushed them open with her head and they closed behind her. I followed as soon as I could get there and they opened easily to my push. Sylvia was just outside the doors. We were in a large grassy yard with several shade trees.

She explained how some of this worked. She said, "We're in a girl pack. Master doesn't want us idle so we work around the estate. It has over a thousand acres inside a tall brick and steel wall. It keeps all sorts of predators and snoops out. There are lots of guards and sensors all over the wall and inside. If you ever need help just scream You'll be amazed at the number of big, armed guards that show up in just a minute."

I asked, "How does a girl pack work in the estate?"

"Simple things. We pull carts for the gardeners and the foresters. Weed the vegetable and flower gardens. Water the plants in the greenhouses. Paint fences. Things like that. There's always someone in charge of each project who guides us. But its not all work. We have a lot of free time to talk and play. There' an exercise session every day for an hour or so followed by training sometimes. All of this is to keep us in good shape for the hunts. They happen every couple of weeks."

"Hunt? What's that.?

The guests hunt us. Its great fun. We get a head start and they hunt us with dogs and horses. The guests usually work in teams. The team gets to use the girls they catch that night. Its wicked good fun. The teams keep a running score. The fastest capture gets the most points. At the end of the year there's a big party and the winning team gets a big prize. Usually a lot of money plus use of all the girls they caught that year for a weekend."

"Sounds barbaric. You sound like its fun. You like being hunted like an animal?"

"Yeah," she said, "Doesn't sound too good when you say it like that. But it is fun. Its exciting and you're competing against all the other girls to be the cleverest and fastest and best sport . Did I say that the girl who takes the longest to be caught gets her name on a plaque as one of the best and she gets a dish of ice cream and she gets to sleep with Master for three nights. Its the best prize ever and we fight like cats for the honor. You know by now that being taken by the Master is the best prize ever."

I did know that. It sounded exciting even if it was the most demeaning sporting event ever conceived. The prizes sounded worth working for. I asked, "Seeing how we're fixed, do the men use us very often?"

She looked dreamy, "Yes, a lot. Master often takes a girl to bed. The staff often does too. The staff can have us any night they want. Some of the staff are married and the couple can take us. Heck, all of the pack are available until lights out at ten. Guests can have us for the night. The staff takes us to their rooms and locks a long chain on our necks to ensure we don't wander and the guests don't take us with them. You can play with anyone who wants to play back. You can even force yourself on a girl if you can pull it off. Sometimes several girls will gang up on another girl who has goofed up and gotten us in trouble. The masters don't mind what we do as long as no one gets hurt physically."

"Sylvia, you said masters, plural. I thought there was only one Master."

"Sorry," she said, "that is sloppy of me. There is only one Master Robert. He owns and runs this place. He doesn't own any of the slaves now, but he could. Any of us not already enslaved to a master would gladly be his.. Any male or free female is a master or mistress to us. All the slaves have owners, most of those here work for Master Robert. You're not one yet. But we have to obey every free person, man or woman. There are only a couple of free women on the estate. They work for Master. More come for the hunts. You are really a potential slave and need to learn the etiquette and protocol of submission. You will be punished just like us if you are disobedient or break a rule."

"I don't know any rules yet," I said.

She said, there are really only a few. Always address a free person as Master or Mistress. Always obey a free person. Always verbally acknowledge an order. You can't use any of the furniture. You cannot speak without permission. You can ask permission to speak but if its denied, shut up. If you protest a punishment it doubles. Whenever a free person enters a room or where you're working, stop what you're doing, face them and kneel. OK, that's all of them. That's enough talking for now. I'm supposed to show you the ropes. Follow what I do." She started crawling toward the nearest shade tree. I followed her and watched how she moved. It got easier the farther we went. She circled around the yards twice and stopped. Then she straightened her legs and got up on hands and feet. There was no way to walk on these boots, but this worked. I awkwardly followed her as she easily sped away from me. This too became easier as I practiced. It was kind of like falling across the lawn. After a lap it was much easier and faster than crawling. I could see how I could learn to actually run this way.

Sylvia stopped and lay down on her side. I tried to lay flat on my stomach but it squished my breasts so I tried so sit cross-legged, but my tail was uncomfortably pushed into me. Eventually I lay on my side like Sylvia. I asked her, "How can we pull carts like this?

She replied, We have different tack for pulling things. We have normal boots and harnesses we use to pull carts and carriages. Yours is in your locker. When we go back in we get to take off the boots and other gear and put it up. We have to wear ankle chains inside. We get our daily assignments from Mr. Alistair or Ms. Johansen in the morning after breakfast. Then we put on the right gear and the people we are working for come get us. Gardeners, foresters, etc. They help us with the things we need where we're going, like bug spray, chaps, sun protection, hand tools.

A man and a clothed woman came into the yard and looked around. They saw us and called, "Sylvia, Cynthia. Here girls."

We scrambled up and got to our hands and feet. She hissed at me, "Don't speak if you can answer with a shake or nod, No human speech. Wag your tail as if you're glad to see them. Smile." I followed Sylvia over as fast as I could on hands and feet. She knelt facing the pair and I followed. I remembered to wag my tail. God, this was demeaning, yet I felt so expectant, so ready to please. I was acting like a happy puppy. There may be a lot to be said for a wagging tail as a mood enhancer.

Mr. Alistair said, "I'm going to order you into a pose. Sylvia knows them and she'll assume the pose. Cynthia, watch Sylvia and copy the pose. Understand?"

I watched Sylvia and she nodded her head and barked, tail wagging. I did the same. When in Rome...

"Stand." Sylvia got up on her hands and knees, tail wagging. I followed.

"Belly." Flat on the ground, arms straight out in front, tail wagging.

"Lay." Roll over, lay flat on back, spread legs open, arms at our sides, hands by our shoulders, palms up.

"Beg." Kneel, hands at our shoulders, palms forward open mouth, tongue out, back arched, breasts out, wag tail.

"Down." Kneel, legs wide, hands on thighs, palms up, body erect, back arched, breasts out, mouths open, tongue out, tail wagging.

"Punishment." Hands straight out in front, head and breasts on the ground, ass high in the air, legs spread wide.

Mr. Alistair said to Ms. Johansen, "Cynthia picked up on all the poses quickly. Let's try her on a leash. Ms. Johansen took two short leashes and clipped them onto the backs of our collars. Mr. Alistair said, "Heel." Sylvia crawled on all fours to his side and assumed the 'Down' pose. I did the same on his other side. I felt him take hold of my leash.

He said, "Walk to heel." He started walking forward. I shifted forward to all fours and crawled beside him. My head was inches from his leg and I watched carefully so I could follow his turns. He walked at a pace I could match on all fours. He walked around the yard then turned and went around it in the other direction. Then he made smaller radius turns and circled the shade trees. I realized I was having fun. It was a great game trying to stay in the right position. I was feeling excited and expectant and happy to be mindlessly playing this game.

He led us back to Ms. Johansen too soon. I wanted to play some more. He stopped and said, "Down. We knelt. He walked a couple of feet away and turned to look at us. I was beaming and my tail was wagging so hard it whapped against my ass cheeks at every wag. He asked us, "Good girls. Would you like to play some more?"

I wagged even harder, nodded yes emphatically and barked three times. Sylvia was almost as enthusiastic. Honestly I felt so good that he had been happy with us.

He said, "Let's play fetch." Ms. Johansen took our leases off and handed him a wooden stick a foot long with tooth marks in the middle. She had one too. They turned toward the open yard and threw the sticks . He said, "Fetch, girls."

I jumped to paws and feet and ran as fast as I could toward one of the sticks. Sylvia was faster and got to hers seconds before I reached mine. I knew she had more practice than me but I promised myself I'd improve. I put my paws on each side of the stick and lowered my mouth around it. As I closed my teeth on it I realized that demeaning didn't matter anymore. I was just so happy to be running and doing what made my master happy. The joy of obedience and submission flooded through me and I almost dropped the stick. I held on and ran back to them. I put my head close to Ms. Johansen and dropped the stick into her hand when she reached for it. She said, "Good girl, Cynthia." I felt tears of joy trickling down my cheeks. This was so good. I think I was high on my own endorphins.

They threw the sticks for us four more times. We were both sweating when they stopped us. We were sitting on our haunches, ready to go again when Ms. Johansen put the sticks back in her bag, She said, "Cynthia, stand."

I jumped to all fours and she walked to me. She ran her hands over my warm body. Her cool hands were welcome. She said, "Cynthia runs well for being brand new and her buttocks and legs are muscular. I don't see an ounce of fat anywhere but her breasts, which are quite nice too."

Mr. Alistair said, "Very good work girls. I agree. I think you will do very well in the hunt, Cynthia. Tonight I want both of you for my bed. Ms. Johansen will bring you to me tonight. Now go play." He and Ms. Johansen walked away.

I asked Sylvia, "Have you been taken by Mr. Alistair before?"

She gushed, "Oh, yes. He's a wonderful lover. When he uses you, you its like you've gone to heaven. I can't wait. I wonder if Ms. Johansen will let us get pretty tonight. I want this to be special for him."

I had been given several truly memorable orgasms last night. I wondered if Mr. Alistair could top that, but I hoped so.

Mr. Alistair, Ms. Johansen. and Master Robert entered the yard and called Sylvia and I over to them. We ran over on all fours and knelt in front of them. I remembered to keep my tail wagging.

Mr. Alistair said, "Cynthia, you look fit. Have you been exercising?"

I barked once for "Yes."

He said, "You look fit. How often do you exercise?"

I had to speak. This was not a yes/no question. I said, "I worked out at a gym three days a week and I run nearly every morning for three to five miles."

He said, "Good. You will continue that program here. Are you a fast runner or just jog?"

"I start out fast and after a mile or so I slow down, Sir."

He said to Ms. Johansen, "Let's take them to the track and time them."

Ms. Johansen replied, "Yes, Sir. I have their shoes here. Girls, Lay and raise your feet."

We lay back and raised our legs. She took off our boots and put running shoes on us. I was surprised to see she had my shoes from my apartment.

Master Robert must have understood my expression. He said, "You signed a power of attorney form when you started. We closed out your apartment and put most of your things in storage. We brought a few personal items you could use here."

Ms. Johansen finished our shoes and said, "Girls, Stand."

We sprang up into standing display. She put a mesh exercise bra on each of us. I was grateful to have some support for my breasts. These provided better support than the best I had found. We followed the three of them out a locked gate. I had not been here before. It was an oval running track with a high railing on both sides. There were some things in the middle I didn't recognize. The track was marked off into lanes with staggered starting points. Ms. Johansen took us onto the track, led us through some stretches, and positioned us on the innermost starting lines. Mr. Alistair said, "Both of you run an easy warm up lap. Go."

Sylvia and I ran easily together. It felt good to stretch my legs. I was warm when we finished the lap and ready for a real run. Ms. Johansen put us on the starting lines again and I got ready to jump. Mr. Alistair said, "Go." and we started sprinting. Sylvia was faster than I had expected but I slowly closed the gap between us. I overtook her in the middle of the second turn but she sped up and we crossed the finish in a dead heat. We slowed and stopped. She put her arms around me and I did the same. She said, "You're fast, girl."

I said, "You're no slouch, either."

She put her lips on mine and we kissed. It might have turned into something heavy but Ms. Johansen said, "Save that for later, girls," and led us back to the rail close to the two men. They were looking at a computer tablet. Mr. Alistair said, "They ran well. Sylvia ran very close to her record and Cynthia matched her. I think we have another Gazelle."

Master Robert agreed, "I was sure she was built for speed as well as looks." He looked at me and smiled.

I blushed and said, "Thank you, Master."

Ms. Johansen removed our exercise bras and said, "Lay. Feet up."

She put our boots back on us and we followed them back into the yard. Mr. Alistair locked the gate and told us to go play. Ms. Johansen said she'd put our running shoes in our lockers.

Girls started coming out through the same door we had used. There seemed to be an endless supply. They came singly, in pairs and threesomes. They all were slim and healthy, like race horses. They moved quickly and smoothly, like Sylvia. They were sleek and their hair was cut a little shorter than shoulder length. Long enough to wave in the breeze and allow the girl to show expression with it, but not long enough to be a bother when she' s working. There were girls with all sorts of skin tones and hair color. I noticed that all of their loins were bare. They must shave their bushes regularly. Mine was the only one visible. Every one was lovely. None had any makeup on that I saw and they didn't need it.

A bell rang and Sylvia said, "That's dinner, come on." She trotted over to a white stripe on the grass. I had seen it but forgot to ask about it. Sylvia sat on he haunches a few feet away and waited. When I stopped beside her she said. "When they rollout the numbers, go wait a few feet back from twenty nine, that's yours, so they can lay your meal out. Don't go close to the food until they give the OK."

Two stainless steel serving carts were rolled out onto the grass by two clothed women, maybe five years older than me. They stretched out a wide cloth strip on the white stripe. Every three feet or so there was a number. even on the other side and odd on the side closest to Sylvia and I. She was almost perfectly placed in front of number eleven. I scampered down to twenty nine. The smell of food wafting from the carts made me ravenous. I watched impatiently as the women set bowls of food and water and desert on the cloth. I guess "No furniture" included "No utensils." I was the last one, number twenty nine. All the girls were lined up, kneeling in "Down" position. All of us were watching the women. Finally, one said, "Eat."

We all moved closer and bent our heads to the bowls. It was rice and beans with bits of chicken and vegetables. A stir fry. The desert was rice pudding, Delicious. When I finished, I sat up and looked around. The others that had finished were in "Down" position, waiting for something. Either an OK to leave or maybe just until everyone had finished. I waited to see what happened next.

After the last girl had straightened up, one of the women said, "You're excused." All of the girls left their bowls. Some went off by themselves, some formed wandering packs, Most found a spot close to a few others and knelt or lay together. I went back to Sylvia to find out everything I could.

I asked, "Are we like, free for anyone to use us?"

"Yep," she said. "There's nearly twice as many staff as there are girls. Most of us get taken three times a week. Its not exactly every other day 'cause some of the staff have favorites. You're new so you'll get used every day. Everyone will want to try you out. Don't worry, you'll have a ball. The men and women who use us are trained before they see us. They are excellent lovers. The ones you need to watch are the guests, especially when they've been drinking."

I looked at the yard full of girls and asked, "Are all of these girls employees, like me?"

She said, "Most are. I only know of a couple who didn't volunteer because of the money. Quinn, the one with the bright orange hair by the plum tree. She chose to be here instead of facing jail. She was caught trying to steal a car. She's only been here for a couple of months. Let's see, Patty has brown hair and is sitting against the far wall with the two blonds. She chose to come here and to be her husband's slave afterwards. She was having an affair with her gardener and was caught. She was poor and married into a wealthy family. She signed a pre-nup and would lose everything if he divorced her. I've heard rumors about a couple of others, but I don't remember who. Any girl with a metal collar has volunteered to be a slave, like me. I don't get paid money anymore. For us the pack is daycare and fitness spa while our masters are working their jobs. At night they take us home and the rest of you stay in the kennels or with a guest."

"What happens to slaves who get too old or infirm to go on a hunt?"

"Same as for slaves who decide to leave. Manumission. Their slavery is revoked. They are freed. They become employees again or they can retire. Off on the other side of the estate, outside this fence, there is a retirement home. All the employees are entitled to free care if and when they want it. When your year's up you'll get a tour before you decide if you want to be a slave. I had mine last week."

"You mean even slaves can leave"

"Yep. Even when you're a slave, you can decide to leave whenever you want. You're an employee now. You are getting paid. I'm a slave. I don't earn money. What I get is retirement credit. If I stay for twenty years I can retire and I'll get a pension worth $100K a year in today's money adjusted for inflation."

I thought it over. "So, a nice retirement, living here, room and board and exercise are what you're getting for being a sex toy for everyone."

""Yeah," she said, "You'll get more and better sex here than you ever imagined. Its a good deal for someone like me who'd be bored to tears and depressed all the time if I had to tend to two whining kids and spend all my time driving them to activities. I'm excited and active all the time here."

Boy, I had a lot to sift through. I had always heard of the terrors and cruelty of slavery. This was pretty benign. I'd have to lose my freedom, but they'd pay me well for it. Another thought occurred to me. I asked, With all this naked female flesh around, do they play with each other?"

Sylvia looked at me and said, slyly, "Why, Cynthia, we play all the time. Remember what we did before eating?"

She was playing with me! "You know what I mean. Do the girls have sex with each other?"

She sat up and looked around. She said, Look at the Ornamental Plum shade tree on the north side of the yard."

I saw the tree. "OK?"

"See the girls under it?"

I focused under the tree and said, "Yes...Oh My God. Right out in the open?"

"Cynthia, Forget all the cultural no-nos. Here we are all sex toys. For each other too. Its really the best way to get to know someone. The thing to remember is that we have no responsibilities to each other. Only to our masters and only to give pleasure, show respect, and obey. Sex games with each other is encouraged, the girls will love you, and they want you to love them.

"Have you ever made love to a girl, Cynthia?"

"Nooo," I said, " I've heard about and read some, but I never did."

Sylvia said, "You don't know what you've missed. You'll get plenty of opportunity here. LAY."

I lay back, put my hands by my shoulders, and she rolled over onto me and put her pussy in my face and her face in mine. I was pinned under her. "Not in public," I protested."

She said, "No one cares. Just sniff me. Learn my scent.' I felt her mouth kissing my nether lips. "You smell sweet, Cynthia." Her warm breath tickled my inner recesses.

I inhaled her aroma. She smelled like the best sex in the world. I had never tasted a girl before. I tentatively stuck my tongue on her dry sex lips. Nothing but faintly salty skin, but her scent was heady. I felt her tongue licking my nether lips. I felt my nipples get hard and my labia lips grow hot.

She said, "Just lick my pussy lips gently."

"No," I said hastily. "I need to work up to it." I was getting more aroused now. I wanted more. I licked her lips softly, bottom to top, one side then the other. I could taste her juices now. Her nectar was sweet and salty. I hoped mine was as tasty.

Soon I was licking hard, wanting more and she was pushing me closer to the edge. I heard a moan and couldn't tell whether it was me or her. It didn't matter. I was so close to coming I should have moaned. In a moment we both came nearly at the same time. By now our moans were continuous an we screamed together. When we had recovered she rolled off of me and we got applause and cheers from the girls who had gathered to watch us.

I looked around me in surprise. and blushed when I saw how many girls had watched us. There were calls of, "Way to go." and ""I'm next." and, "I want the one on the bottom/top."

Sylvia said, "Enough. Now you've seen how it should be done. The rest of you go practice." They dispersed with some ribald cheers.

"Now, that wasn't so bad, was it? Remember all of us are free for any of the staff or guests to use. Women too. If you don't give anyone using you a good time, you'll be punished."

This was a revelation. Previously I had been a little revolted at the thought of eating pussy. But now I wanted more. Did all girls taste like her? I would wonder now every time I saw a girl's cunt. I would look forward to tasting her and I wanted them to eat me. Why didn't girls talk about this more. It was good clean fun our bodies were designed for and there was no problem with unwanted pregnancies, either. I could have as many women lovers as I wanted and here they were abundant and friendly. I said, "Not bad at all."

Chapter 4

Anal Training

Ms. Johansen collected us just before lights out and took us to the bath. She washed out our insides and lubed our asses. She reinstalled our tails. She clipped our wrists behind us and put leashes on our collars. She led us out of the kennel area and into what I guessed were staff quarters. She knocked on a door and Mr. Alistair called, "Enter."

She opened the door and led us into a nice, spacious living room. He took our leashes from Ms. Johansen and said, "Thank you, Christina. I'll take them back in the morning."

She said, "You're welcome, Mr. Alistair," and left.

He led us into another room, slightly smaller and I saw several items of furniture obviously designed to hold girls where he wanted them. He dropped my leash and said, "Stand, Cynthia."

I adjusted my pose and watched him put Sylvia in place. He strapped her legs to the feet of a tall "X" shaped item attached to a wall. He unlocked her hands and strapped them to the uprights. He said, "Struggle. Try to get loose." I watched the muscles in her arms and legs bulge as she pulled and tugged each limb, to no avail. He came back to me and picked up my leash. He led me to Sylvia and said, "Kneel in front of Sylvia. Get as close as you can."

I saw what he was doing and I was helpless to stop it. I knelt and scooted closer until my breasts were touching her thighs. He passed my leash between her legs and pulled it tight so my nose was buried in her crotch. He fastened the leash in place and I couldn't move my nose away.

He said, "You must give a good experience to all who use you. I understand you are inexperienced in loving woman.

Remember you don't have to like what you're doing. The one using you must have a great time or you will be punished. Sylvia is your client now. She will tell you what she wants and you must obey. Is that clear?"

I said "Yes, Master." My voice was muffled by the flesh surrounding my mouth, but I guess he heard me.

He said, "OK, Sylvia. Instruct your pupil."

She said, "Start licking my outer lips. One side, then the other."

Her scent filled my nostrils with a musky note. I stuck out my tongue and tentatively ran it up one side and down the other. I repeated this a couple of times.

Sylvia said, "Start lower down and go up higher. Run your tongue from bottom to top on both sides."

I obeyed and she said, "Good. Now speed up. And stroke harder."

I worked faster and harder. I started to feel moisture on her outer lips and tasted her essence. I was less musky and sweeter. I heard her moan softly and I knew I was succeeding.

She gasped, "Now. Push. In. Me. All. The. Way."

I hesitated. This was too much. I didn't want to be inside her. I felt a searing pain on my bottom. I couldn't move my head at all so only my body jumped.

"Mr. Alistair said, "Deeper, Cynthia."

I felt another harsh blow on my ass. I shoved my tongue inside her and found more moisture. I licked all around in her love canal and her moans crescendoed. My face was getting wet with her dew. This wasn't so bad. She tasted good and was moaning continuously. She was pumping her cunt up and down as far as she could go. Her excitement was starting to affect me. I could feel my loins getting hotter and a great itch forming in my pussy.

He said, now suck, Cynthia, get all her love juices. Suck her clit into your mouth. Nibble on it. Tickle it with your tongue."

I sucked her clit into my mouth and I felt Mr. Alistair's fingers in my pussy. It was wonderful. I nibbled her clit and she came with a scream of pleasure. My climax was right behind her and we both relaxed together. When I was recovered he released my collar from the cross and I adjusted my pose into a proper kneel.

Sylvia said, "Thank you. See what I mean?"

I said, "I never knew. Thank you Mr. Alistair and Thank you, Sylvia."

He released Sylvia from the cross and clipped her hands behind her. Then he put me in her place and strapped me tight. He said, "You need to experience the other end now. Sylvia, make her come. She scooted up and put her nose in my cunt. It felt great right from the start. Needles to say, I was already warmed up and she drove me over the moon with her experienced tongue in less than a minute. I moaned and gasped and screamed just like she had. It was a mind-blowing experience. Why hadn't anyone told me how good it could be. I don't know if he helped her to a second orgasm or not. My eyes were clamped shut and I don't think I would have noticed the second coming anyway.

He released me, picked up my leash, and led me to a low trestle. He strapped my legs to the legs on one end, so I was spread wide. He lay me on the top. There were cutouts for my breasts, closer to the end than I would have thought. My ass stuck out over the end a foot or so. My waist was right on the end. He put a strap across my locked arms at my waist and another cross my back, about even with my breasts. My chin rested on the other end of the table. I could lift my head but that was all.

He moved my tail from side to side and I felt the now familiar movement in my ass. He said, "I understand you are unfamiliar with sex in your bottom. Is this correct?"

I said, "That is correct, Master."

I'm going to remove and insert your tail. I want you to relax your muscles as I do both of these actions. I tried to relax. I felt him pull on the tail. My muscle was gripping the narrow part and I felt him slowly pulling and twisting the tail. My muscle relaxed enough to allow the big end to pass and it left me out with a wet, plopping sound. He immediately pushed it back in. I tried to relax and I think I did. He cycled it in and out of me several more times and I managed to relax a lot more.

Then I felt his finger slide into me. I yelped and jumped a little. He said, "That's just my finger, Cynthia. Feel it slide around and rub you inside."

He didn't have to tell me that. I felt every mover he made. I was uncomfortable and my muscles were clenched tight, trying to expel him. Of course that didn't work.

He said, "I can feel how tight you are. If a guest felt this, you'd be punished for refusing service. Don't think about who is using you or how they're using you. Think only about what you are doing. You need to learn to exercise conscious control over your muscles. Relax your muscles. Relax every muscle in your body. Accept everything."

I managed to relax into the table.

He said, That's good. I feel you relaxing. Now tense just your bottom. Squeeze my finger."

That part was easy.

"Good. Now relax."

Better. Keep tensing and relaxing. Control what your body is doing."

I kept exercising, Open. Close...

After a dozen or so, he said, "Good. Tighten up on me. I'm going to remove and insert my finger. I want you to be relaxed and welcoming when you feel me at your opening. Tighten up once I'm well inside you. Make me feel like you don't want me to leave. I'm the best thing you've ever felt. Smile while I'm in you. Feel disappointed after I've left."

I smiled and tightened up on him. He slowly pulled his finger out. When I felt him leave, I worked on disappointed. Then when I felt him outside me, I relaxed and he entered me again. I smiled and tightened up. He left, no smile. He repeated this exercise five times. The next time I felt outside and relaxed, his cock slipped easily into me. I could easily tell the difference because his rigid cock was much bigger than his finger. Nonetheless, he slipped inside with little effort. I tightened up and he gave me a good ride. His hands grasped my dangling breasts and tweaked my nipples as he slid in and out. I felt the heat rise in my belly again. I was getting aroused. One of his hands slid to my pussy and his fingers slid into my wet lips easily. His fingers went in and out in time with his cock in my ass. I was going to come again. I felt him stiffen and his hot sperm flooded into me. His burst threw me over the edge and I came nearly simultaneously with him.

I slowly recovered and he was still in me, smaller, but still a presence. I realized he was a welcome presence too. I never would have had that last orgasm without him. And now I looked forward to my next "Bottom Sex." My God. In my ass. I couldn't believe it. All these pleasures my body was capable of giving me and they had been hidden from me all my life. If my mother had been still alive I would have kicked her ass. No more. I was going to enjoy everything my body had to offer from now on. I was still strapped down tight and gripping Mr. Alistair tightly. He pulled out of me and said, "Excellent work, Cynthia. How do you feel about a person using your bottom now?"

"I liked that a lot, Master. I understand what I should do and how I should feel. I'm going to have to work on dissociating the act from my user though. It still is very personal. That bit about smiling was good advice. It really helped."

He left the room for a moment. When he returned he took Sylvia out and was gone a few minutes. He came back alone and unstrapped me from the table. He led me into the bath and unlocked my hands, He undressed and took me into the shower and we cleaned off. I got aroused again as he cleaned my breasts and pussy. His fingers were magic. He got stiff again as I cleaned him. He was only a few years older than I and in good shape too. We dried off and he lubed my ass and pussy, "Just in case," he said. I think he already knew I'd need it. He locked my hands behind me again and sat on the edge of the bed. He turned me over his lap and put a leg over mine to hold me in place. With one hand he lifted my hands and with the other he gave me six slaps on my ass. Three on each cheek. The first two hurt and I squeaked. The last four just fanned the fires in my belly the first two had ignited. I was on fire. He let me up and said, "Kneel. Service me."

I jumped into place and slid my mouth around his already rampant cock. I licked and sucked for a few moments before he said, "Enough." He threw me on the bed and I spread my legs wide. He mounted me and threw my legs back over my head while he thrust into me. He wrapped his arms around my legs, pinning them back and leaving his hands free to control me. The lube wasn't necessary. I was sopping wet from the spanking and oral sex. He pumped me up and I orgasmed. He gave me no chance to savor it. He kept pumping and I felt the flame in my belly start up again. One of his hands was fondling my breasts roughly while his other had grasped my neck, above the collar. His furious onslaught was shoving me to the brink of another orgasm. I loved his powerful body taking control of me. I felt like his slave already. I loved the feeling of helplessness and submission. He exploded in me. His hot spend flooded my cavity and threw me over the edge into my next orgasm. I screamed as he grunted and we both went still for a moment as our bodies enjoyed a shared pleasure.

He let my legs down and stayed in me. "Do you want to clean up again," he asked?

"No, Master. I want to lay here with you in me and just enjoy the feeling. I have a wet spot under me and I know its both yours and mine. I want it to dry around me so I can smell us all night. I'd like to shower again in the morning, if that's OK."

"Of course. You deserve all the pleasure I can give you.."

He pulled out and rolled over. He got out of bed and locked a chain on my ankle. "To keep you from wandering," he said.

I didn't mind. I wasn't going anywhere and I was practicing to be a slave, wasn't I? I slept the contented sleep of the well fucked girl.

In the morning He took me back to the kennels and I showered. But when I came out to get my paws and boots Ms Johansen stopped me. She clipped my hands behind me and put a leash on my collar. She took me to a hallway that was bigger than most rooms. She had me kneel on one side and locked a long chain to the back of my collar. She released my hands and took off the leash. Above me on the wall was a sign. It said, "Cynthia is new and needs to practice her sexual servitude. Please use her freely." A six foot padded bench was against the wall behind me. There was a bucket of water and a waste pail with a lid beside it.

She said, "Just obey anyone who stops. You aren't allowed to use the furniture without orders." I saw there were a couple of folding screens standing against the wall. I guess some of my "Clients" might want privacy. More ominously, there was a riding crop hanging on a hook.

101

Beside the hook a box was mounted on the wall. Both were out of my reach. She left me there waiting for someone who might want some sex in the morning.

I didn't have to wait long. A sweet looking woman in her fifties, I guessed turned into the hall, saw me and came over. She glanced at the sign and said "Good morning, Cynthia."

I replied, Good morning, Mistress." She walked over to the box, looked in and took out a lock and a small square metal something on a chain. She locked my hands to the back of my collar and said, "Look up."

I tilted my head back and she stuck the thing up to my nose. It was a clamp. It fit around the bottom of my septum and she tightened it until it was snug and wouldn't fall off unless my skin tore. She sat on the bench, spread her legs, pulled me around to kneel between her legs, and lifted her skirt. "Service me, Cynthia."

I knew what to do. She pulled my nose into her crotch with the chain to my nose. I opened my mouth and licked and sucked like I had been taught by Sylvia. When the woman started moaning I took her clit in my mouth and nibbled gently. She was a quiet one. Her moans got a little louder and she kind of gasped/chuckled as she came. I,

102

unfortunately, wasn't sufficiently aroused to even moan. Still, I felt pride in a job well done. She pushed me away and wiped my face with a hanky she had moistened in the water bucket.

She said, "Very satisfactory for a new girl, Cynthia. Thank you." She unlocked my hands, dropped the key and lock back in the box, and left. She left the clamp in my nose, likely intentionally for the convenience of my next client. I crossed my hands behind my back and waited.

Several more people passed by and looked at me, but nothing else. Then two young, large men entered the hall and stopped in front of me. One asked, "How new?"

I replied, "This is my second day, Master."

He asked, "Have you been trained in oral sex?"

I said, "Only with a woman, Master."

"A real woman loves to suck cock. Are you a real woman?"

I replied, "I would love to suck yours Master."

He strode up to me and pulled out his cock. It was big and already semi-rigid. He took the chain from my nose in his hand and gently pulled me toward him. I don't know if I would have wanted to do this two days ago, but now it was the most natural thing in the world. I knew just what to do. It was almost like the inverse of Sylvia. I opened my mouth and licked his tip. It was already moist with his juice. It was salty and thick. I put my mouth around his tip and sucked and licked. He grew larger and I had to strain to get him in. Then he was in all the way and thrusting against the back of my throat. I was so full of him. Then I heard a grunt from him and knew he was about to come. I wondered if I could swallow it all. Then he spasmed and my mouth was full of his hot spend. I swallowed as fast as I could and I managed to only let a few drops escape my lips. He pulled out and said, "That was excellent, Cynthia."

His friend stepped up and said, "Out of the way, John. Its my turn."

John stepped aside and let go of my nose chain. The new man stepped in front of me and took hold of the nose chain. He said, "I hope you have room, Darling." Then he took out his cock. It was an identical experience, except that John had knelt behind me and roughly fondled my breasts as I blew his friend. It was distracting but I didn't get close to coming. After they left I rinsed my mouth out and spit it into the waste pail. They tasted good but it left a salty taste in my mouth.

I serviced a total of nine people, three women and six men before lunch. There was a rush and I had a line waiting to use me, New meat, I guess. I serviced ten people at lunch, then things slowed down again. Only twelve more until dinner time. In all I gave orgasms to ten women and twenty one men. I got ten orgasms myself. OK its official. I am a slut.

Ms. Johansen came and got me about five and took me back to the kennel. I got to shower, wash my hair, put on a little make up. She helped me get my tack on and it was just about dinner time when I got in the yard.

I saw Sylvia and trotted to her. She asked, "How was it?"

I said, "Lots of sex. I enjoyed it and I think my partners did too. But I'm tired now. It takes a lot out of you. I had thirty one partners and got ten orgasms myself. I guess I'm experienced now. I'm certainly a slut."

She laughed, "We all are, Cynthia. Want to do it again?"

"Not tomorrow. I need to recuperate. And I think only ten a day is adequate."

Chapter 5

Work

It was my first full day in the pack. After we had put our bedding away and eaten breakfast, Mr. Alistair lined us up and gave out assignments. I was in a small group of three girls assigned to help the garden crew. We were told to put on light cart harnesses with our tack. and to assemble at the garden carts. I just followed my group. We helped each other get dressed. Boots first then a wide belt with oversize rings sticking our on the sides. A thick layer of sun screen all over. Sun hats then our paws. Ms. Johansen helped with the paws since once they were on our hands were mostly useless. She locked our hands behind us and let us out in the garden. I followed the other two to a sort of small garage for garden carts. A gardener was waiting for us and he fastened the carts to our harnesses. The carts were just boxes on two bicycle wheels with two poles sticking out that were run through our harness rings and strapped in place.

The gardener copped a couple of feels while he was hooking us up. He was a good looking guy so we all flirted with him. Harmless fun and maybe he'd ask for us in the evening. He led us to the area where the weeding crew was working. They all had sun hats, boots, and plain work gloves on their hands. I saw Sylvia in the weeding crew and she waved to me. Their wrist cuffs were linked with six inches of chain and the ankles by twelve inches. They had orange plastic spades and hand rakes. They were linked into three strings of four girls by about five feet of chain between their collars.

I didn't see any physical reason for their chains. The whole estate was enclosed and patrolled. Why would a girl run away. All she had to do was say she wanted out and she'd be out. It had to be psychological. To make all of them feel the submission and loss of freedom. Unless, maybe I hadn't been told the whole story. Maybe there were different kinds of slaves, some less voluntary than others?

The gardener supervised everyone. Each girl had a couple of white five gallon buckets. They would pull weeds and drop them in a bucket. When a bucket was full they would put it on one of our carts. When my cart was full I would pull it to a compost pile. A single girl whose collar was locked to a large tree close by dumped the buckets and put the empties back on the cart. When I had all the empties, I'd pull them back to the weeding crew. The gardener would give me a drink of water when I came back from the dump.

The gardener stopped us in the early afternoon. We took our carts back, were disconnected and put back in the kennel. Ms. Johansen unlocked our hands, took the sun hats, and put us in the yard. I got a drink and sat under a shade tree. We had some free time until dinner. Sylvia came into the yard with the other members of the weeding crew. She was later arriving because it took a few minutes to remove all their chains and they got to shower.

I asked her, "Sylvia, are there any girls here who can't just leave when they want? I was wondering because of all the chains they put on your crew."

She was slow to answer and finally said, 'I've wondered about that too. Our ankles are always chained on a work crew. Sometimes our hands too. But there are a couple of girls who always have their ankles chained. I've asked them if they know why and they always say they like it and asked for them. Maybe that's true. I've never seen them treated any differently. Don't turn your head, but look over in the middle of the long wall, just to the right of the fountain. There are two girls sitting and talking. They are always chained and they hang out together most of the time. The raven haired one is called Jasmine and the red-haired one is Nylla. They don't talk much to the rest of us, as far as I know."

I asked, "Can I go talk to them?"

"Sure. I've never been told not to or anything like that."

"Want to come?"

"OK."

We got up and went to the two girls. We knelt in front of them and I said, "Hi. I'm Cynthia. I'm new here and I wondered why you two are the only ones with chained ankles?"

The black haired girl said, "I'm Jasmine and my friend is Nylla. I guess someone thinks we might try and escape."

"I'm confused. I was told that all anyone of has to do is say we want out and we'll be released. Isn't that true for you too?"

Nylla said, "That's true. We could do that. We asked for our feet to be chained. We like them that way."

I was surprised. What girl would want her feet chained? I said, "Why in the world?"

Jasmine replied, "When we first came here it was a revelation for me. I had always dreamed of being the slave of a powerful man. This is the closest I could come to that. I want to feel my submission as much as possible. It arouses me. Every step I take makes me hot. I find I'm more intensely alive when I'm completely controlled. Sometimes they take the chain off because I need my feet free for a job. Its terrible. I quite literally get depressed when I'm free. OK. I know how it sounds. Nylla and I are just natural slaves. Girls like you are involved with slavery. Its a financial lark, a game for which you're paid. We're committed. We'd do anything to stay slaves. The money is irrelevant to our hearts."

Nylla said, "Jasmine said it best. We're natural slaves and the more we're restrained the happier we are. These trinkets on our feet don't stop us from doing anything but run and we would never run anyway. We get just as much sex as you do and I bet we enjoy it more. We get the full joy of submission while you, as you said, can always leave. Try it yourself. Ask Mr. Alistair if you can try it for a week. I'll be interested what you think afterwards."

I was intrigued. I was training to be a slave and I was having fun. It was like a vacation from responsibility with a load of sex thrown in. Would I feel the "joy of submission" as she called it, if my feet were chained, or something else?

It sounded no crazier than what I was doing now. I looked at Sylvia and said, "You're a full slave now and I'm just an employee. This is intriguing to me. Would you consider a week with chained ankles with me? You're my best friend and I'd like a friend on this ride."

Sylvia said, "Why not. I'm in this for the long haul and like Nylla said, a chain on my ankles won't stop me from doing anything I'm doing now. Sure. sign me up. A week only, at first."

I stood up and said, It was nice to meet you and you've given me a lot to think about besides my feet. Sylvia and I'll go see if we can get our chains too. Either way, we'll come talk to you again."

Sylvia stood and we trotted to the kennel door. We knelt and barked until Ms. Johansen let us in. She let us use human speech and laughed at our request, "Been talking to our 'Natural Slaves' I see. Sure. Turn around and I'll put the chains on you. Come back in a week and tell me if you want to keep them." A couple of clicks later and we were hobbled. We crawled back outside and played with our chains like they were new toys. We could still run on all fours, but our steps were shorter. Other than that we didn't find any difference.

There was a psychological impact, just like Justine had said. I felt more subjugated. There wasn't a Master holding my leash and making me obey. This was more subtle. It just felt right for me, who wanted to learn to enjoy being a slave. Sure I could leave. But now my feet were controlled by something outside of me. In a very real sense, it was just jewelry. A lot of women's adornments are in the form of chains. Necklaces, bracelets, anklets, belts. A lot of this was functional to fit any shape, but a big part was not. It was symbolic of women being possessed by men. There was a joy from wearing chains. I wiggled my feet and watched the chain shimmy and glint in the light. I had asked for this so it was jewelry. I liked the way it flowed and changed with my steps. It was a beautiful accent as well as everything else. I also realized that was a load of rationalization horseshit. It was a further abdication of responsibility. I was even less in control of myself. Whoever held the keys to my chains had taken responsibility from me. Of course I would be humiliated if a free woman saw how helpless I was. But I was already naked, I couldn't stand up, and I had a puppy tail in my ass. Ok, I couldn't be much more humiliated.

Sylvia looked at me and said, "You know you have a stupid grin on your face?"

I realized I was happy and retorted, "Well, you do too, puppy girl."

She said, "Girls are silly. I like this feeling. I hope it lasts."

I spent the rest of the day playing and talking with Sylvia, Jasmine and Nylla. Despite our attire and circumstances, it felt like we were young girls again. The world had just opened up a new country for our exploration and wonder. We were all giggling and wondering at flowers and ourselves. I had never had such un understanding of my own sex organs and where my nerves were. We spent hours examining each others pussies and touching each other. It seemed that I had awakened my senses since I had come here. The world was a much different place now than a week ago.

At night the slaves would be returned to their masters. The new girls, like me were locked in our kennels.. Tonight, however, after everyone else had been locked in, Ms. Johansen locked my hands behind me and put a leash on my collar. She took me to Master Robert's quarters and handed my leash to him.

He said, "I wanted more time with you."

"Thank you, Master. I need to understand you if I'm going to be your personal assistant."

"Right. Tonight we're going to learn about our reactions to each other. Mr. Alistair tells me you've had your anal training and enjoyed it. He also said you were a very pleasurable companion. I'm going to try you and you me." He led me down a short hall to another room fitted with many devices for bondage games. He took me to a weird stationary bicycle. There was a seat and pedals under it. No wheels. The pedals drove a reciprocating horizontal shaft behind the seat. Instead of handlebars it had a pillory sized for a girl's neck and wrists. He took the ankle chain off and unlocked my hands. He lifted me up and lowered me onto the seat. I put my feet on the pedals. "Put your wrists and neck in the grooves."

I had to bend over to put my parts into place. He lowered the bar and I heard it lock into place. The wood was snug on my wrists and loose on my neck. I felt him insert a phallus into my pussy. It was a rather large one and actually felt very natural. He removed my tail with a wet plop. I felt his fingers grease my bottom hole. He stood behind me, grasped my pendulant breasts, and said, "Pedal."

I started pedaling and was startled to feel the dildo in my pussy start moving. The pedals caused it to ram into me then retract. It was very realistic feeling and my pussy started getting wet. My body didn't care if it was real or not. It just knew I needed lubrication. After a few cycles I felt Master's stiff member probe my bottom hole. I remembered Mr. Alistair's lessons and relaxed my sphincter muscle. He slid in without too much effort. I tightened up when he started to withdraw. Mr. Alistair had schooled me well. I managed to make my "Squeeze - Relax" match his in and out. Meanwhile I was keeping the pedals turning at a steady and quite pleasant rate. My arousal steadily grew until I had a wonderful orgasm. I stopped pedaling but Master kept up his rhythm. When I recovered I realized I was close to coming again. I started pedaling again, but I went over the top before I had made ten revolutions. Still he kept on. Another orgasm a minute later. Finally he came and filled me to the brim. And I blew again. After a while I felt him leave me alone, still locked to the bike. I recovered and realized I still had the means for more orgasms. I started pedaling and felt my arousal growing. I pedaled myself into yet another orgasm. He took me off the bike and into the shower. He scrubbed me all over and I did him. He locked my hands behind me and put the chain back on my ankles.

We lay in bed and looked at each other. He said, "Goodnight, gorgeous." It was so incongruous. I was helplessly chained, lying bed with a hunk of a billionaire and he said goodnight like we were an old married couple. I just smiled.

He said, "I've found I love seeing your smile, it brightens my day every time." I blushed and my smile broadened. Sleep vanished from both our minds and we made sweet passionate love again. It didn't matter that I was chained. They were his chains. I slept through the night. He took me in the morning before getting up, making sure I orgasmed too. Ms. Johansen took me back to the kennels for exercise and breakfast.

Today I was put on the weeding crew. There were several large gardens and we were a handy source of labor to maintain them. I think Mr. Alistair was rotating us around so we got to get experience with all the jobs and overseers. So today, more sun protection, barefoot, work gloves instead of paws, and chains. I was chained to three other girls by my neck and my wrists were joined by a short chain. My ankles still wore the chain I had asked for. Jasmine was in this crew on another coffle.

The coffles were in adjacent rows. There were grass strips between each row so we knelt on the grass and removed weeds from either side of us. When we finished everything we could reach, the gardener looked over our work and if it was adequate he moved us on to the next twenty foot section. I pulled weeds and dropped them in a bucket. When the bucket was full the gardener put it on a cart and gave me an empty one. When the cart was full he would send the cart girl to the compost pile. We had water bottles the gardener would replace if needed. We all had our puppy tails in place so no solid waste was allowed. If we needed to pee we just moved to the side away from where we knelt, squatted and watered the grass.

We had short breaks every hour and we worked until about 2 pm. When we were done the gardener took us back to the shed where we put our tools away. He took us back to the kennel area and Ms. Johansen took our chains off and sent us to clean up. I appreciated the shower. I had been sweating in the sun for hours and didn't smell good.

We were put back in the yard to wait for dinner. I wanted to meet some of the other girls so I went to several and introduced myself. Every girl asked about my ankle chain. I always gave the same answer, "I asked for it. I like the way it feels and I think it looks good on me. What do you think?"

They usually showed surprise at first, then admitted it looked good on me. A couple asked it I thought it would look good on them. My answer, of course, was enthusiastic, "Of course, It would accentuate your slender ankles," or, "It would go with your skin tone," etc. I always meant it too.

One thing I noticed was that most of the girls wore earrings and had one or more tattoos. I knew we women decorated our bodies to make ourselves more attractive. I put on makeup and had my hair styled, and bought expensive shoes because they made me feel better. I guess that was because I thought they made me more attractive. I had considered a discrete tattoo of course and even experimented with temporary tattoos. Never took the plunge into tattoos or body piercings. Except earrings, of

118

course. I wondered why I hadn't got rings like Julie. I thought she was beautiful with them. I wonder if I could get some here. I'd have to ask Julie where she got hers.

One girl had a phoenix covering most of her back. It was gorgeous on her. It must have hurt for a long time. But now any pain was gone and she was very happy she got it.

I wondered if Master would let me get one?

I tired of meeting new people and wandered over to Sylvia, Jasmine, and Nylla. They were discussing the finer points of orgasm control and how delaying made it better. I listened to their techniques and finally said, "I could never delay an orgasm. I'm totally out of the loop when I get close. I just whimper and watch it blossom in me. How can you do anything when every nerve in your body is screaming 'Now. Now. Do it now?'"

Nylla grinned and said, "The trick is to start thinking about it as soon as you feel the heat rising. I do something physical my user won't notice, like cross my toes and tell myself I won't come until I uncross my toes. Doesn't always work, of course, but when it does, the fireworks are spectacular."

Sylvia agreed, "I do something similar. I clench my fists and don't let go until I'm bursting with need. Then when I can't wait any longer, I slowly open one fist and keep the other clenched. I open my hands one finger at a time and I don't start on the second one until all my fingers are wide open. Like Nylla, it only works sometimes. If he or she's gotten me warm enough before the main act, I just fling both hands open and other times he comes in me first and that triggers my orgasm."

Jasmine said, coyly, "Every orgasm is my best one yet."

We finished dinner when Ms. Johansen called to me, "Cynthia, come here." I trotted to her and knelt, keeping my tail wagging vigorously.

Chapter 6

Rachel

She said, One of the guests has asked for you. Come inside and I'll get you ready."

Someone asked for me by name? I wondered how they picked me. I wasn't well known outside of the staff. How did a guest know me? Was it a recommendation from one of the staff people who had me yesterday? I was dying to know but wasn't sure if I would get punished for asking. I knew the general rule was slave girls don't ask questions, they just obey. Maybe I could ask the guest. I bet he wouldn't mind if I was a little curious after he fucked me.

Ms. Johansen took off my paws then I took off my boots and I put them in my locker and showered. After I dried my hair and put on a little makeup and lipstick, Ms Johansen locked my hands behind me, put a leash on my collar, and led me into the guest wing. She stopped in front of a door and knocked. A woman opened the door and looked me up and down with a smile. She said, "Yes, Cynthia is quite lovely. I'll take her."

The woman was small and cute. Her hair was dark and pixy cut. She was slim and dressed in expensive clothes. Her expression was not the happiness of having a living sex toy delivered to your door. It was more like seeing your plan come together.

Ms. Johansen handed her my leash and said, "Just ring the kennel when you're done with her and I'll come pick her up."

The woman led me inside and said, "I'm Rachel, but you have to call me Mistress."

I said, "Yes, Mistress. I am yours tonight. I hope I will please you. May I ask why you chose me. I'm new here and I've never served a guest before."

She said, I saw your picture in the catalog and recognized you." She waved to a large format book open on a coffee table. She led me to it and I saw two glossy letter sized photos of me. One was a head shot and the other was of me naked and chained.

I said, "Recognized me? I don't believe we've ever met."

She said, no, but I've seen your picture. When you were dating my husband Allen Swartz."

Oh shit. This is the Allen's wife who found out about me. She'll kill me. I said, "Pease, He told me he was divorced."

She tied my leash to a wall ring. The knot was close to my neck so I had to stand facing the wall. She said, "I'll be right back. Don't go away. Don't worry. I know it was Allen's fault."

 I wondered if Allen was there too or if it was just her. She came back and untied my leash. She had taken off everything but a slip. She had a great figure and face. She could have been one of us easily. She held up one of the nose clips I had worn yesterday. I groaned inwardly, but I kept the smile on my face. She asked, "Know what this is?"

I said, "Yes, Mistress. Its a clip for my nose."

She asked, "Have you worn one before?"

"Yes, Mistress. Just yesterday."

"OK," she said, "hold still while I adjust it." She slipped it onto my septum and tightened it until it was at least as tight as yesterday. I squeaked at the last turn. She said, OK." and put the tool down. She took my leash off my collar and clipped it onto the end of the short chain dangling from the nose clip. She tested it by jerking down on the leash. I fell to my knees instantly and her hand was still high and the leash jerked my nose up painfully. Tears formed in my eyes.

She asked, "You will obey me, won't you?"

I choked out , "Yes, Mistress."

She said, "Crawl to the chair. She walked in front of me and pulled on my nose leash. I crawled as fast as I could. She reached the chair, sat down and pulled up her slip. The pull on my nose was relentless until it was firmly planted in her pussy.

She said, "Start licking my pussy lips. Both sides."

Her scent filled my nostrils with a musky note. I stuck out my tongue and licked up one side and then the other. I repeated this a couple of times.

She said, "I have always been small and very submissive. For once in my life I am in control and you have to do everything I say. Isn't that right?"

I could only mumble with her smothering my mouth. "Yes, Mistress."

Were you always submissive, Cynthia?"

"No, Mistress."

"How does it feel to be so helpless?"

"Wonderful, Mistress." I wondered where she was going with this. I wanted to give her an orgasm and hoped for one myself. Talking was not the way.

She said, "Lower and longer, slut."

I obeyed and she said, "Good. Faster and harder."

I worked faster and harder. I started to feel moisture on her outer lips and tasted her essence. I was less musky and sweeter. I heard her moan softly and I knew I was succeeding.

She gasped, "Now. Deeper."

I pushed inside her labia lips. I felt a searing pain on my bottom. I couldn't move my head at all so only my body jumped.

"She said, "Deeper, slut."

I felt another harsh blow on my ass. I shoved my tongue inside her and found more moisture. I licked all around in her love canal and her moans crescendoed. My face was getting wet with her dew. This wasn't so bad. She tasted good and was moaning continuously. She was pumping her cunt up and down. Her excitement was starting to affect me. I could feel my loins getting hotter and an itch forming in my pussy.

She said, now suck my clit. Nibble on it."

I sucked her clit into my mouth. I nibbled her clit and she came with a scream of pleasure, but her grasp on my leash didn't relent at all. I was pulled tight into her so I could hardly breathe and her juices washed over my face.

She finally recovered and loosened her grip on my nose. She stood up and said, "Stand up slut."

I stood and she led me to a bench just like Mr. Alistair had me on the night before last. I guess they are useful for everyone who wants to use a girl. She bent me over the bench and shoved my breasts in the holes. I felt the strap go over my arms and back and pulled tight. My ankles were still chained so she just pulled my knees apart and strapped them in place.

She said, "I found out you were screwing several of the men at the firm besides my husband. How did it start?"

"I graduated from college and applied for a job at your husband's firm I was offered a job and it came with an apartment they owned that they subsidized for new hires who couldn't afford to live in the city. After I moved in I found out it was really owned by several executives and I was supposed to keep it clean and disappear if they wanted to use it for a couple of hours. Pretty soon I was who they wanted to entertain. They told me they all were single or divorced. I liked them all and it seemed harmless."

"So, " she said, "you were taken in but when you found out, you decided you liked it."

"Yes, I guess so. I was poor and they gave me nice things and took me to places I couldn't afford. They were all good to me. I didn't see any harm since none of them were married."

She said, "I don't believe you didn't suspect some were married. Any man will lie to get a pretty woman in bed. You're not that naive."

It was true I had suspected a couple were married, but I was never sure. I said, "I never suspected Allen was married. He just didn't act like it. I'm sorry."

A line of fire erupted on my taut, exposed ass. The sound of the sharp crack followed close on the pain. I screamed at the pain. It was the worst thing I had ever felt. I had been wounded. I could feel the burst skin on my bottom. She was cutting me to pieces. I pleaded, "Please, Mistress, not so hard. You're hurting me. Please stop."

She said, Count them and thank me for each one. I'm going to give you ten. If you don't count and thank me, I'll start over."

Ten. Oh No, I can't stand the pain. Ten will kill me. But if I don't obey, I'll get hit more. Shit. I focused through the pain and said, "One. Thank you Mistress."

128

She hit me again, so hard. It felt like she was flaying me alive. I screamed loud. I hoped someone would hear me and save me. I faintly heard her through my uncontrolled sobbing, "Count or I start over, bitch." She was so angry.

I had to count or this would go on forever. "T...Two, M..M...Mistress. Thank you. "

She hit me over and over. I think I passed out. I heard her say, "Too bad you didn't count. I have to start over"

Then there were more voices in the room. Men's voices. Someone took me off the bench and I was put on something flat. Everything went black.

I was just getting the bitch to feel the pain she had caused me when the door opened and men rushed at me. Two of them grabbed me and took my cane away. They were strangely silent. They forced my arms behind me and another cuffed my hands together. I yelled at them, "What are you doing. She's mine tonight. I get to beat the bitch for what she did to me."

They ignored me and didn't say a word. They released her from the whipping bench and put her on a gurney. One pushed her out of the room. Two of them grabbed my arms and took me out too. "Where are we going. Let me go. I'm a guest here. My husband is Allen Swartz. He'll have your jobs when he finds out what you're doing to me. At least let me get dressed."

There was no response.

They took me to a stark room like they show on TV when the police are interrogating someone. There was a table and four chairs. The table had a short chain laying on it. They moved my hands in front and cuffed them there. They sat me in a chair and locked the chain on the table to my cuffs. I lifted my hands and found the other end of the chain was fastened to the table. The table didn't move when I pushed on it. I pulled and twisted the cuffs to no avail. I was going to stay here until someone unlocked me. I swore at the men and once again demanded release.

No response. They just walked out of the room. Shit.

They left me alone for a long time. I cursed and swore they would pay for this. I saw two cameras in the corners of the room, at the ceiling. I knew they were watching me.

I sat still for a while. There had to be some way out of these damned cuffs. I inspected them. They were snug on my wrists. I couldn't slip them. I yanked and made my wrists sore and drew a drop of blood from my lacerated skin.

After a while I stood up and tried to move the table. It was solidly attached to the floor.

I yelled some more. Eventually I sat back down in the chair. I yelled I needed water. One of the men came in and gave me a water bottle. I drank it and was soon sorry. I needed to pee.

I yelled, "I need to use the restroom."

No response.

It got urgent. I yelled some more.]

No response.

Finally, I went around the table, hiked up my slip and peed on one of the other chairs. "Sorry," I said. "I really needed to go."

The door opened and, without a word, a man came in and moved all he chairs I hadn't peed on over to a wall, out of my reach. The only chair left for me was the one wet with my pee.

More time passed. Finally, My husband and a big man I didn't know entered. They took two of the chairs and sat across from me. The stranger lay a briefcase on the table. Allen looked angry and resigned. The stranger's face was neutral. Allen said, "Hello, Rachel."

was angry and scared, I said, angrily, "I've been handcuffed here for hours. Where have you been?"

"Trying to keep you out of jail, Rachel."

I was really scared now. I said, "I was told I could spank her. She entered my room voluntarily. What's the problem?"

The stranger took a tablet computer out of his case and touched the screen a few times then he held it for me to see the screen. It lit up with a view of me hitting Cynthia with a cane. I saw the bleeding slash it made on her ass. She was fastened down and helpless. She was screaming and pleading with me to stop. I hit her again. It was pretty bad. I felt rotten now. The stranger stopped the video. He said, "Two counts of assault with a deadly weapon. Unlawful imprisonment. Three felonies. Witnesses plus the video. Cynthia is an employee and is free to press charges. If the police become involved you face a lengthy prison sentence. Allen and I met with a colleague who is a former prosecutor. You are virtually assured of being convicted and put away for many years. Would you be interested in a less severe alternative?"

I could have killed myself right then. I was guilty and many people knew it. I asked, "What alternative?"

Allen said, "If Cynthia agrees not to press charges right now, you will become my slave and undergo a year of training here. When your training is over you will come home and live as my slave. I will take you in public as a slave. You will tell everyone who asks that you want to be a slave."

I didn't believe him. I said, "You're kidding. You would never do that."

He said, "I don't have a choice. I agreed to keep you as a slave because it was the only way Robert would agree to not call the police. If you don't agree then I can't help you. Robert has the power to break me and you if we don't fulfill this agreement. If you agree, I will keep you in chains and treat you as a slave from now on. Don't think you can get out of the agreement once you're home."

I shrank back from him. "But Allen, why would you do this. I was a good wife. Can't we go back to that?"

The stranger chuckled. "Rachel, because of what you did to Cynthia, you're getting a new chance to be Allen's lover as well as his wife. You drove him to seek outside affection and blamed Cynthia when he did. This place will show you how to regain and keep his love. If you don't accept, you'll be locked up for many years and lose him forever. Do you accept?"

My mind was awhirl. All because I recognized her in the catalog. "Can I have some time to think it over?"

He said, "I'll give you an hour. We'll be back then to see what you want."

Both men stood up and left the room. One of the guards came back in and removed my handcuffs. He left and closed the door. I was sure he locked it.

I thought about the choices. I had decided in ten minutes. I thought about how Cynthia had looked when I took her into the room. She was like the statue of Venus. She was smiling and beautiful. She was naked and chained. She was compliant and malleable. She gave me a wonderful orgasm and let me fasten her to the bench. She was a perfect sex toy, eager to please and give pleasure. If I had been male, she would likely have been rewarded with her own pleasure. I spent the rest of the hour trying to find a reason to change my mind. What would it be like to be her? To offer yourself to give sexual pleasure to others? To be always displayed for others to look at and desire? She looked happy while I was full of bile. I wanted to be as happy and carefree as her. Its got to feel better than I've felt for the past few years.

Robert and Allen went to Robert's office in back of the Pub. "I'm really sorry about Cynthia, Bob," Allen said, "Rachel can be intense, but I've never known her to be mean or violent. I've never seen that part of her before."

"Cynthia will be OK in a few days. Nothing was broken. What do you want to do with Rachel if she agrees to my condition."

Allen looked confused. "What do you mean. I thought she'd be just like all your other girls."

"Maybe, maybe not. Most of mine are volunteers who already know they're submissive and are familiar with the lifestyle. Rachel may be submissive, probably is, but may have never thought about it. She has pursed the urban dream. You know, find a husband, plan a family, be a housewife. Now she's faced with prison or being your slave. Either way she loses the housewife vision. As your slave she still has you but in a different situation. If she accepts my deal we'll enslave her. Teach her the positions, the reactions, how to give you pleasure. Obedience. Do you want her to be anything else?"

"I see," he said. "Rachel has always been a little cold to sex. She'll do her wifely duty at night, in the missionary position, but that's all. Is it possible to make her really need sex all the time, or at least learn to behave that way. I have a lot more need for sex than she has."

Robert said, "Yes, that's possible, but you need to help by learning how to manipulate her body. We can give you a quick course. Probably only take less than an hour since we have the instructors and the girls to practice with. If you're sure, I can get it going now, before we go back to Rachel."

"Yes. I definitely want her vibrating with need all the time. Let's get started."

"OK." Robert picked up the desk phone and called a number. He explained what he wanted and hung up. He stood up. "Let's go to the training room and get you started."

When the men came back, they stood in the doorway and looked at me. I had removed my clothes after I decided. I was already kneeling in front of the door. I bowed my head. I said, "Allen, I would like to be your slave. I want to give you great pleasure and have you display me to others that I may show them how proud I am to be your property. Please enslave me, Master."

Allen said, "I accept you as my slave, Rachel. You will stay here for a year of training. I will visit you and you will write letters to your friends and relatives which I will review. Think of a story that will keep them happy for a year. Remember at the end of the year you will become a publicly revealed slave. There is some preparation for you and I will see you tonight. Obey them." He turned and left.

The stranger left and then the two men who brought me lifted me up, cuffed my hands behind me, put irons on my ankles, and took me out of the room. They took me into a long room and walked me up to what looked like a barber's chair and put me in it.

A smiling woman walked up and said, "Honey, I'm Suzanne. I'm going to do your piercings and put your rings in. You can't be moving around or I might make a mistake.

Suzanne was young, just a year or two older than me. She had a slim build, red hair and nice breasts. She looked friendly. and, curse her, she was fully clothed.

She walked behind the chair and I felt a leather strap buckled around my upper left arm. Then the right. Then the straps tightened and my arms were pulled back hard. I was now attached to the chair. Suzanne then used another strap to bind my head to the chair. Finally, I felt her putting more straps around my thighs. She pulled until my knees were spread as wide apart as my shackles allowed.

I asked, "Suzanne. Is this going to hurt?"

"A little. I do it every day to girls who want exotic piercings. Some of them yell a little, but its over real quick. I'm going to do your nipples first, so I need to get them to stand up."

I was actually pleased to get nipple rings. I had wanted them since I first saw them on a model. They looked so erotic. I had hinted to Allen I would like some, but never followed through. She put a hand on each of my breasts and started rubbing my nipples. It felt pretty good, then she said, "My, that was quick."

She painted an orange liquid on both nipples then she pushed a big needle through my left nipple. It hurt a little,

138

but not near as bad as I expected. She picked up a big ring from a tray and used it to push the needle back out and then the ring was the only thing in my nipple. It was open and she used a large pair of pliers to squeeze it shut. I heard a sharp click as it closed. Now it was a solid gold ring. In my nipple. Heavy.

She did the same for my right nipple. Then she put a pair of rings in my labia lips. One in the left and one in the right. They looked identical to my nipple rings. The labia didn't hurt at all. I wanted to see them. I thought she was done and all I seen were glimpses around Suzanne's hands.

Then Suzanne told me, "just one more to do. This one is a little different because I'm going to put a grommet in first."

"A grommet, what's that for?"

"It lines the hole where the ring goes. Makes it stronger and the ring won't bind on your skin."

"OK, but where else can you put it?"

"In your nose, honey. It will look great there."

I was not happy about having a ring in my nose. I know it was becoming more popular. I had even seen ads for nose jewelry from big name designers. Still, I felt uncomfortable. "Suzanne do you have to put it there?"

"Honey, that's where I was told to put it. If you don't want it, I was told to ask you if you want out?"

"Oh, No. I don't want out. Go ahead."

"Good," Suzanne said, and brushed some of the orange liquid inside my nose with a q-tip. My nose got numb and she stuck a big metal thing in my face. Big parts stuck in my nose, then there was a snap sound and pain erupted in my head. It was much worse than my nipples. I thought I had been shot. I screamed and she pulled the thing away from my face. I saw my blood on it and felt faint. I couldn't move. She brushed some more stuff in my nose that stung. She stuck something else up my nose and moved it around. Everything she did hurt. Then I felt pressure squeezing in the middle of my nose. I felt a click and she took the things out of my nose. I still felt the pressure. She inserted another gold ring, threaded the end link of a light chain on one half, and squeezed it together with large pliers. Another click. Then I was left alone with my pain, another heavy ring, and a four foot length of light chain dangling from my nose.

She released the strap holding my head. I shook my head and felt the heavy ring and the end of the chain swing back and forth like the clapper in a bell. I wanted to see myself so much. "Can I use a mirror?"

"Just a minute Honey. Let me get these straps lose and you can look in the mirror on the wall to your right." She took all the straps off me and I sat up. I felt all the new metal moving in my most sensitive areas. I stood, shakily. I was still shackled and all the new movement in my body made me unbalanced. Suzanne took hold of my upper arm and let the chain leash dangle. She steered me toward the wall. I was grateful for her help. Then I saw my reflection in the mirror. It didn't look at all like me. I knew what I looked like. I was OK, I guess. But the girl in the mirror was gorgeous. Her rings shone in the light. Her breasts were high and firm with erect rosy nipples and pierced by those huge gold rings. She was the most sexy and erotic creature I had ever imagined. She wore her chains with distinction. Their graceful lines enhanced rather than shamed. I watched the creature in the reflection smile. I realized I was smiling. I could have stood there the rest of the day, but I was also impatient to be done.

I turned to Suzanne, "Suzanne, thank you for giving me these rings. They are beautiful. What's next?"

She took my arm, picked up my leash, and led me to the other end of the shop.

A middle aged man watched us approach. Suzanne said, "Mark, this is Rachel."

He looked me up and down, Appraisingly. He said, "Hello, Rachel. You're beautiful. You're going to get a complete set of irons. You'll look even more beautiful when I'm done."

I didn't know if I was expected to say anything, so I just said, "Thank you, Master."

He took the leash from Suzanne and locked me to a ring on his workbench.

He said, "Sit on that stool and lift your legs up here," pointing to the bench. He removed my leg cuffs and set them aside. He tried a couple of anklets on me until he found a set that fit. A chain, maybe fourteen inches long, joined them. They were rather elegant in their shining simplicity. They looked refined and stylish like a Scandinavian designer had made them for me.

In a short time, Mark had somehow made them secure on my ankles and he had me stand. They were snug, implacable, and elegant. I could see no joint, no lock , no hinge. They appeared to be a single, continuous band of metal. They were smooth, shiny, and there was no keyhole. I loved them. Yes, I could no longer run or kick, but I had not done that for ten years, anyway. They took nothing from me. They looked like unusual jewelry, but what they added was subjugation. Anyone who saw me would know I was not free. Well, I wasn't, for a year, at least. At best, who knew.

In a little while, I was chained and quite helpless. I wore a tall metal collar, and bands around my wrists and belly. The waist band was tight, like a corset. All the others were just snug. It had fixed staples in front and back holding steel rings. There were several more fasteners around its circumference, folded down, into the band. They could be stood up if my masters wanted to lock something there. I could detect no hinges, locks, or keyholes in any of my bands. They looked both elegant and permanent. Mark was an artist. He locked my wrists to the back of my waist band.

He released me from the bench and led me farther down the shop and through a door. It was a bedroom. He said, "Rachel, one of the perks of my job is that I get to play with all the girls I work on. Do you have any problem with being used by anyone who wants you?"

I had expected to be used freely by anyone. It was still a surprise to have it done. Up until mow it was academic, now its real and personal. I had read the rules. I knew I was now available for anyone. I better start enjoying it. I said, No, Master, may I service you or would you like to take me?"

He grinned, and said," Service me, Rachel. Let me help you since your hands are 'tied up.'" He opened his fly and took out his erect penis.

I looked at it in awe. It was long and thick. It would pose a challenge for me to take it all in, but I was determined to try. "Master" I said, you have a grand penis. I will try and do it justice." I started licking the tip, tasting the salty, sweet pre-cum. It was a good taste, so masculine and full of promise. I took the end in my mouth and sucked in several inches, preparing my mouth and throat for the whole thing. I moved my head in and out, going deeper each time. I felt it grow even larger. I wanted it in my belly. This was a waste. I wanted a climax from this artist.

I couldn't stop. I knew if I kept on like this, I would shortly receive his whole load, and I wanted it. My pussy was screaming in my brain, 'NO. I WANT IT.' I had never had this happen before. I kept on thrusting and sucking because I didn't want to stop. But I wanted to stop and have him fuck my pussy instead. I knew I could only have one, but I wanted both. Damn it. At last, he came. I managed to swallow it all. It was wonderful, but almost too much for me to handle. I wished again it was in my pussy, but there was nothing I could do. I was helpless, and heaven help me, I loved it. Was having my body locked up all it took? I had not felt this good since my wedding day. I could see whole new vistas of erotic use laid out before me. How could a few bits of metal suddenly make sex joyful again?

I licked him clean, swallowing it all. He wiped my nose for me. I was crying and he said, "Was it bad?"

I sobbed again, and said, "Oh, No, Master. It was wonderful. I loved giving you pleasure. I am just so happy. I am glad you put such beautiful metal on me and made me so helpless. I hope you can fuck me hard some day."

"I hope so, too, Rachel," he said.

He took me back out to the shop and gave my leash to Suzanne.

Suzanne and said, "You are mine now, Rachel," and taking hold of my chain, led me to the back of the shop.

She took me to a small apartment at the end of the shop. I could see a kitchen, bath, and bedroom off the main room.

She led me to a couch and used the chain from my collar to lock my ankles to a couch leg. She said, "Kneel there," pointing to a spot.

I knelt and she lifted her skirt up. She was not wearing anything under the skirt and was shaved. She had a tattoo in a minimalist style of a Cheshire cat's face right above her slit. It was very erotic.

Suzanne took hold of my nose leash and pulled me to her loins. She smelled clean and fresh. She put her finger through my ring. Boy, did I feel helpless. I loved it. She held the ring right up against her skin, just above her slit. Just like I had done with Cynthia. I started licking her lips. I am experienced with bringing a woman to climax. I am small and have always been willing to follow others. I used to worry about being so submissive, but I realized it was what I am. I realized during high school that I was a natural slave. I identified with all the subjugated women I read about in history and novels. I couldn't imagine a better life than belonging to a strong master or mistress. I knew myself well and soon the other girls in my classes learned too. I was always ordered to do dirty, demeaning tasks and I loved doing them. Oh, I didn't like the work itself. That stank. But I wanted so much to hear, "Good Girl," that I would obey any command.

That was the story of my life after school, too. I wanted to be used, ordered, commanded. I looked good and was attracted to take charge men like Allen. He knew what he wanted and I loved following him. Things got rough for us when he wanted to set up a threesome with other women. It wasn't that I didn't enjoy other women. My school days were filled with other women making me eat their cats. I was afraid he would find someone he liked better than me. I was afraid of invidious comparisons. I loved being taken any way, but I was a fucking expert with oral sex, anal sex, complete helplessness. I would come soon and often. All my partners loved my heat. Of course I did too.

I started slow with her, just licking her labia lips. Soon she began moaning and I sped up. I felt her lips becoming engorged and starting to spread apart for me. I sped up a little more and thrust my tongue between the lips. I tasted her love juices. I loved that taste. Like sweet, thin honey. I started sucking and her moans turned to gasps. When I thought she was ready, I took her hard nub into my mouth and sucked hard. She exploded, flooding my mouth with her love juices and screaming. I sucked in everything I could, thinking I was going to gain weight this way. As she relaxed, I stopped licking and sucking. I used my tongue as best I could to clean up around me. Suzanne still held my nose ring against her body so I was trapped. I waited until she pushed my head upright. She now held my nose leash clasped in her hand.

She said, "Rachel, you are amazing. I don't want to see you go. I hope your master lets me use you again."

Chapter 7

Assignments

I woke laying on my stomach. My hands were free and someone was rubbing a cold cream on my bottom. I heard Ms. Johansen say, "You have some beautiful marks on your bottom, Cynthia. You'll be fine in a few days. You can get up if you want, but don't sit or lay on your bottom today."

"Yes, Mistress. What..."

She stopped me with a finger on my lips and said, "Master Robert will be in to see you in a few minutes. He'll answer your questions." I heard her walk away and a door close.

My ass still burned, but it was much reduced. I was afraid to move for fear I would make it worse. Finally I rolled carefully off the table and got to my feet. It wasn't so bad. I saw I was in what looked like an infirmary in a prison. I was in a cell with an exam table and a mirror. There was one just like it with a bed next to mine separated by a wall of bars. Both cells were separated from the rest of the room be a wall of bars with barred doors. There were Doctor's office type things around the walls in the rest of the room. I looked at my bottom in the mirror. Ugly. I had ugly red gashes across both cheeks, glistening with an ointment. The skin on both sides of the slashes was a glorious shade of purple fading to pink further away.

Master Robert entered leading a much changed Rachel. No longer elegant, she was naked and heavily chained. Master said, "Cynthia, Rachel has agreed to become a slave as penance for her unconscionable behavior. Her period of punishment is two weeks. After that she will be a pack member and stay here for her training. Rachel, apologize to Cynthia." He locked her in the cell next to mine and left the room.

She stood there and looked at me. I looked back, angry. I said, "Come here." She walked up to the bars. I reached through and took hold of her nose leash and pulled her face to the bars. "What did you hit me with?"

She said in a very soft voice, "A cane, Mistress."

"Because I made love to your husband?"

"Yes...No, Mistress."

"Which is it?"

"No, Mistress."

"Well, why did you light into me so hard?"

"Mistress, I was angry but now I realize I was angry with myself. You were just ..available for my anger. I know it is my fault he was looking for other companionship.. I am so sorry I hurt you."

Well, now what do I do? I asked, "Are you a submissive?"

She answered slowly, "Yes, Mistress, I am. I'm sorry."

"What for. Almost all women start out submissive. Nature designed us that way to find strong men. Why do you think women are smaller, weaker, slower, and less aggressive

151

than men? Its hard not to be submissive. Master Robert says you're a slave. Why aren't you kneeling? Don't you know I'm not a slave?"

She stammered, "M..Mistress. I thought all of the women here to be used were slaves. I didn't know. If you'll allow me, I will kneel."

I loosened my grip on her leash and allowed her to kneel. I said, "Some women come here of their own free will, Like me. I'm an employee. In a year I will decide if I want to stay permanently. If I do, I'll be a slave like you. Spread your legs as far apart as you can. Arch your back. Stick out your breasts, Hold your head high. Keep your eyes on the ground." I watched her adjust. "Wider, slave. Now stay there. That's your position unless told otherwise."

I tied her leash to the bars.

"Slaves don't speak without permission unless acknowledging an order. If you want to say something, ask permission to speak. If its denied, shut up. Do you know any slave positions?"

"No, Mistress. Except the one I'm in now."

"OK. Stand up. Like kneeling, everything else the same. Spread your knees wider."

I ran her through all the positions I knew. "OK. Kneel."

She knelt in good form and said, "Yes, Mistress."

Ms. Johansen entered the room and took Rachel out. She came back a few minutes later and came into my cell. She looked at my bottom, added a little more ointment, locked my hands behind me, and took me back and put me in my kennel. They let me sleep late in the morning and told me I was off the duty roster today. I was left in the yard with my paws and boots on. I was bored. I'd rather be working in the garden or something.

. . .

The attendant woman, Ms. Johansen, came and took me out of the infirmary. She said, "Your Master wants you to wait for him, Rachel." She untied my leash from the bars and led me out of the room and through several halls. I recognized it when we got to the guest wing. She took me into my old room. Allen wasn't there so she locked my leash to a wall ring. There was enough slack I could kneel and wait.

I wondered how he would treat me. He was always in charge at home. I wondered how much worse it could be? I was helplessly chained. He had never played bondage games before, now it was all I could do. It was so strange

153

kneeling there, helpless to do anything. I couldn't get a drink or do anything with clothes. I had nothing I could do. I could think of what I'd like to do, but that was useless. I couldn't tell Allen unless he asked. I was sure he'd already been coached on how to handle me. I was here for a year to learn I could only do what I was told. That's what slavery is all about. No choice, only obedience. I can do it. I have no choice, I must do it. It was my mantra now. "My duty is obedience. My duty is obedience..."

I heard a key in the lock. I started to get up and then I remembered. I adjusted my pose and stuck my breasts far out. Allen entered the room and looked at me. I lowered my forehead to the floor in submission. He walked over to me and said, "Kneel." I raised up into proper kneeling position. He looked at me and said, "Rachel, you're stunning. I've never seen you looking so erotic and tempting before."

I blushed and said, "Thank you, Master."

"Stand up."

I stood and he kissed me. I wanted to put my arms around him too, but they were lost to me right now. I opened my mouth to his tongue and accepted his control. When he broke the kiss he unlocked my leash from the wall ring. He unlocked my wrists too. He took off his coat and tie and handed them to me.

"Put these up."

I had never acted as his valet before. I guess it was a reasonable task for his new slave. I took them and said, "Yes, Master." He grinned at me and I went to the bedroom. I held his coat up and looked at it. I had made him go to a good men's store downtown to shop for this suit. He hated shopping. I had picked this suit out and it looked nice on him. His wide shoulders and athletic body made it impossible to get anything off the rack for him. How could I do this in the future looking like I did now. Well. I'd manage. That's what women had to do. I buried my face in the material, inhaling his scent. My nose ring was a discordant note. I loved him so much. I hadn't realized how much until I was faced with separation and prison. Husband or master, or both, I realized, I loved him.

I hung them up, threw my leash back over my shoulder, and went back to the living room. He had sat on the couch and was flipping through TV channels. I sat beside him and he said, "No, No. Slaves are not allowed to use the furniture. Kneel beside me."

I stared at him. No furniture?

He said, "They gave me this too." He pulled a small silver and black object from his shirt pocket. It looked like a miniature TV remote with six or seven buttons and a small LED screen. "Its your controller. If you need correction I can just push a button and you get punished. It does a few other things as well. Since you haven't gotten off the couch yet, I'll give you the lightest punishment."

I said, No, Master. I'll.." and then I got a powerful shock. It hurt and I jerked like a fish on a line. My hands flew to my neck. I screamed wordlessly. Then it stopped. I was still seeing stars. I slid off the couch and knelt in front of it. I said, "That really hurt, Master. Please don't do that lightly."

He smiled and said, It hurts but it won't harm you. That was the lightest setting of five. Five will knock you unconscious. Remember, no furniture. Come around here and kneel beside me."

"Yes, Master." I crawled around and knelt beside him. He pulled my leash back to my front and held the end of it loosely. He said, "Let this hang in front of you. I like the way it looks." He put his hand on my head and ruffled my hair. It was late and we didn't stay there long. He turned off the TV and we went to the bath. We brushed our teeth, he undressed, and we went to the bed. I hadn't noticed it before, but he pulled a chain out from under the bed and locked it to my ankle chain. He said, "Its long enough to reach the toilet if you need it tonight. He locked my hands behind me and pushed me back on the bed.

He shoved my feet up against my ass and pushed my knees wide open. He rubbed a finger down between my nether lips. It felt so good. Either he had improved or I was easier to please. I suspected the latter. I moaned and asked, "Please, Master. Take me, fuck me hard."

I saw his rigid cock between my spread legs as he knelt over me. He had pushed my feet up over my head and held them there. God, I didn't remember him being so big. He was erect and ready for me too. He put his member at my pussy and I closed my eyes. I wanted to feel everything. He stroked my pussy lips with the tip of his member and it drove me crazy with need. I begged him, "Please Master, take me now. I need you in me. My cunt was spasming hopelessly.

I wanted it in me so bad. I couldn't help staring at it as another moan of lust slipped from my lips..

He lunged forward, his weight fell onto my body, pinning me to the bed as his stiff cock impaled me. I felt his thick shaft split my lips apart and I nearly swooned as his ribbed penis slid into my hungry loins. My muscles clenched around his shaft, straining to keep him in me even as he withdrew for another thrust. Twice more he impaled me on his thick shaft and then I felt him explode in me, filling me with his hot spend. It was wonderful, but not enough. I hadn't orgasmed. I prayed he'd continue, but he didn't. He pulled out of me. "Please Master, keep going, fuck me more."

Again, I wished my hands were able to hold him. He lowered my legs to the bed and went to the bath and cleaned his member. I just lay there. Used but unsatisfied. I tried to ignore the aching need in my belly. I wondered if this was what he felt all the mornings I had refused him. I was careful not to move since any motion at all caused my chains to rattle. I wanted to cum so badly I hurt. I also felt such overwhelming love for him. He was my Master and he was strong. Stronger than I remembered. Was having me as his slave making him stronger than when I was just his wife? I felt submissive and wonderful despite my need. He was in charge and he would make damned sure I served him well. I knew I was owned, property. I lived only to serve him and I felt so alive, so excited. I was happy. My need forgotten in my zeal to please him, I felt tears of joy pooling in my eyes. I shook my head and felt them fly onto my cheeks.

He went into the bath and cleaned himself. He came out and got in bed, naked himself. He had always worn pajamas before. I guess now both of us were ready for sex whenever he wanted it. I'm his possession and my only job is to please him. Well, I've doe my duty, trying to ignore the terrible ache in her loins. I'm so frustrated I would rub myself off on a doorknob. I hope I'll be allowed to cum if I'm good. I held that prayer as his hands turned me on her side and fondled my breasts. His fingers slipped inside my new rings and took a good grip on my boobs.

It was hard sleeping in all this metal. I couldn't move without making a lot of noise and with my hands locked behind me I couldn't adjust the covers except a little with my mouth. I finally fell asleep an hour or so after Allen. I guess I should start thinking of him as "My Master" now. If I ever addressed him as Allen or Honey I'm sure he'd push that damned button and shock me. I couldn't blame him. He'd kept me out of jail and he'd have to spend more time handling his nearly helpless slave. I wondered what he had in mind when he said I'd be a "publicly revealed slave?" Would he take me naked and chained into bars and restaurants? Maybe just invite our friends over and show me in our house? I got a thrill thinking of my friends seeing me like this. Was I an unknown exhibitionist? Whatever he did, I'm sure I'd hate it. I might like part of it too? I knew I should be horrified, but I was relaxed. He would do whatever he wanted with me. He was my Master and I wanted to obey and please him. This submission was new to me and really quite pleasant. Nothing would ever be my responsibility again. It felt freer than I ever had before. No one else mattered to me save my Master.

In the morning he let me use the bathroom then he took me into the shower with him and cleaned me. He let me have my hands back so I could fix my hair and do some makeup. I heard him order room service breakfast. He made me answer the door and accept the breakfast cart, I set the table and served him breakfast then I knelt beside him and he fed me bites from his plate. I didn't get much food. I'm not sure if he wants me to lose weight or just wanted me more dependent on someone else for everything. When I was cleaning up he warned me that if I snuck any food from the leftovers I'd spend the rest of the day gagged. I was careful to stay away from the food.

When everything was clean he took me into the bedroom, locked my hands behind me, and had me sit in the middle of the side of the bed. He unlocked my ankle chain from my left anklet and let it dangle from my right foot. He brought some rope from the closet and tied a piece to the ring on both ankles. He tied my feet to the posts at the foot and head of the bed and tightened the ropes until my feet were spread so wide the tendons in my legs stood out. I was stretched very tight. I could feel moisture forming on my pussy lips.

Allen said, "You never let me have sex in the morning before, did you?"

I shook my head and softly said, "No Master."

"Do you know why?"

"I shook my head again, "I just didn't feel like it. Master, I'm sorry."

"It wasn't your fault. Women's sex hormones peak at night and are very low in the morning. Men's do the reverse, though they're still high at night. Lucky for me, what you want doesn't matter anymore, does it?"

"No, Master."

"Beg me to fuck you, Slave."

Suddenly I wanted him in me so bad. Was it my body responding to his command? Could that even be possible?

"Master, please fuck me. I need you so bad. Please Master, fuck your worthless slave. Let me give you pleasure."

"Very well done slave. I almost believe you want to be fucked."

"Master," I pleaded, "I do want you. I need you in me more than I ever have before. Your command made me need you. Oh, Please believe me Master. I do need to be fucked. Please. Please"

He ran a finger down inside my slit. It felt so good. I needed more. I moaned at his touch. It made me hotter

He held his moist finger up and examined it. "You are well lubricated, slave. Clean my finger."

He held his finger to my mouth.

"Yes, Master." I sucked it clean of my musk laden juices. I had never tasted myself before. I had assumed a woman's juices would be distasteful. I thought it was heavenly.

He stripped off his pants and shorts. His cock stood out stiffly, almost touching his belly. I wanted it so bad. My lust knew no bounds. I couldn't help staring at it.

He said, "But first..." I tore my gaze from his cock and saw he held a narrow cane in his hands.

The first blow hit my straining breasts and it stung but not enough. I needed more. I sad, "Harder, Master, Please, harder."

The next stroke was harder. He hit my open thigh and I almost came. The pain inflamed my lust, made it shiny and irresistible. "Again, Master, please"

But no, he dropped the cane and impaled me on his thick shaft and I nearly swooned as his ribbed penis slid into my hungry loins. My muscles clenched around his shaft, straining to keep him in me even as he withdrew for another thrust. Twice more he impaled me on his thick shaft and then I felt him explode in me, filling me with his hot spend. It was wonderful, but not enough. I hadn't orgasmed. I prayed he'd continue, but he didn't. He pulled out of me. "Please Master, just a little more."

He looked down at me and reminded me, "Rachel, slave, your only goal now is to please me. You have given me pleasure and succeeded in your goal. I won't need to punish you now, You've done well. It is not my goal to pleasure you, but to ensure you learn to be an excellent slave. If you continue your excellent performance, I may reward you. Later. Good job this morning." He leaned over and kissed me. It was hard and passionate and rather harsh. The kiss of a master to a slave. It was the only reward I was going to get. It was enough for now. I knew I would have to work harder to get more.

He went into the bath and cleaned himself. He came out and donned his dropped clothing. He smiled at me and left me tied to the bed. This is what I've been reduced to she thought bitterly. I'm a pet, his possession, being trained to salivate at his presence. Its working she thought, trying to ignore the terrible ache in her loins. I'm so frustrated I would rub myself off on a doorknob. Undoubtedly why I'm still tied. I'd much rather be caned than left feeling like this. But that was exactly what he wanted. I'm sure I'll be caned tonight, but maybe I'll be allowed to cum if I'm good. He thought I did well. I was a "Good girl." I held that thought until Ms. Johansen came and released me later.

She took me back to the kennels. A tag with the number 30 was put on my collar and I was locked into kennel number 30 with just a thin blanket to separate me from the concrete floor. I wondered how long I would be locked in here? I was left alone for a little while, then Ms. Johansen took me into the yard.

 Mr. Alistair was waiting , He asked, "Rachel, you look a little soft. Do you exercise any?"

"No, Master."

"OK. We will start you with some private exercises to get you up to the pack's level. If you don't work hard, you'll be punished." He held up a riding crop in one hand and a remote in the other. He motioned to Ms. Johansen who took off my ankle chain and unlocked my wrists. She wrapped my leash loosely around my neck and clipped the free end to my collar. She took the remote from Mr. Alistair and said, "Get on your knees. Pushup position. Start doing them and don't stop until you can't do any more.."

She exhausted me over and over using different muscles. When she finally stopped I could barely move. hen she took me to an oval racetrack with a high railing around both sides. She took me onto the track and said, "Do one lap as fast as you can.. Go"

I started running, but quickly tired and slowed to a jog at the first turn. I slowed to a fast walk at the second turn and was down to a normal walk when I got back to her.

"Well, that was pretty slow. Don't worry, I'll make you faster. Walk around the track until I stop you."

I walked as fast as I could. My legs started burning on the first lap. When I passed Ms. Johansen, she was sitting in a chair watching me. Damn her. I walked until I was

165

exhausted. Ms. Johansen stopped me and put the chains back on my ankles and locked my hands behind me. She unwound the leash from my neck and used it to lead me back to the kennels.

She said, You're to be punished for two weeks for how you treated Cynthia. Stand still." I froze.

. . .

Cynthia

I was alone in the yard when Master Robert entered it. I saw him immediately and watched him walk to me. I knelt properly and made sure I was wagging my tail vigorously. I really was glad to see him. When he got close I lowered my head to the ground and stretched my arms out toward him in obeisance.

He said, "Hi Cynthia, Kneel." and I did. I smiled as prettily as I could. He clipped a leash on my collar and led me out the back gate into the back lawn. He led me across the lawn and into the woods. The estate was vast. These woods had arts like a park with all the unsightly undergrowth tamed by the gardeners and the pet girl pack. We passed parts full of heavy stands of timber and dense undergrowth. He led me around and described the features . A couple of shallow ponds, a bridge over a stream. There were covered seating areas scattered throughout. As we walked further back the undergrowth took over with walking trails wandering through the woods. There were a couple of gravel roads used by heavy carts and security patrols. He took me close to the outer wall. It looked enormous. He told me it was twelve feet high and almost twenty miles long. As we got close he pointed out a white line on the ground. Beyond that all the vegetation up to the wall had been removed. He told me there were two things I needed to know about the wall. First was that I wasn't allowed to cross the white line. He said if I did I'd be shocked and he'd be notified. I could expect punishment if he was notified.

He said, "This is a demonstration." He led me closer to the line. When I was maybe ten feet away, my collar began to vibrate and buzz loudly. He stopped and said, "You're being warned away from the line. There are some other areas this will happen. Heed the warning and stop where you're heading." He led me closer. He stopped me just short of the line. He took a remote out of his pocket and did something with it. He said, "I've put your collar in demonstration mode. This reduces the shock to a very low level. Cross the line"

I cautiously advanced. When my head crossed over the line, the buzzing and vibration increased and I felt a mild shock. I stopped.

He said, "Keep going."

I did and the vibration, noise, and shock continued. I reached the end of my leash and knelt.

He said, "Come back now."

I got to all fours and returned. The shock ended and the buzzer quieted as I crossed the line. He led me away from the line until the warning stopped. He stopped and I knelt beside him.

He said, "The shock lasts as long as you're inside the line." He did something else with the remote. "I've turned off demonstration mode. Don't test it." He led me on into the trails.

After a while he said, These woods are large but they are quite safe. I don't mind spending funds on good security. Most of mine are hired from Israeli special operations forces. They are very skilled. Your collar does more than warn and correct you. It also has systems to protect you. It tells me where you are and some vital signs. If you ever need help just scream or yell and security will be with you in a minute. If you are needed to return to the house, it will vibrate in a pulsing pattern: on off on off. If you don't return in a minute you'll be picked up. I'm giving you the grand tour because these woods are the venue for our hunts and you'll be what we're hunting. Your job is to give the hunters a good run for their sport. I know you're fast, but speed alone won't let you escape capture. You need to be cunning. The hunters will ride horses and use dogs to track your scent. You'll have a fifteen minute head start, but they will be faster and you can't get out of the estate. You should talk to some of the experienced girls and find out how to double back and break a scent trail and there are several other tricks available." He looked at me and I nodded my head and barked to show I understood. He rubbed my head and said, "Good girl." I didn't consciously do it, but I felt my tail wag vigorously.

"Now," he continued, "I want you to help me do something different. The hunters are too good. They always catch all the girls. Everyone enjoys the hunt but its become too easy, too routine. I want you to get the girls to work together and find a way to make the hunters work harder for their reward. This is your first assignment as my personal assistant. I've pulled together some information on how tracking dogs work and I'll give you time to study it when you're with me."

I sat up straighter and looked questioningly at him, my tail wagging furiously. I wanted him to say more about that. He just smiled beatifically down at me. I whined piteously.

He laughed and said, "OK. Use human speech. What do you want?"

"Master, I asked shyly, "am I going to be spending more time with you?"

He laughed again, "Cynthia, you're my personal assistant. I expect you to be nearby at all times, ready to get me a paper, or have my clothes pressed, or get the President on the line. You will be chained to my desk or bed all the time. You're just undergoing a little training now. Are you ready to spend your nights chained to my bed?"

Well this didn't take a lot of thought. "Let's see. I may have to think about this...Yes. Take me to bed Master. Please." My tail was wagging all by itself.

He smiled, "Good choice. You'll still spend your days training and working on my project for a while. I'll have Alistair bring you to me instead of your kennel tonight. Oh also think of what we should do with Rachel."

"Yes, Master. Thank you , Master."

He said, "OK, no more human speech."

I barked and wagged my tail harder.

He used me well in the woods. I was happy and tired when he left me in the yard. I was anxious for the day to end. There was a wooden structure in the yard near the house that wasn't there when I left. I went and looked at it. It was a low platform with a pillory in the middle with a backstop. The wood looked new. I moved the securing bar on the pillory. It was sturdy. There were some spiked balls attached to chains laying behind the pillory along with some wooden pieces. I heard an excited commotion inside and went to the door. Ms. Johansen saw me and motioned me in. She was holding a blindfolded Rachel's leash and the girls had armed themselves with crops. They were lining up in two rows. Ms. Johansen motioned for me to get with them. I got a crop from the rack and stood last in one row. Sylvia was across from me, last in her row.

Ms. Johansen led Rachel between the two rows. Each girl struck her somewhere one time. It looked like they were swinging hard. Sylvia whispered to me. "Aim for her nipples." I hit her square on a nipple with the crop. I had swung it hard. Rachel collapsed on the floor in between Sylvia and I. God help me, I really enjoyed that. I'd likely burn in Hell, but it was worth it. After watching Rachel squirm futilely on the floor for a few seconds, I motioned Sylvia to help me and we got her on her feet.

Ms. Johansen led her outside and put her in the pillory. I watched the balls being hung in front of Rachel's boobs and pussy and understood that my Master was very angry with her. When Rachel was secured, Ms. Johansen had me come to a white line on the ground in front of Rachel. She handed me a ball of red stuff in a waxed paper shell. She said, "You get to go first, Cynthia as you're the aggrieved party. Aim for a ball."

I was only twenty feet away. I took the ball and threw it hard. It hit the ball between her boobs on the nose and the ball rammed into her soft breasts. The paper burst and red goop coated her chest and face. The other girls cheered and Ms. Johansen handed me another ball. Blue this time. My aim wasn't quite as good this time and it hit a glancing blow to the lower ball. The waxed paper burst, coating her left side with blue goop and knocking the ball into her other inner thigh. She yelled at that too. I reluctantly relinquished my spot to another girl and got in line for another turn. There were two throwing stations with boxes full of missiles. I waited and took another turn but it wasn't as satisfying to add more goo to the fully covered girl. We mostly wandered away and watched a few girls throw a few balls. Rachel was sobbing in the pillory, hopefully

172

regretting her vicious attack on me. Two weeks of this should cure anyone of repeat offenses.

. . .

Rachel

Ms. Johansen walked around behind me and locked a chain to the back of my collar. Then she freed my hands one at a time from my waist band and pulling it high on my back, locked it in place. She put a blindfold on me and led me somewhere close. Is heard a babble of female voices and heard her say, "Girls, this is Rachel. She is to be punished for two weeks then join you. Its time for the gauntlet. Everyone get a crop and line up. Two rows. When Rachel passes you, give her a hard smack on her ass, thighs, pussy, or breasts. Only one."

I heard the rustling and giggling as the girls armed themselves and lined up. I felt the leash pull on my nose and I started walking. I had taken only one step when I felt a sharp pain in my left breast, then another in my right ass cheek. I squealed and pleaded but to no avail. The blows were raining on me in a staccato drumbeat. All the places Ms. Johansen had named were struck repeatedly and viciously. I was sobbing and felt the tears leak out of my blindfold and trickle down my cheeks. The last two blows were hard smacks delivered directly on my ringed nipples. The pain was terrible. I screamed and crumpled to the floor, unable to stand. Several pairs of hands pulled me up. Good thing. I don't think I could have risen by myself.

Ms. Johansen took off my blindfold and led me out into the yard. The girls followed us out. I saw a large wooden platform, only a foot high was sitting on the grass. On the platform was a wooden structure I didn't recognize, but I was sure I wouldn't like it. She led me onto the stage and sat me on a plank so I was facing the front. She unlocked my hands and clamped my head and hands into a pillory rotated ninety degrees so they stuck up in the air. She unlocked my ankles and spread my legs wide then they were locked in place. Two balls with stubby spikes were hung six inches in front me. One between my breasts and one in front of my pussy. She whacked the one between my breasts and it swung into my breasts, spikes hitting both breasts. I yelped. It hurt. The blindfold went back onto my head. In a moment the missiles started flying. I learned later they were wax paper covered balls of vegetable oil and chalk mixed to a thick, gooey consistency. All I knew at the time was that things that felt like ripe tomatoes hit me all over one or two at a time. If they hit my skin they stung and hurt,. If they hit one of the spiked balls, those hit me and it hurt worse. Soon I felt the slimy concoction running

174

down my body. I only hoped it wasn't honey or tar. I could feel lingering sore spots forming on my breasts where the balls hit repeatedly.

I couldn't see what was happening. The initial onslaught of missiles lasted an hour or so. Accompanied by a lot of taking in loud voices. Then the missiles thinned out. I hoped they were out of them. It turns out that most of the girls had other things to do and only late arrivals or returning girls threw them later in the day.

Just when I thought everyone was tired of pegging projectiles at the dirty girl in the pillory, Some men came to play. I heart male voices and groaned. They would probably hurt more when thrown with male strength.

The first missile knocked the breast spikes into me much harder than the ones thrown by the girls. I could tell bruises were forming where the spikes smashed into my tender boobs. I wasn't hit with as many missiles, but they hurt more. It turns out only four men came to torment me versus the twenty or so girls.

Ms. Johansen took me down from the target pillory in time to get cleaned up for dinner. She put the full set of chains on me and I ate that way. I couldn't keep the leash on my nose ring from falling into my food. I learned to eat around the chain. Ms. Johansen wiped my face and leash off after I ate then put me in my kennel with bedding. She said, "You'll stay in there until your Master wants you."

Hours later Ms. Johansen took me out of my kennel. Unusually, she tied my elbows together so my breast stood out at full attention. She took me up to the guest wing and knocked on Allen's door.

He opened it and taking my leash, said, "Thank you for delivering Rachel, Ms. Johansen. Was she a good girl today?"

She replied, "She was obedient and well punished."

"OK. Thank you for tying her elbows too."

He pulled me into the foyer, closed the door. and led me into the living room, my ankle chain clinking happily. I hoped he would let me have an orgasm tonight.

Chapter 8

Displayed

Oh My God. Around the large, well-appointed room were a dozen women from our neighborhood. People I talked to every day. Well dressed women with husbands of importance, and my sister, Ruth.

I had nowhere to hide.

If you've had the nightmare about finding yourself naked downtown, I don't have to describe my feelings about standing naked in a room full of people who knew me. In a nightmare you wake up. Sometimes you know you're going to wake up. But I was already wide awake.

So were all the women looking at me.

I faced a sea of delighted faces. I don't think anything could have been more intriguing or delightful than me standing there naked and helpless with gold rings everywhere. I was very aware of my breasts. My tightly tied elbows made them stand out so far. I must have looked like I was half breasts with rings in my nipples. Every way I turned my chained feet I saw sparkling eyes and open mouths. I became one huge blush. I knew everyone of them by name. It surprised me that not one of them seemed embarrassed by their treat.

Hungry eyes feasted openly on my ringed nipples and labia. No one looked me in the eye except my little sister Ruth.

Ruth said, "My, my, Rachel. My big sister seems to have gotten herself into a pickle. And you were always so straight-laced. Allen only told us that you had had a big change and we should help you celebrate. I've got to say, you have exceeded all my expectations. Was all of this, the rings, the chains, the collar, the lack of clothes, your idea?"

Allen said, "Rachel, answer her truthfully."

I said the only thing I could say without being punished, "Yes, Master. Mistress, none of this was my idea beyond declaring myself Master Allen's slave."

Allen said, "Rachel has agreed to become my slave. From now on she will only wear these chains and the minimum clothing the decency laws allow. This is her first public appearance and there'll be more. This is my celebration, not hers. I'm hoping you will all help her to fully understand her new position and that she is not allowed to have any privacy, dignity, or choice. She needs to get over any sense of humiliation or shame. Do not harm her but pain is appropriate. I've been denying her orgasms, so that might be a good place to start. There are rope, crops, whips, and various clamps and sex toys in that cupboard. I'm going to leave her with you for a couple of hours. I hope she is chastened and glad to see me when I return." He left the apartment to my dismay.

Ruth took my leash and led me around the room, past all the women so they could get a good look. She asked me, "How do your rings feel, Rachel? Does it hurt when I pull on this leash?"

I had to tell her the truth. I was a slave. I felt the thrill of submission jump through me like an electric shock. I said, "No, Mistress, my flesh is still tender where I was pierced. They were put in my erogenous zones so I would get aroused when my movement causes them to sway and tug on me. My nose ring only hurts if I feel a hard tug. They put a grommet in my nose first so the ring passes through that instead of my flesh. I try very hard to follow my leash so it doesn't pull hard."

"So, how do you like being a slave girl?"

"I know it must sound strange coming from me, but I like it. I'm scared of what all of you might do to me, but I love the excitement of never knowing what might happen to me. And I love my Master and am glad I can serve him. And the sex is incredible."

Ruth said to the audience, "Let's go to the game room. There's more room and some things we can use. She led me down the hall and into the well equipped bondage dungeon. She led me to each piece of equipment and explained its purpose. All the women found seats.

Ruth paraded me around the room in front of the others, one more time. She continued questioning me like a prosecutor too. "Were you always a submissive?"

"Mistress, I don't know. I liked being tied up as the captive princess or captured settler when we played as children. So, I guess so."

"But you were always bossing me around when we were growing up."

"Mistress, you were my little sister, I had to keep you from getting hurt or in trouble>"

"Yes, but not when I was in high school!"

"Mistress, old habits are hard to break. Besides, you never complained."

"Rachel, I complained all the time. You ignored me. Its hard to ignore me now, isn't it?"

"Yes, Mistress. I can't ignore you."

"You'll do everything any of us tell you?"

"Yes, Mistress."

"Why?"

"Because I am a slave and I must obey."

She took a slender cane from the cupboard and put it in my chained hands. "Show us 'Punishment position.'"

Master must have told her about the positions. There was no avoiding it, despite my feeling of impending pain. I knelt in the middle of the room, spread my legs wide, put my forehead on the carpet and raised my ass high in the air.

"That's a handy position, isn't it girls?"

There was a loud chorus of assent: "Damn right," "Lovely," "Beautiful."

Ruth commanded, "Crawl to each of your mistresses, Greet her, tell her what you are, put the cane in her hands, ask her nicely to cane you and assume this position in front of her, ass toward her. Thank her after."

"Yes, Mistress." I straightened up and crawled to the closest woman. "So good to see you Margaret, I am now Allen's slave and must be kept in my place." I turned around and raised my locked hands toward her. I continued, "Mistress, I beg you to cane my bottom to help me learn my place." She took the cane from my hands. I assumed the punishment position.

I heard a rustling behind me then a bright line of pain erupted on my ass. I yelped and jumped a little. She had struck me hard on my taut skin. I would have a bright red welt now. But it wasn't enough. I needed more. I said,

"Mistress, You have such a strong arm. Might I feel it again, please?" I wiggled my ass.

"Of course, dear. I didn't know you liked this sort of thing. You should have told me earlier." Another fiery line erupted on my ass. I was so close to coming. I was panting and a tiny moan bubbled up and out of me. I said, "Thank you, Mistress. I would love to have some more," I said hopefully.

Margaret asked, "Ruth?"

Ruth said, "I'm afraid not, Margaret, She's close to an orgasm and her Master is denying her release right now."

Margaret said, "Sorry, Rachel. Another time." Damn, damn, damn.

 She put the cane back in my hands. I straightened up and turned to face her. I smiled wistfully and said, "Thank you Margaret. That was kind of you."

Margaret, leaned down and kissed me on the lips, hard. It surprised me, but after a moment, I returned the kiss. She pulled away and said. "That was lovely. I'll be glad to cane you anytime."

"I would like that Mistress, if Master permits."

I crawled to Denise. I had to be careful not to put my knee on my leash. That would hurt. I went around to all the women and got a variety of stripes. None worse than Margaret's, but many similar. One girl. Alice, gave me a love tap and apologized profusely. I assured her it was what I wanted, then apologized again for not doing it hard enough. Ruth said, "Alice, she really needs this. Do it again, harder."

I said, Yes, please, Mistress," and took up the punishment position again. This time she put all her strength into it and I screamed and fell to the floor, trying to reach and sooth my scalded flesh with my hands, but I couldn't reach it.

I was on my back and looking up at Alice. She smiled and said, "That was better, wasn't it?"

Ruth said, "Much better. Stand up, Rachel."

"Yes, Mistress. It was hard getting up with my hands and feet chained. Ruth encouraged me with a steady pull on my leash.

She turned me to face the women. She asked, "Rachel, how did that make you feel?"

That was easy. "Mistress, My bottom is sore and I feel good. I wanted to please you all and demonstrate I am really a slave now. This is not a role for me, it is my life."

Ruth said, "Good. Let's all give Rachel a round of applause. I think she's earned it."

I blushed anew as everyone clapped and cheered me.

Ruth raised her hand to stop the noise and asked, "Will everyone here who has made love to another woman raise your hand?"

Six hands went up. Some slowly and cautious, most eagerly. I was surprised at some of the strait-laced and happily married women that raised their hands.

Ruth wrote down names. "All right. I know Rachel is inexperienced at this and we need to help her get better." She pointed to Alice. "Alice, you're first. Rachel is going to make you come. Sit in that chair," she pointed, "rise your skirt and lose your panties."

Alice protested, "No. I'm not that kind of person. I love my husband."

"He's not here, Rachel needs your help. You'll enjoy it."

"No, I won't," Alice said. I'm leaving."

Ruth gathered up the women who had raised their hands with her eyes and said, "You need a little help too, Alice. Strip her."

The experienced women grabbed Alice and had her naked in a flurry of hands and protests. Ruth took bondage gear out of the cupboard, cuffed Alice's hands behind her, put a leather collar on her neck, and strapped a black ball gag in her mouth. Margaret and Joyce sat her in the chair and held her shoulders. Sue and Francine pulled her legs out and spread them wide. Ruth led me to her and said "Eat her pussy, Rachel."

I knelt between Alice's legs and Ruth grabbed my leash in her fist, touching my nose ring and held my face in Alice's pussy.

Alice was protesting through her gag and bucking her hips. I licked her labia lips and felt her stiffen. I kept licking and thrust my tongue between her nether lips as far up her love canal as I could and waggled the end of my tongue. A moan escaped past her gag and I felt a trace of moisture as she began to lubricate. I doubled my licks, moving faster and harder. Her moans grew louder and she began to flow in earnest. I loved her taste. I sucked in all I could and greedily swallowed it. She was humping my face now, no longer trying to escape, but seeking release. I sucked her clit into my mouth and sucked. She exploded and her flow increased. I sucked as hard as possible and she swooned with a tiny scream.

Ruth relaxed her grip and I pulled my moist face back and knelt, glad I had pleased Alice and waited for orders.

There was more applause and calls. Ruth said, "Good girl, Rachel." I was inordinately pleased with myself.

Ruth motioned to the four girls holding Alice who released her. She asked, "Alice, was that good?"

Alice, unable to speak, nodded her head "Yes."

Ruth said, "Good. Bring her over here."

Margaret and Joyce dragged Alice over to a wall ring. Ruth locked her leather collar to the ring with a padlock. She said, "Later."

The other novice lesbians gave in gracefully and I serviced them under Ruth's watchful eye. Margaret stood behind me with a cane. She promised that if I didn't do a good job, she would "Correct" me. I got the feeling she envied me.

That encouraged me to work hard.

All of the other novice lesbians complained, but eventually they complied and no more were sent to join poor Alice. I got two unearned stripes from Margaret. I think she just liked whipping girls.

After I had serviced the lucky novices, Ruth, Margaret, Joyce, Sue and Francine went to a corner and conferred. They came back and announced it was time for me to get a proper whipping. My hands and feet were unlocked then they used the rooms many bondage features and stretched me into an "X" in the middle of the room. I had never been so exposed.

Another conference ensued, followed by Alice being brought over and joining me in my "X." We were fastened face to face, our breasts squeezed together. A tight rope around our waists assured full pussy contact.

Ruth said, simply, "Twenty five each." The audience applauded.

Margaret took a long, single strand whip from the cupboard and started walking around us. One stroke apiece at each turn.

It was painful being whipped on the back. Each stroke bit and stung. I knew the whip wouldn't cut the skin, but it hurt. An it was unpredictable. The tip of the whip would fly around Alice and hit the side of my breast when it wasn't my turn. I kept myself from screaming but Alice started screaming on the fifth stroke. They had taken her gag out when they out her up with me. Her piercing screams stung my ears as bad as the whip on my back. I turned my face and tried to muffle her mouth with my cheek with limited success.

Mercifully, after Ruth watched us for ten strokes, she stopped Margaret and put the gag back on Alice. The whipping continued. I was proud of myself. I didn't scream. I didn't like it, but my mistresses could do what they wanted with their slave. There were other compensations.

Finally it was over. Alice sagged against me, whimpering a little. Margaret and Ruth conferred a moment and Margaret replaced her whip in the cupboard and took something small out of it. "Oh no, I thought. They aren't done.

Ruth came back to us and said, "And ten more for a special treat."

I couldn't see Margaret as she was behind me. Then the lovely little slender strand of leather struck straight up into the place I least wanted it. When it lashed into my tender flesh its tiny tip struck Alice in her nether lips. It was excruciating and I felt Alice stiffen. I lost it and screamed. "No," I said, "its the wrong place. Don't hit us there please. Margaret must have loved the effects of the tiny whip. Both Alice and I danced in our bonds, shaking them and adding the vocal accompaniment I could no longer contain. The tiny whip struck our tender inner thighs as well as our pussies. Alice and I were whipped with precision. Our tenderest flesh was rosy and covered with thin red stripes.

The end of our whipping marked the end of our evening's entertainment. Hugs and kisses were exchanged, luncheons arranged, parties confirmed. Alice and I hung in our bonds, ignored by the rest. Margaret came over and kissed my cheek and patted Alice's bottom. She said, Rachel, I enjoyed this more than anything. If Allen will let you, I'd like to show you another good time."

Finally, only Ruth remained. She came to us and took the gag from Alice. She went out and left us hanging there.

Alice said, "Why isn't she untying us?"

"They usually leave me tied after a punishment session. Helps reinforce our feeling of helplessness. They could leave us here all night." I was being mean, but she deserved it. I think I would have gotten off easier if she wasn't here.

She asked, "Does this happen often?"

I said, "I'm punished daily. I earned punishment and I'm going to be punished for another week or so. I deserve it and I don't like it. Slaves must expect to be disciplined. There are worse things than a whipping. It will be over soon."

"You mean they aren't going to let you go after this?"

"No Alice. I'm a slave for life. I can only go and do things my Master lets me. I volunteered and, strange as it sounds, I volunteered because I think I love obeying my Master."

She was quiet after that. Eventually, Ruth took her down and out of the games room. She came back in a few minutes and said, "You made quite an impression on Alice. She asked if she could borrow you sometime."

"Oh, I wonder if she just wants to whip me?"

I got the impression she wants to know more about being a slave. She may be a convert."

She took me down, locked my hands behind me and put the chain back on my ankles. She led me to the living room and locked my leash to the ring by the front door.

"Kneel properly. When Allen enters, say 'Welcome, Master,' and kiss his feet. Then go back to kneeling."

"Yes, Mistress."

I knelt and waited. I asked, "Mistress, may I ask a question?"

Ruth said, "OK."

"Mistress, does Master really intend to take me out in public like this?"

"Why? Don't you want to be exhibited as his woman?"

"Mistress, I don't object to anything Master wishes for me. Its just that I want to make him proud and I could stand to lose a few pounds."

"Rachel, you're gorgeous just the way you are. He's already proud of you. But don't worry. The staff here has told him they are exercising you to increase your fitness. I'm sure he won't take you public until they think you're ready."

"Thank you, Mistress. Are you going to stay for a while?"

"Sis, Allen has hired me to be your babysitter when he's away. I'm here to learn about your training and to make sure you become the best slave girl for your Master. I arranged this little soiree for a couple of reasons. You need to get used to other people seeing and handling you. You're no longer in charge of your body. Another reason was to dilute whatever pride you still had. I have a copy of your remote too, so be respectful."

"Yes, Mistress. Thank you."

She said, "I envy you in many ways. You have responsibility, you're beautiful, and you are the most erotic and sexy creature I've ever seen. Of course you have to obey everyone and can't even move unless Allen or I free you. Tell me, Rachel, was it a good deal for you?"

I thought about it. I loved Allen and I loved obeying him. I was calmer, and had no gripes about anyone or anything. My rules were simple, and easy to follow. They were strictly enforced with pain to my ass if I disobeyed. I had quickly learned to obey. No doubt about it, as long as I didn't mind being the lowest one in a room, I could be very happy. Of course Everyone used me as a sex toy, but that was sort of fun too, watching the goofy expressions on the women and men I got off. My only regret was wanting to get more sex. "Mistress, it was a very good deal for me. I love everyone now and Allen loves me. I wish he'd let me climax more, but its his right to control me."

She looked at me. "Rachel, "she asked, " if I was in your place and you in mine, would you be nice to me?"

"Yes, Mistress, I love you and Master."

"Would Allen be nice to me?"

"Mistress, I think so. He takes good care of me and he's never mean. I think he only takes the crop to me when I need correction.   I'm sure he would not treat you differently. Remember, I can leave whenever I want. So could you. We share the same genes and experiences, so I'm sure you would like this life too."

"Rachel, how do you feel about being displayed publicly now?"

"Mistress, Its scary and exciting. I liked it with my friends. I only saw a few other people in the Pub and I showed off for them. Its like Master is my clothing. When I'm with him, Its fun to tease strangers."

I thought about what she told me. She was in charge of me. I wish I had been more considerate of her when she was in high school. Master was going to show me off in public. Would I always feel so humiliated when a strange woman saw me?

Master came back in a few minutes and I did as ordered. He ordered me to stand and kissed me deeply. I was so glad to have his arms around me. I loved him more than ever after my group therapy. He unlocked me and sent me to put his coat away. When I returned he had me kneel beside him while Ruth and he talked.

It was about me, but I didn't really listen. My opinion didn't count so I just watched Master and dozed, waiting for an order.

. . .

Cynthia

That night at lights out, Ms. Johansen said, "Cynthia, come here." My hands were locked behind me, of course and a leash held me to a wall ring while she put everyone in their kennels except me. After all the doors were locked she took me to Master Robert's suite. He took my leash off, removed my ankle chain, and unlocked my hands. I was free! He kissed me for the longest time. I was able to hold him this time and it was grand. He took me to his desk and knelt me beside his chair. Jeb came up to me, sniffed my pussy and lay down beside me.

Master handed me a thin sheaf of papers and said, "This is what I found on scent tracking dogs. You'll see there are some conflicting opinions and no scientific studies. I suggest you choose a theory and work up a plan to exploit it. If it doesn't work this time, there will be other hunts. I'm not going to change the rules or anything about the hunts. I just want you to get the girls to cooperate and use what they have and what you can learn about the dogs."

"I said, I understand, Master. I'll do my best. Can I have a map of the estate since I am not familiar with the grounds."

He said, "I thought you might like that, here." He handed me a topographic map on letter paper.

I studied the articles and had some initial ideas. I needed to run them by some experienced pack girls. Master finished his work around ten and we went to the bedroom. He stripped and left his clothes on the floor. He led me to the center of the room and said, "Since your bottom isn't fully healed, we're going to have to play a little differently tonight. He put his arms around me and kissed me. For the first time in this sexually loose madhouse, I was able to fully participate in the kiss. I threw my arms around his neck and had a spectacular kiss. I felt his stiff rod pushing into my stomach. I don't know if it was that or the kiss, but I also felt moisture wetting my pussy. When he finally let my mouth go he said, wrap your legs around my waist. He lifted me up so it was easy. He put his hands around my legs and lifted me over his stiff cock. He lowered me onto him and he slid in like he was made for me. He was. He was. He lifted me and lowered me like I weighed nothing. God, he was strong.

I released my arms and leaned back. The shift in angle made his shaft's movement even more effective. I was floating toward an orgasm before, now I was soaring. I pulled myself back up. He bent his head and sucked my left nipple into his mouth. My orgasm exploded through me And my scream of pleasure was piercing.

My soaring joy didn't stop him at all. He kept pumping me up with his mighty arms and soon I was on my way to heaven again. This time it was even quicker. I felt him erupt in me, filling me with his hot cum. The hot fluid filling me drove me over the edge and into a mighty shared orgasm. When I felt anything else he was still in and holding me up. He lifted me off him and set me on my shaky feet. I clung to his wide chest crying at the joy of having someone like him loving me.

He said, "Thank you, Cynthia for a memorable evening. You were a wonderful partner."

I was crying and sobbed, "Thank you, Master. You're the kindest, strongest, sexiest man alive. Thank you."

"Let's shower before we retire, OK?"

I followed him into the bath and we scrubbed each other in that opulent shower. When we were dry me both got in bed and I remembered something. I said, I forgot something and scurried into the living room. I looked all over and finally found it on a small table. I scooped it up and ran back to the bedroom. I jumped into his lap and handed it to him, "Would you do this for me, please?"

He said, "Its not necessary, you know."

I said, "I like it." I rolled back and raised my feet above him and he locked the chain back between my ankles. I held my feet up and admired my hobble. It was beautiful and even more significant now. I rolled over and slipped under the covers. But he wasn't done.

He said, "You've made me stiff again. What am I going to do with you?"

I said, "Master, I seem to suffer from the disease of lechery. I think you have to use your staff of manhood to scourge the demon from me." I rolled over onto him. "Now would be good."

He said, "Since I can't spank you, I think I have to sentence you to ride St. George."

He lifted me up and I bent my knees. He set me down on his lap impaling me with his rampant prick. He was a very good shot with my body. He hit the target both times with a bulls eye. I took over and rode the heck out of St, George until we both had come again. This time we forgot the shower and fell asleep quickly.

Next morning I sat on his lap with my hands locked behind me as he fed me breakfast. It was the best way ever to eat breakfast. Then he sent me back to training. I was looking forward to starting to gather my troops to discuss the problem. I hope they are as excited about it as I am. I know I have to convey a sense of adventure and excitement to the girls, most of whom are familiar with the hunt already.

Chapter 9

Puppy

Whenever my Master and Ruth were away I slept in a kennel. Mine had "Rachel" on the wall outside. I was punished for two unending weeks. Every day I walked the gauntlet then was displayed as a target on the pillory. It never got any easier. I cried a lot in those two weeks. After punishment came exercise. I was worked harder than I thought possible. But I improved. After two weeks I could run around the track twice before having to walk. I was able to do ten pushups. I improved and lost weight as well. Mr. Alistair pronounced me adequate for the pack after my punishment was over.

Mr. Alistair took the chains off my ankles and wrists. He left the bands and rings and that damned leash on me. He put what he called paws on my wrists. They were like stiff gloves so I couldn't bend my fingers. They clipped onto my bracelets. He put light boots with steeply angled soles on my feet. I couldn't stand in them since my heels were far above my toes.

He said, I'm going to install your tail now. It won't hurt so don't move. He had me kneel, put my head and hands on the floor and raise my ass in the air. I did as he ordered and felt helpless and tiny. I felt his fingers at my bottom hole. They slipped into me and spread grease on the outside and around the inside. Then he pushed something bigger in me. It didn't fit easily. He pushed and rotated it and slowly my muscles relaxed enough it slipped in and I felt my sphincter contract around its narrow part. I knew about butt plugs, and now I knew what one felt like. I felt full, but in a different way.

He took my leash and led me into the yard. I felt the tail shifting inside me as I crawled. He said, "Kneel."

I knelt, squeezing my legs together and hunching over. I felt the sting of his crop when he hit my back. It wasn't too hard, but it stung.

He said, "Straighten up. Arch your back. Stick your breasts out. Farther." His crop landed on my shoulder and I arched my back as fart as I could. My breasts bobbed in the air before me.

"Spread your knees wide. I want to see your pussy lips separate. Cross your hands behind you. Head erect. Eyes on the ground in front of you."

I tried to follow his commands exactly. I must have satisfied him since I didn't feel his crop again.

"This is your kneeling position. When a person is near, assume it unless ordered otherwise.

I said, "Yes, Master."

Ms. Johansen brought another girl out. She had the same paws and boots I did. She didn't have the rings in her flesh or a leash on her nose. I was special and I guess I deserved to be. She also had a tail like mine, the same color as her hair. She sat on her knees with her legs spread wide and her hands crossed behind her back. She was shifting her ass making her tail wag several inches. She was smiling.

He said to the new girl, "Peggy, you've seen Rachel before. Her punishment is over. She is a pack member now. She needs to learn her positions and how to behave. I will order a pose and you will be my model. She will learn from watching you. Understand?"

The girl nodded her head and barked. She barked.

He said to me, "Rachel, you are playing the role of a tiny, helpless puppy. Don't speak if you can answer with a bark, shake or nod. One bark for 'Yes,' two for 'No.' No human speech. Wag your tail when a person is with you. Smile. Go over beside Peggy and copy her moves." I crawled to Peggy as fast as I could on hands and feet. She knelt facing Mr. Alistair and Ms. Johansen and I followed. I remembered to wag my tail. God, this was demeaning, yet I felt so expectant, so ready to please. I was acting like a happy puppy. There may be a lot to be said for a wagging tail as a mood enhancer.

Mr. Alistair said, "I'm going to order you into a pose. Peggy knows them and she'll assume the pose. Rachel watch Peggy and copy the pose. Understand?"

I watched Peggy and she nodded her head and barked, tail wagging. I did the same. When in Rome...

"Stand." Peggy got up on her hands and knees, tail wagging. I followed.

"Belly." Flat on the ground, arms straight out in front, tail wagging.

"Lay." Roll over, lay flat on back, spread legs open, arms at our sides, hands by our shoulders, palms up.

"Beg." Kneel, hands at our shoulders, palms forward open mouth, tongue out, back arched, breasts out, wag tail.

"Down." Kneel, legs wide, hands on thighs, palms up, body erect, back arched, breasts out, mouths open, tongue out, tail wagging.

"Punishment." Hands straight out in front, head and breasts on the ground, ass high in the air, legs spread wide.

Mr. Alistair said to Ms. Johansen, "Rachel picked up on all the poses. Let's teach her to heel. Ms. Johansen took two short leashes and clipped them onto the backs of our collars. Mr. Alistair said, "Heel." Peggy crawled on all fours to his side and assumed the 'Down' pose. I did the same on his other side. I felt him take hold of my leash.

He said, "Walk to heel." He started walking forward. I shifted forward to all fours and crawled beside him. My head was inches from his leg and I watched it carefully so I could follow his turns. He walked at a pace I could match on all fours. He walked around the yard then turned and went around it in the other direction. Then he made smaller radius turns and circled the shade trees. I realized I was having fun. It was a great game trying to stay in the right position. I was feeling excited and expectant and happy to be mindlessly playing this game.

I slept in Allen's room for the first week but he never let me orgasm.

I was desperate and plead for release so much he gagged me after feeding me dinner. I had to wear the gag all night and until Ms. Johansen took me back to the kennels. When dinner was over and everything put away he'd kiss me hard. The kiss of a master to his slave girl. I longed for that kiss. It was so good, so full of meaning. But I came to dread it too, for after it he'd put the big black ball gag in my mouth and pull the strap tight.

He used me once or twice a night and once in the morning. He had somehow learned to read my body very well indeed. He could tell when I about to come and stop. Once I was so close that stopping wouldn't keep me from an orgasm. He pinched a nipple and the sudden pain killed my arousal dead. I cried and cried. I was so close.

He told me if I was very good he might let me orgasm on my birthday. My birthday. It was over a month away.

Chapter 10

Gardening

Mr. Alistair announced, "Twenty one through thirty, gardening duty, no shoes, no paws. Sunhat, sunscreen. Get greased up and line up by the south gate. Use lots of sunscreen, its going to be hot today. I took pity on Rachel and spread a thick layer of sun block where she couldn't reach, which was a lot of skin due to her chains. I had her do me then. I made sure she had a sunhat when I got mine. She followed our group to the gate. I had her line up in front of me. We were put in two coffles of five girls . The gardener took us to the shed and gave us stacks of shallow boxes and gloves. We were picking strawberries today. He led us to the berry patch and we got on our knees and crawled along the grass strip between two rows of strawberries. I saw there were twenty long rows of strawberries. We probably wouldn't get done today.

We had two cart girls working with us today. When I filled a box I left it on the ground and started on a new box. Every now and then the gardener gave me more boxes. Someone picked up the boxes and put them on a cart. When the cart was full the cart girl pulled it away and came back in a little while.

Rachel worked hard and almost kept up with the rest of us. She had more difficulty because of the short chain joining her wrists.

The gardener stopped us when we had finished half the strawberries. I was tired of strawberries. I hope a different crew got to finish them. We were sweaty and dirty when we got back to the kennel area so we showered and fixed our hair. A little makeup made us all feel better. In the yard we found all the other girls back from their chores. We had an hour before our meal so I found Sylvia, Rachel,

Jasmine and Nylla. I gathered them under the plum and asked about the hunt.

Sylvia said, "Its exciting and fun exercise, filled with wild activity, danger, the thrill of being chased, and it ends with intense sex. Its like what prehistoric women had every day."

I said, "sounds like fun. But how does it work? Do we all just run into forest and try and hide?"

They filled me with details for some time. everyone had a bit add to everything anyone else said. I just listened as hard as I could, trying to sort them into order. When they ran down I said, so here's what I heard:

Nothing unusual happens until the day of the hunt. We all rest the night before.

The dogs won't hurt us, just flush us out.

We get up early and put on our group's body paint.

All the pack girls participate.

There are three groups of girls painted alike:

Gazelle are the three fastest girls, brown backs, white fronts, black stripe on our sides, and worth ten points,

Deer are the ten next fastest girls, beige body paint, and worth five points,

Rabbits are slower girls, have dark brown paint, and worth three points,

The body paint covers our chest and belly.

We get running shoes and bare hands.

We can go anywhere inside the white line except the house.

The dogs get our scent by smelling our pussies before we start.

We get a fifteen minute head start.

A capture occurs when our hands are cuffed behind us.

We'll be used a lot when captured and the rest of that day.

We may be punished if we don't run well.

Is that about it?"

They all nodded their heads, obviously impressed I remembered it all. I was getting some ideas. Maybe it was possible, if the girls worked together, to let some escape capture. I still had a couple of details to work out.

After dinner Mr. Alistair and Ms. Johansen lined us up and put us in a coffle, all thirty girls. He told us we had all worked hard for the last couple of days with no problems, so they were taking us to the Pub. Mr. Alistair led the first girl out and the rest of us followed the girl in front of us. He took us outside, around the side yard, across the front and in a door on the far side. Several of us wore hobbles so we set the pace for the string of girls. We went in the door, down some stairs and into the Pub. We stayed on the coffle. There weren't enough chairs to accommodate all of us and the regular customers too. A couple of guards moved the tables and chairs away from the long wall and we knelt with our backs to the wall. We each got a cold beer in a tall plastic glass. Heavenly. It had been days since I had tasted any liquid save water.

The place was packed. I saw Sylvia and Julie at a table with their masters. I had been introduced to Brian earlier, but I guess the other man was Henry Oldman. Sylvia saw me and mouthed "Hello" and blew me a kiss. Julie was facing the wrong way. I saw at least three free women in the Pub. They were naked and wore handcuffs, but were allowed to sit in chairs. We were talking to our neighbors when Ms. Johansen came over and took me off the coffle. She said,

"You're wanted," locked my hands behind me and put a leash on my collar. She led me into a back hallway of the Pub then through a door.

It was a study. Big desk, several upholstered chairs and cushions, books on the wall and a laptop computer on the desk. Master sat behind the desk. He smiled and said, I'm glad Alistair brought the pack to the pub. This is my private office where I go to avoid most people. We will spend a lot of time here."

I shifted into standing pose and stuck my breasts out proudly. After all I was pretty enough to be owned, at least someday.

Ms. Johansen handed him my leash and he said, "Free her hands, please."

When she did he thanked her and she left. We looked at each other with smiling faces. Finally he stood up and walked around the desk, still holding my leash.

He stood tall in front of me. I had to look way up to see his eyes. When his lips touched mine I realized I had been holding my breath. He was the best kisser I had ever met. I had his undivided attention. He wasn't thinking about a business deal or getting me in bed. I was his universe. It was overwhelming. I had had some good kisses in the past, but his kiss was passion itself. Kissing can be more intimate and personal than sex. Sex can blow your mind but touching lips is closer to touching your soul. I'm a slave to my animal instincts like all the other girls here, but while he kissed me our souls were commingled. We were one.

When he finally broke the kiss I noticed my arms were around his neck, his arms around my back, and my feet were off the floor. We continued to hold each other and he asked, "How are you coming on the Hunt? There's only a few days until the next one."

"I've got all the data I need and some ideas. Do you want to hear them or wait until I have a plan?"

"Give me the high points now then you can stay here and work up a plan. I have to meet some people in a half hour. The meeting shouldn't be too long. I'll come back here to hear your first draft."

"OK. The dogs track us by our scent. Some comes from our pussy scent and from our sloughed skin cells. The scent blows on the wind. We wear body paint, mostly on our chest and back. The hunters only follow the dogs, they don't help them like real trackers, so we don't have to worry about footprints and broken vegetation. Several girls should be able to lead the dogs away from others if they carry their scent and we conceal the scent of the protected ones. I've got some ideas and I'll need a little while to put a plan together."

He positively beamed at me. "I knew I could count on you. You're going to make me proud. I've made a bet with a friend, a pompous friend who loves th hunt, that some of the girls will evade capture. He is so proud of his team that he doesn't think any girl will ever avoid capture."

"I hope its not too large a bet, Master."

"its huge and public. We've disagreed for years and everyone knows it. It would destroy my friend if he had to pay."

"Is it really that large, Master?"

"Relax, its only a dollar, but its a very significant dollar."

He kissed me and said, "I'll be back soon and I'm anxious to see your plan. There's paper and pen in the drawer." He strode out of the room.

I sat in his chair and stroked the arms until I realized with a start I wasn't supposed to use the furniture. I jumped up and got a pad and pen out of the drawer. I was tempted to snoop but refrained. I wanted him to trust me. I knelt in front of a coffee table and started working.

I was done in less than an hour. It was a simple plan. I had sketched a map of the area from memory, omitting the non-essential stuff. I had a timeline from the start of the day until the dogs were let loose. I wrote what each girl involved in the plan was going to do and where using map reference points. I had a list of materials and all were available to the girls. I really had two variations of the plan to account for wind direction. I only had a few days experience with local wind. I hoped Master could give me a wind forecast the evening before the hunt. I couldn't think of anything else, so I put the materials down, turned around to face the door, and crossed my hands behind me. I waited.

I didn't have long to wait until he returned. When he opened the door I said, "Welcome back, my Master."

He said, "All done I see. Explain it to me."

I picked up the plans and handed them to him. He sat at his desk and motioned me over. I stood beside him and explained the plan. It only required six girls to protect three from discovery by the dogs. All the materials needed were on site and readily available to the girls. I told him I needed wind information the night before to make the plans specific, but if I didn't have it the girls would only have to make a small correction.

I finished and he thumbed through the sheets one more time. He swiveled his chair around and pulled me into his lap. "Cynthia, This is fantastic work. I don't see any reason why it should fail. You need almost nothing but some cooperating girls. I am going to win the bet this hunt. Steve is a bit self righteous and he's is going to be beside himself with disappointment and chagrin. It will be wonderful to see. If even one girl evades capture, I'm going to give a reward to the girls who help you."

I shivered as I realized I had pleased my Master. He was proud of my work. I felt the heat rise in my face. I earned praise for my work not my body. This was the first time in my life I had done well. I was in front of the pack for once. My Master appreciated me for my work. It was a wonderful feeling, like an orgasm without the juices. Now I had to make it work. As he was pulling me onto his lap, I was thinking of the girls I needed to get to help me. Sylvia, Julie, Jasmine and Nylla were certain. I needed one more, the other Gazelle and I didn't know who she was.

I stopped thinking about the plan when his lips found mine. I hoped he'd keep me with him tonight. Heck, every night.

We didn't get a lot of sleep that night and I walked a little bowlegged at first in the morning. I was fine by the time I was back in the kennel. Ms. Johansen picked me up in Master's rooms and delivered me in time for exercise and breakfast. I was assigned to gardening again. Today the crew was picking green beans and cucumbers in the greenhouses. We were had just our boots since we needed our hands and were inside, out of the sun. Mr. Alistair and Ms. Johansen put ten of us in coffle and handed us off to the gardeners.

There were five long greenhouses side by side. They took us off the coffle two at a time When I was led into the greenhouse if was like being in a long conservatory. Plants reaching to the ceiling from warm, rich soil. The smell of compost. Fans blowing warm, humid air around me, cooling my naked skin. It was a sensuous environment. The chain on my collar was locked to a chain hanging down. I looked up and saw it was threaded on a long steel cable that ran the length of the greenhouse. There were two long rows stretching the length of the greenhouse with plants on both sides. There was a cart with two shelves beside me , covered in empty wicker baskets. We were to pick the ripe vegetables and put them in the baskets. We had to cut the cucumber stems so there was a knife fastened to the cart with a long chain. I guess they didn't want to let us take the knives with us. Strange.

My body was covered in a glistening sheen of sweat within minutes of entering the greenhouse and the blowing air was a pleasure. There were many vegetable and I filled my cart twice. When full I pushed it back to the end of the greenhouse, pushed it outside and took an empty cart back. My tether was just long enough for me to step a couple of feet outside the greenhouse to change carts. When I was finished I took the last cart back and knelt in the greenhouse entrance. The gardener checked my work periodically and showed me how to tell if a vegetable was ripe for picking. Many weren't and I knew a pack crew would be back here in a week. The work was pleasant. There were two girls in each greenhouse so we could talk while we worked.

The girl in the greenhouse with me was Megan. She told me she had been in the program for eight months and was looking forward to having her own Master. We talked about the life she expected as a slave. She readily admitted she wasn't sure, but she had a man in mind. He was a computer tech in the security department. He had taken her to his room the first time a couple of months ago and now she was the one he asked for every night. When she wasn't available his second choice was always different. She thought the two of them just "Clicked." She liked that he was both careful to make sure she orgasmed and strictly controlled her. She liked wearing his chains which was good, since he always kept her completely helpless when they were together. She said he liked to keep her hands locked behind her head when they were alone as well as in the Pub.

My feelings on bondage were more complex. I enjoyed having the chain between my ankles. It reinforced the joy of submission every step I took. I knew I enjoyed being helpless with Master, but I also enjoyed being able to do things for him which usually required using my hands. Maybe the best part of bondage for me was having Master changing it around to suit his desires and needs. I wasn't stuck in any one mode, but serving my Master as he wanted.

Chapter 11

The Hunt

I was strapped to the bicycle machine, my neck and wrists clamped immobile by the pillory. I was pedaling hard making the big, purple, ridged dildo pump in and out of my pussy. I felt Master's even bigger member reaming my bottom hole, his big hands holding my breasts. I could just barely get enough air past the bit in my mouth. I was pumping as hard as I could but my orgasm wasn't happening. I was sweating and needed to cum, but even with Master helping, I couldn't. I opened my eyes and saw a faint light coming through the barred door of my kennel. I was lying on the cold floor beside my bedding. My fingers were in my pussy and sticky. It had been a dream of frustration. Undoubtedly because I was in my kennel instead of getting my accustomed nightly orgasms in Master's bed. It was hunt day and all the girls were getting a night's rest.

The morning of the hunt dawned clear and calm. Master had told me last night that the forecast wind was from the south and only one or two knots. There were six girls in on the scheme. The last one I found was Gina, a lithe, leggy raven haired beauty. She was the last Gazelle. The three Gazelles, myself, Julie, and Gina had our "Tools," one tampon apiece still in their insertion tubes. Our "Pit Crew," Sylvia, Jasmine, and Nylla knew what to do.

We were awakened early to get ready. Ms Johansen had collected the ankle chains last night. Mostly to allow time for us to don our body paint. Sylvia and I were a team. Likewise Julie and Nylla and Justine and Gina. Gina and Julie followed my lead. First I took the tampon out of its tube and rubbed it all over my body, hard. I wanted every loose skin cell I could find on it. I shoved the string end back into the tube but left it half exposed. Then I put the tampon in my vagina and stuffed the string out of sight. I

221

wanted one half to suck up all my pussy scent. Next I showered and left a thick layer of conditioner on my scalp. I tied my wet hair in a tight coil around my head, and dried off well. Now I was ready for the body paint. Sylvia had showered when I did and she was ready. She applied my body paint in the approved Gazelle pattern but made sure that every inch oh my skin was covered with a good layer. Usually the paint only covered half of a girl's body. We needed to cover up all the sources of skin cells that could slough off. My reading indicated that dogs often used these wind borne skin cells for tracking. I didn't want any in the wind today. Then she was done I put on my running shoes and did her paint job. It took a lot less time.

When we were both done I checked the other teams. They were near done. Sylvia and I inspected Gina and Julie. They were perfect. I took out my tampon and shoved the absorbent part back into the tube. I handed it to Sylvia and she hid it in her vagina, stuffing the draw string inside too. Gina and Julie followed suit. Then it was time to line up. We assembled in the yard in a straight line and took up a standing pose with our legs spread extra wide. I was surprised I was so nervous. I couldn't hold still. The excitement was overwhelming. I was about to run into the woods, a collared slavegirl intended to be the sexual prize of whoever caught me. The idea should have been repulsive, disgusting, but my excitement grew. Would my plan work or would some stranger catch me and take me in the woods. If caught I would be his plaything all night long. My plan would work. I was sure of it. But there had been no opportunity to test it. It was all theory.

I rubbed my fingers deep in my slit and felt my nipples harden and stand up tall. I looked at the other prey and saw the excitement and anticipation in their faces. I smelled the scent of their ready, excited cunts. I was in a sea of rock hard nipples.

The dogs began baying as soon as they were let into the yard. I had been assured they were well trained and wouldn't hurt but it was still nerve wracking. I felt the cold wet noses on my pussy and felt dirty, used. I looked around me and saw nothing but excitement. I realized with a start that everyone else here thought this was perfectly normal. What a strange world I had thrown myself into. Yet I was happy, excited, and in a hurry to get going and show them all how good we were. I would show them. I would elude them all and spend the night with my Master, not a stranger.

The handlers had the dogs on leashes and made sure that every dog stuck their noses in all our pussies to get our smell. When they were done they assembled off to the side of the yard. Mr. Alistair yelled. "Give them a run for their money girls. Go."

We trotted easily through the gate past the hunters mostly standing beside their horses. We ran into the woods on the main road. Once out of sight of the hunters we got back together with our "Pit Crew" and stepped out of the pack at the first cross road. They pulled the tampons out and started waving them in the air like fans. Julie, Gina, and I trotted down the side road to the north, downwind of the woods. I threw a kiss to Sylvia. She, Nylla and Justine trotted off to the south. It was their job to spread our scent upwind so the dogs chasing us would go that way. Julie, Gina and I walked north. We didn't want to sweat. The body paint was porous enough for our skin to breathe, and therefore to pass loose skin cells into the air. We hoped that having our scents blowing on the slow wind from the south and ours concealed by the body paint we could evade detection. We walked to the white line and found some tall trees with a lot of foliage. We each picked some kind of evergreen and climbed until we couldn't see the ground. I had cautioned them to be careful and not wipe off their body paint where it could be seen from below or expose skin. I was halfway up the tree before I heard the dogs baying. I kept having giggling fits as I thought of the frustrated hunters unable to find any of the Gazelles. A couple of times We heard horses and dogs walking in the woods below us. The men and women were talking in low voices. I couldn't make out the words, but I thought they sounded frustrated. It was quiet and we were still safely hiding in the trees when my collar started vibrating the recall pattern. I climbed down the tree and met Gina and Julie. They were all smiles.

We started back to the road and heard a vehicle. It was one of the security team driving a large ATV . He was all grins too, "Excellent work, girls. The hunters are fit to be tied. You are the first ones to ever evade them. How'd you do it?"

Julie grinned at me and said, "Good teamwork, Mike."

We drove up to the crowd in the yard triumphantly. All of us were standing up through the open roof and pumping our hands. All the girls cheered as we pulled through the gates. So did most of the hunters who appreciated a good quarry. There were a few glum faces among the hunters, in particular one man standing beside Master. Master was holding a dollar bill aloft and waving it. He was grinning happily. I was so proud and so happy he had given me this chance. As we got closer I suddenly felt a chill. The unhappy man next to Master. The one who lost the bet. It was my brother Stephen. I remembered Master said

"Steve" had made the bet. I saw him looking at us and a shocked look appear on his face. He'd recognized me!

The ATV stopped in front of Master and Stephen. I put the smile back on my face. I wasn't going to let anything spoil my victory. We walked over to Master and knelt before him.

He said, "Great job girls. You've shown the hunters what smart prey can do." He turned to look at Stephen, Steve, this clever girl here, Cynthia," he indicated me, me, "formulated an ingenious plan using only the materials available to a pack girl, and snookered all the hunters, including you. I told you a clever girl could evade the dogs."

Stephen, without a bit of humor in his eyes, said, I've known Cynthia for years, Robert."

Master was surprised at this revelation.

Stephen said to me, "Hello, Cynthia. You're Robert's slave girl now I see. In all the years we've known each other, this is the first time I've seen you naked. Robert, is she available for me to use tonight?"

Master was watching me and saw the flicker of fear in my eyes. He said, Sorry, no, Steve. Cynthia is exclusively mine to use. She's special and I'm keeping her for myself. You can see why."

Stephen said, "Pity. We have a lot to discuss. I need to see to my horse and team. See you at dinner?"

"OK, dinner."

Master said, "Really exceptional jog, girls. Who else was it who helped you?"

I said, "Sylvia, Nylla, and Justine were our "Pit Crew." Without them this couldn't have worked."

Master asked Mr. Alistair, "Would you get Sylvia, Justine and Nylla up here?"

"Right away, Sir." He went into the crowd of hunters and prey and soon returned with the three girls. They knelt beside us.

Master said, "The six of you are to be commended. You showed that clever, selfless girls can upset a system that has been stacked against them for years. The Hunters expected to have full use of all the girls they expected to catch tonight. Now some of them are going to have only cold beds to look forward to. Sylvia, Justine, and Nylla, do any of you want to avoid tonight's partying?"

All three said, "No Master." Sylvia said, "We enjoy being used, Master."

"OK, so be it. Cynthia, you're mine tonight. Julie, I know Brian will be glad to have you in his bed tonight. Gina, I don't recall, do you have a master?"

She said, "Oh yes, Master. Allen Jennings is my master. I'd like to be his tonight."

"Good. Allen it is. The rest of you go find your users for tonight. Cynthia, stand up."

After they left he kissed me and said, "Tell me about Steve."

"He's my older brother. I was born almost ten years after him. I was an accident. We don't like each other. I think he's a pompous ass who treats women badly. He thinks I'm a lazy, self centered brat. We're probably both partly right. I was friendly with his first wife who was closer to my age. He cheated on her and she killed herself after the divorce. We stopped talking after that. Please don't let him use me, Master. I think he'd like to finish what Rachel started."

"Don't worry about that, Cynthia. I saw the friction between you two. I'll keep you away from him in the future. You know, you probably just cost him and each member of his team more than a million dollars each. They were in first place and good hunters, plus they bet a lot on themselves to win the trophy. With this drubbing they can't win and maybe won't finish in the top three. Anyway I meant what I said about keeping you for myself. From now on you'll sleep in my bed. I want you to finish the training though, so Ms. Johansen will take you to the pack classes in the morning. I've rewarded the other members of your team. How can I reward you?"

"Master, would you give me a set of rings like Julie's? I've envied her ever since I saw them."

"Hmmm. You did very well, but girls don't usually get rings like Julie's until they become full slaves. It would set a precedent. I'll think about it. In the meantime, is there anything else you want?"

"Master, you have much better breakfasts than the pack. Can I eat with you?"

"No. I don't want you getting fat and I need to get you out of my sight as soon as possible each day so I can get some work done. You are far too great a distraction to let you tempt me too long."

I waved my eyelashes at him and said, "But Master, After training is done, I'll be with you all the time so I can

"Personally Assist" you. Shouldn't you be practicing your resistance to temptation?"

"Minx. I suspect I don't have that much willpower. Maybe I should have you stay in another room and just talk to you on the phone. Or maybe I'll have a nose ring put on you so I can keep you from getting 'Underfoot' too often."

"Master, I don't think its your foot I'll be under."

"No, I agree. So you think a nose ring is a good idea?"

"Master, I didn't say that. They are becoming more popular, its true. Most of them are removable, but I don' think that's what you had in mind, is it? In any case, I don't get to make choices anymore. Its all up to you." I had thought about getting one after school. I wanted to confound tradition, but never got rebellious enough to do it. Besides if he ringed me, I hoped it would strengthen his feeling of owning me. What girl wouldn't want to be the property of a billionaire hunk who's shown a tendency to care for his charges?

"No, its not what I had in mind. OK. I'll think about it. Now there's a party in the Pub. Stand up."

"Master, should I lose the body paint first?"

"By all means no. Its expected that the prey will appear as they were hunted. Its a badge of honor. And you Gazelles have much to brag about."

We spent a couple of hours in the Pub, talking and retelling our tales to everyone who would listen. The girls were allowed one beer or glass of wine, so we made it last as long as we could. Master took me back to his quarters and helped clean me. The stuff was waterproof and he had a cream that wiped it off easily. Then we went to the games room and he put me on the bicycle. I remembered my dream this morning and this ride was much better. That dildo that the pedals pumped was just right. It was all I needed to get an orgasm, but it was easier and the orgasms were better when Master used my bottom hole too. He let me have five orgasms on the bike then I got another one in bed.

When he was ready to get in bed to sleep I asked, "Master, would you mind doing my hands and feet first?"

He grinned and said, "You feel the joy of submission, don't you?" He went to get my chains and locks.

I said, "Yes, Master. I feel safe with you and when you lock me up I feel happy and cared for. I know you'll take care of me. Its like the first blush of love that makes the day brighter." I held up my feet for him to hobble. When they were secure I rolled over and held my hands together above my back. When the lock clicked I rolled onto my back and said, "Thank you, Master."

After breakfast the next morning, Master took me to see Mark. He told Mark, "Cynthia has done well and she's told me over and over she wants to be my slave. So, while its too early yet, I'd like you to give her a metal collar and cuffs."

I could hardly believe my ears. I squealed and jumped in front of him. I couldn't hold him since my wrists were locked behind me, but I could rub against him. I was crying and said, "Thank you, Master. Thank you so much. Would you unlock my hands so I can hold you, please, Master?"

He turned me around and freed my hands. I jumped into his arms and kissed him..

When he set me down, I ran to Mark and asked him, "Can you do me now, Master?"

The next couple of weeks were memorable only for their routine and my regular orgasms. Master started teaching me to orgasm to pain. I spent many hours dangling from my arms while he used a whip to take me to orgasm. He never broke the skin, but I was usually pink and striped on my back, legs, ass, and breasts the next day.

He liked leaving his mark on me and I liked his attention. It got so I started to ask him to make it harder. I learned my orgasms came quicker and were stronger if the pain has stronger. My favorite though was being spanked. One swat and I felt him stiffening under me and that kicked me into high arousal. I was such a slave.

He sent me to exercise with the girls every morning. He wanted me fit because I was going to keep running in hunts. He told me if anyone ever caught me besides him, I'd be sore for a month. I didn't want to be caught, and this gave me a real incentive to improve the girls hunt tactics. After exercise I'd work beside Master learning his contacts and companies, being a useful PA. I was under the same rules as all the other girls: no furniture, speak only with permission, never any clothes, etc. Of course I had to answer the phone and do scheduling, so speaking was allowed for that, but never to person.

His office had an executive washroom, but I wasn't allowed to use it. I had a litter box in my little room. I was used to that from my time with the puppies.

Chapter 12

Stephen

I was sitting in the backseat of a silver limousine, waiting for my Master. He was taking me to watch a hunt at another estate. He said he wanted to broaden my knowledge of the hunts and the hunt network. Ms. Johansen had taken me to Julia this morning. She was head of HR and one of the first slave girls I had met here. Ms. Johansen delivered me naked, of course, my hands locked behind me and still wearing my beloved ankle chain.

Julie hugged me and said, today you are getting a treat. She unlocked my hands and handed me a large box.

"Here," she said, "put these on."

I opened the box and found a beige Dior suit, a salmon colored blouse, and a matching scarf. I hadn't worn clothes for almost two months and I wasn't sure I wanted anything on me. I liked showing off my body.

Julie saw my concern and said, "Its just for the day. Master is taking you to see a hunt on another estate. He wants you to be an elegant observer and take notes. See if there is anything you see from your unique perspective that we could use to improve our hunt."

She handed me another, smaller box. "Here are some new shoes. You'll can wear your ankle chain for this trip and these boots will cover your anklets and still permit the chain."

If Master wanted it, OK. She removed my ankle chain and put it on her desk. I donned the crisp new clothes. I put the boots on last. The boots were knee height black patent leather with fuck me heels and decorated with three gold rings at the ankle. Front, back, and outside. The placement seemed odd. I looked and saw a slit where the one on the inside would be, but it was missing. They zipped up the back and as I unzipped one I saw the slit on the inside was finished, like a buttonhole. I slipped it on my foot and saw the ring on my anklet aligned with the slit. I slid the ring through the slit and zipped the boot up. The ring was a perfect match for the other three. I put on the other boot and stood up. Julie came around the desk and locked my ankle chain back in place.

Last, Julie wrapped the scarf around my neck and tied it in a loose knot. She removed the band from my ponytail, freeing my shoulder length hair. Ms, Johansen had trimmed it yesterday so it was even. Julie brushed it out and pronounced me ready. I looked in the mirror on the back of her door. I was amazed. I hadn't seen myself for months. All the exercise and enforced diet had made my waist even slimmer and my cleavage more pronounced even without a bra. I turned to Julie and said, "I guess this life of slavery agrees with me."

Julie said, "One more thing, sit down."

I sat in the chair in front of her desk.

She handed me a couple of pages full of colorful printing and logos. I looked at it and saw the heading was of a national bank.

"What's this?"

"Its your bank statement."

I looked at the word." My name was under the bank logo. The column of numbers was short and started with my original thirteen hundred and some odd dollars. It had two more deposits of twenty thousand dollars. Holy shit. I now had over forty thousand dollars in my savings. I looked at Julie.

She said, "Mr. Olander pays the income tax on his PA's earnings. The amount you were quoted is yours to keep. Give that back and I'll file it for you. You won't have anywhere to keep it until you finish training next week. Now its time to go.

We both stood up. I picked up my ankle chain from the desk and dropped it in my pocket. Julie watched me and just smiled. She escorted me to the car and said, "Master will be right here."

I sat in the car and pondered my future. My slave training is almost over. Next week I start really being Master's PA. I have a small office off of his. Really just a big closet with a desk and a bookshelf and a small window I can retire to when he has a private meeting. My normal place is a cushion next to his desk. He says he wants me close to him in case he needs something done quickly. He promises I will know all but the deepest secrets of his far-flung organization. It causes flutters in my stomach just thinking about the scope of my job. I never dreamed of anything like this when I was getting coffee and picking up the dry cleaning for Ralph. I might be able to make a difference here. I resolved to try and understand the big picture passing in front of me. I knew I'd have the menial jobs most of the time, but I would try. I wanted to be the most useful PA my Master had ever had.

I extended my feet out in front and studied my ankle chain. The people at the hunt would get a mixed message from me. I was clothed so I wasn't a slave. I was chained so I wasn't free. Master brought me so I was his. Did this strange society of wealthy hunters love women or just loved controlling us? Or were they misogynists? Master was a wonderful lover, but was he typical?

Master got in and kissed me full on the lips. "Cynthia," he said, "I'm sorry for the wait. I received a call at the last minute. I fixed the crisis, or at least delayed it as soon as I could." The driver started the car and we moved smoothly off on our trip. Little did I realize how much of an adventure I would have.

He looked at my feet and said, "You are lovely. I see you have your hobble. Was it your choice?"

"Julie put it on me after I dressed, Master. But I want it."

"Good, you'll fit in perfectly."

"I will. Will there be other women there like me?"

"Cynthia, there are no other women like you. You are absolutely, astoundingly gorgeous, and that's the least interesting thing about you."

I blushed and said, "Thank you, Master. I hope I will always please you." I slid close until our legs were touching. I half turned to him, slid my arm under his. and soaked up his scent. I memorized his face, his ear, and I knew i was in love. I breathed into his ear, "Master, I want to be your slave."

He kissed me even more thoroughly than before. "Cynthia, I won't accept your submission until your year is up. Its the only way I believe is fair to you...and me."

"I know, Master. But formalities don't matter. I'm already your slave. I'll remind you every time we're together. I also love you. I'll be quiet now so you can work."

It was not a short trip. He had brought some reports to read. He made notes and I watched the beautiful rolling countryside go by, my arm around his.

I knew we had arrived when the driver turned onto a driveway guarded by massive steel gates and two armed guards. The driver stopped and exchanged a few words with a guard who opened the gate for us. Master put his work away and said, "I hope seeing a hunt run by others will give you some good ideas, Cynthia."

"I will try to be observant, Master."

A man in footman's garb opened the door. Master exited first them helped me out. Because of my ankle chain, I had to stick my feet out first then pivot onto them. Master helped me do this dance with elegance. I realized how exotic it must appear to an observer to watch my chained ankles emerge from the car, followed by a girl in an expensive suit. Were those real or erotic jewelry? Of course they were both to me. Master extended his arm and I took it and followed him into the front door.

We were greeted at the door by, presumably, the master of this house. Master and the man greeted themselves as long separated friends. Master introduced us. He said, "Jonathan Reynolds, this is Cynthia Lukens, my new PA and friend.

Mr. Reynolds kissed my hand and said, "You are welcome to my house, Cynthia. You are gorgeous and I envy Robert that he has such a friend.."

I blushed furiously, "Mr. Reynolds, Thank you and I am honored to meet you."

A woman only a few years older than me came up with a clatter. She was wearing a designer gown with what had to be Blahnik heels. Her ankles were chained like mine, except the chain was both heavier and longer, guaranteed to drag on the floor. She had a twinkle in her eye and said, "Hello, I'm Alex, Master Jonathan's current slave. Come meet the other girls and tell me all about Master Robert. We have so many rumors to dispel."

I looked at Master and he smiled and said, "Go on. Have fun."

"Thank you, Master. I linked arms with Alex and she took me through the house and onto a covered patio full of other young women. All were very pretty and wore some sort of restraint. They were all dressed in nice clothes and it looked like a bondage cocktail party. There were some serving girls, but they were naked except for tiny French maid aprons that covered nothing. Most of the clothed girls wore ankle chains, a few had wrist chains, and one girl

241

wore a sirik (a long chain running from her collar to her ankle chain with her wrist chain attached to it at waist height).

Alex said, "Girls, this is Cynthia. She's Master Robert's PA."

The girls clinked over to me and introduced themselves. Last names weren't used.

The first question was , "Were you one of the girls that escaped the hunt?"

I admitted I was.

"How did you do it?"

My Master wanted his hunt to be more sporting, so he let me study how tracking dogs work. Then he encouraged me to make a plan to help some girls evade capture. It wasn't that hard. I don't know any way to let even most of the girls escape capture, but we got a few away."

"Tell us more."

"If I tell you, then you'll tell your Master's and they will know what we did."

"Didn't you tell your master?"

"Well, yes, but it was his idea. Tell you what. I'll ask my Master if its OK to tell you and maybe he can make a deal with your masters. Don't ask me about it until I ask my Master. OK?

They reluctantly agreed. They knew they would fall all over themselves to tell their masters should they be questioned. A girl had to answer truthfully. I asked a question, "Are all of you slaves?"

Alex answered, "Of course. We aren't wearing these chains because they're pretty. We love being slaves, but it would be nice to not have to wear the chains all the time. Why do you ask?"

"I guess my Master does things a little differently. Right now I'm just an employee training to be a good slave. He says I can't be his slave until I've been there for a year."

A chill an through the girls. Alex said, "Please forgive us Mistress. We didn't know. "

I was taken aback. What had I said? "Girls, I'm begging my Master to accept me as his slave every day, but he's adamant. Not until the year's up. I'm not free in my heart. I've been taken already. I gladly wear his chains, but he has to make it official."

One of the girls said, "Mistress, our Masters are very strict. We have to treat you as our Mistress or we'll be punished. It doesn't matter that you want to be Master Robert's slave. It only matters that you're not."

"Oh, all right. I order you to all address me as 'Cynthia,' from now on."

Alex said, "Thank you, Cynthia. We know its not your idea, but we have to follow the rules or risk punishment."

I saw the drinks lined up at the bar and asked if I could have something. It was hot out already.

Alex said, "Slaves are only permitted to have iced tea or water, Cynthia. You're free so you can have something with alcohol if you want. Your ankle chain will tell the serving girls you are a slave, though. Better ask for an iced tea or you'll probably get them in trouble."

Shit. I would kill for a martini, but I didn't want to cause a ruckus. It would reflect badly on my Master. Besides, I needed to learn to be a slave, especially the restrictions I was accepting. Alcohol wasn't needed for me to be a good slave, only love and obedience. "Iced tea is fine."

A uniformed footman came to me and said, "Mr. Olander would like you to join him in the library, Ms. Lukens."

244

I excused myself from the girls I was talking to and followed him into the house. I had to hurry just a little with my hobbled ankles to keep up with him. He led me down a couple of hallways to a room and knocked on the door.

A man said, "Enter." and he opened the door. I entered and found a dozen men seated around a large oak table. I found Master and went to stand beside him. Master said, "Cynthia, these men are all masters of the hunt for their estates. They agree with me that they should make their hunts more sporting. They have agreed not to inform any hunter about the methods you developed. I would like you to explain what you learned and how you exploited that knowledge to let you enable some girls to evade capture. I might add that I have refused several generous offers from these men to purchase you. Please sit in this chair beside me and tell them what you did."

I sat down. I was a little nervous. I had not been allowed to sit on furniture for two months and I was a little afraid of punishment. But my Master ordered me to sit, so.

I said, "Masters, my Master gave me access to data on tracking dogs... I finished, "Once you know how the dogs track a girl's skin cells through the air, we covered the skin with paint, our 'Pit Crew' provided a deceptive scent trail, and we hid downwind. We could only make this work for a few girls so we chose the most valuable girls, point wise, to conceal. May I answer any questions?"

One of the younger men said, "So simple. And they completely fooled the best team of the year." He started clapping, slowly. Soon every man in the room was matching him. I blushed and wanted to hide.

Master stood up and used his hands to signal for quiet. He said, "Today I refused your generous offers to take her off my hands. Now you know why. Cynthia is a very intelligent woman who was never allowed to blossom before. She has repeatedly asked to be accepted as my slave. I have never owned a slave before. Cynthia Lukens, I accept your petition to be my slave. Kneel and submit, before my friends.

I slid off the chair and into kneeling display, my limbs straining to maximum extension. I crossed my hands behind my back and held my head high.

I didn't have any prepared words so I just said what came to mind. "I am Cynthia, your slave. I am your property forever and will obey you completely in all things. You may do anything you wish to me, with me, and I will obey you completely. I will delight your senses with my skill. I am your sex slave. I will orgasm at your touch to please you. I hope to bring you pleasure every day of my life. . I am proud to wear your chains so I may display my submission to the world. My throat is proud to wear your collar so that the world may know I belong to you. Master, every part of my mind and body exist only for your pleasure. Please take me as your slave and command me, Master."

All the men cheered and clapped. Shouts of "Bravo" filled the room as if I had given a grand performance.

Master looked down at my tear filled eyes and smiled. He said, "Cynthia, I, Robert Faris Olander, accept you as my slave. You are now my property. I will keep you safe and cherish you. When I discipline you, or pleasure you, it will be from love. I will treat you as a rare and valuable treasure, and you will never be free of my chains."

I leaned forward and kissed his feet. I was such a slave. I was filled with submission and joy. I wanted to be taken right there on the floor as a slave by my Master.

He said, "Stand."

I stood as gracefully as I could and took up the standing display pose. He smiled and took the scarf off me and said, "Wear my collar proudly, slave."

"Yes, my Master, always."

He kissed me and took me to the door. He opened it and asked he footman to return me to where he had found me.

"Alex. Master solved our problem for us. He accepted me as his slave. I'm no longer free."

She beamed at me, "I'm so happy for you, Cynthia. He's a good man and its taken him years to find the right woman. I'm sure you'll be very happy." "Girls, she called, come here, quick."

They all hurried over and Alex spoke again, "Cynthia has been accepted as Master Robert's slave. She's one of us now."

There were squeals of joy and girls hugging me. One tall redhead grabbed me and gave me a full, open mouthed kiss, with lots of tongue. I found myself facing the girl in the sirik. She was slim and short and couldn't get her hands higher than her waist so I took her in my arms and kissed her hard for a moment. When I released her, she looked at me with undisguised lust and said, "Please" with such longing I can see why her master keeps her heavily chained.

We talked about our Masters and the hunts they had been in. We were admiring each other's clothes when Master and several other men came out. Each of the men talked to their slaves. Master said, "Cynthia, I've agreed to let you run in the hunt here. Several girls have come down with the flu and can't run. The rest seem healthy, but don't get near them. Jonathan's people will get you ready. The hunt starts in an hour so be sure and warm up first. I'm sorry you won't have time to help this pack prepare. The hunters have been told that there won't be any nightly use for several of you, but they will expect to use you well if you're caught. Just like home. Run well for me."

"Yes, Master. I'll do my best." I didn't want someone else using me for the first time as a slave, but I had no choice.

I followed Master Jonathan's man to his kennels. I hung my clothes up carefully, hoping they would look good when the hunt was over.

I had one of the other visitor girls paint me in Gazelle markings and made sure all my skin was covered. I didn't know how much good it would do without someone to carry my deceptive odor far from me. It was all I could do in a strange kennel.

We ran around a track several times to get warmed up. Then we were lined up in the yard in front of the hunters in their fine garb and ordered into punishment pose so the dogs could get a good scent from us. I was excited and ready to go. I would give them a good run, anyway. I was sort of looking forward to being caught arte used thoroughly. The thrill of the chase was getting me horny. I felt the cold snouts of the dogs jamming themselves into my pussy. It was making me very aroused. The dogs were pulled back and Master Jonathan said, "Girls go."

All of us straightened up and jogged into the woods. I found a clearing and felt the breeze. I licked a finger and held it up. I tried to move as a steady pace, just below where I would start to sweat. I headed downwind and slightly away from the manor house. Every now and then I stopped and rubbed my pussy on a tree to try and convince the dogs I was treed. Several times I spied a broken branch the right size and rubbed it in my pussy and tossed it upwind. I heard the baying of the dogs when they were released.

I started to run. I stopped myself. Speed wouldn't help. It would just reveal me to the dogs quicker. I kept moving downwind and away from the manor house. A couple of times I found a fallen tree and used it to double back on a scent marker. Then I heard what I most feared. Some dogs were getting closer. Now I started running hard, knowing it was just a matter of time and I wanted to cover as much ground as I could.

I heard the dogs baying increase to a continuous howl as they caught sight of me. I ran as fast as I could, dodging trees and leaping bushes. One of the dogs caught my shoe and I went head over heels. Before I could get up they were all over me, pinning me down. They were careful not to break the skin, but they were relentless. At last the riders came up and two men grabbed me. One of the riders tossed treats to the dogs for their reward. They locked my hands behind me, threw me on my back and spread my legs wide. I closed my eyes and felt four men in succession take me. They were so quick I didn't have a chance to orgasm, but I was close. They stopped and I opened my eyes. Stephen was standing over me with an angry look in his eyes.

"So, you are the bitch who cost me over a million dollars. And the rest of my team, too. Now that we've caught you and had our way with you, you're going to return our losses. He laughed happily. I didn't say anything. It would only make things worse. They gagged me, tied a bag over my head, tied my feet together and threw me over a horse. A most undignified way to travel. We rode for half an hour. They stopped and I was dragged off the horse and dropped in the back of a car. They tied my feet to my hands and slammed the trunk shut. The trip was long before I was taken out and dropped on a hard floor. I was miserably uncomfortable but all I could do was moan through my gag. It seemed forever, but eventually my feet were untied from my hands and I was hauled into a chair. More time passed and I heard muffled voices.

One of the men took the bag off my head. I was in what looked like a big, empty warehouse. He took the gag out of my mouth and held a water bottle to my lips. I sucked it down eagerly. Two men were busy a little ways away. They had two sawhorses and were nailing a plank across the top of both of them. There were ropes hanging down above it. I recognized what they were building. It was a horse. An ancient device for torturing women. I was powerless to stop them Suddenly I knew what they were doing. They were going to extract ransom money from Master. He might be more willing to pay and forgive them if I were suffering loudly. Well, from what I've read about the horse, I'd be suffering a lot and if they didn't gag me, I'd be very loud. Shit.

I said, Hey." He looked at me.

I said, "I know what you're going to do to me. I will yell and scream even louder and more fervently if you just let me stand beside that thing and yell. It'll get you the same result and You won't feel bad about torturing me."

He said, "You cost us several million dollars. We want to torture you."

Shit.

The two men finished their work and one left the room. The other walked over to me and my guard. They talked in low voices. Stephen and the fourth man returned. Stephen said, "Give me Robert's phone number and I'll call him. See if he wants you back."

I needed to gain some time for Master to find me. I knew he was looking. I said, "Tell me how you found me. I was sure I'd gotten away again." I was sure he wanted to brag about how clever he was.

Stephen smiled and said, "Bob recognized you when they brought you girls out. We told our dog handler to only let his dogs get your scent. We held them back until all the others were well away. We didn't want ours confused. They were like guided missiles when we let them go. They ignored everyone else."

"Stephen, " I pleaded, "you don't need to torture me. I'll be plenty convincing. I want to go home at least as much as you want your money. Master Robert won't even miss your money. If you torture or kill me you'll be running for the rest of a very short life. He has more money than many countries and he'll hire every bounty hunter in the world."

Stephen said, "I've been waiting years to get even for my wife. Your latest stunt makes your suffering sweet music to my ears. Of course I'll torture you. I'm betting if I give you a lot of pain but don't harm you, Olander will forgive me. He knows the power money holds. Cynthia, you're stalling. I'll give you a little incentive to expedite this."

Shit. I knew what kind of incentive Stephen thought of. He took something small out of his pocket and reached toward me with something black and silver in his hands. He took my left breast in his hand and moved his other hand toward it. I recognized what he was holding. It was a spring metal clamp like I use to hold papers together. Oh No. He let it close on my nipple. The pain was sharp and biting, like a small animal was chewing on it. I screamed, "Please, Stephen. I'll obey you, but I don't know his number. I never call it. Please take it off."

He smiled and said, "I don't believe you, sis. You are his PA, you must give out his number every day."

The pain was punishing but I could bear it for a little while. I stalled again. I asked, stupidly, I guess, "You're just going to call him? The police will be all over you in minutes."

He replied, "I'm not that stupid. Its a satellite phone I've routed through three satellites and five Asian countries who aren't friendly to the US. Give me the phone number."

I knew the number. Eidetic memory, remember. But I wanted to delay Stephen. I said, "I don't know his number. He's always been in the same house since I've been there. Besides, I sleep in the kennels, remember. No phones."

Stephen knew me better than that. He said, "OK. Put her on the rig. She'll tell us pretty soon."

I whined and screamed that I didn't know. Stephen stuffed the gag back in and tightened it. They lifted me up and one of them untied my feet. I kicked but he just grabbed my feet. I was lifted onto the evil thing and my feet retied. I hurt, but not as bad as I expected. One of them held me up and another tied one of the hanging ropes to my wrists. They pulled my wrists up and my torso was forced forward. Stephen tied a rope to my collar and the other end to the end of the plank I rode. Now it really hurt. My labia lips spread around the plank and I slid down until I rested solely on my inner lips. The pain increased every second. I screamed into the gag, "I'll tell. I'll tell. Let me off, please Stephen."

He pulled the gag out and said, "What's the number, Cynthia?"

I told him and he dialed. I heard him say, "We have your girlfriend. We want ten million in unmarked bills by tomorrow....Don't give me that, you have that much in petty cash. We also want your word you won't harm us or tell the police. I know you won't break it."

The pain was incredible. My pussy was about to break. I wouldn't be able to have sex again. I screamed, "Please Master, give them the money. I can't stand the pain."

Chapter 13

Hunter

"Define 'Missing,'" Robert said in a low voice.

Jonathan said, Robert, I'm so sorry. She wasn't captured and a hunter team is missing too."

"Which team?"

"Venator. The team captain is..."

"Stephen Lukens," said Robert, "I know." He took out his phone and dialed a number. "Brian, Cynthia has been kidnapped. I believe Stephen Lukens is responsible. The other members of the Venator team probably helped him. Get the flight crews up. I want both choppers in the air with the mobile tracking systems and a fire team. Get the G5 ready, too, just in case. They are at most an hour out from my location. Get your best analysts looking for property in the area owned by Lukens, his team members, or their employers. Call me back when everything's rolling."

He turned to Jonathan. and said, "You heard my call. I need to go back to my car and change. I'll have a chopper pick me up when they're close. Is your pad lit?

Jonathan said, 'Of course I'll help. I can get you six men immediately who are all ex-military and well armed. I can get more in the morning."

Thanks, Jonathan. I don't think Lukens will be a threat once we find him, but have them get ready and stand by just in case.

"Can you find her?"

"I think so. Unless he had an aircraft on standby and close, she's still in range of her tracking unit."

He went to his car and told the driver what had happened. Both of them put on Kevlar gear with titanium/ceramic inserts and dark jackets. Next were the utility belts with Glocks , flashlights, and spare clips. The driver chose an M-16 from the trunk emergency gear and Robert picked up his M40A5. They were putting on their encrypted SSB headsets when Robert's phone rang. He just said, OK. Pick me up at Exeter's landing pad. He turned to the driver. Bill, listen on the command channel and take the car and follow us. We don't have an address yet, but we know where she is. I'll have the pilot relay the address when we know it."

Robert ran to the sound of the landing helicopter. The blades were still engaged and ready to lift when he jumped into the open front door. The pilot applied takeoff power immediately and the powerful craft leapt into the sky.

"What do we have?"

A voice came over the team comm headset. "Cynthia's location is two miles south of Accord in what the map calls Allen industrial acres. I looks like a warehouse."

OK. Where's the other chopper?

"A mile away from there and closing. Brian has command. He plans to set down on a pasture a half mile from her and approach on foot. He has four shooters with him."

"Give me a map."

One was handed over his shoulder. He studied the map and said, "Pilot, land as close to the target building as you can." He changed channels on his headset, "Brian, Robert. We're seven minutes out. We'll land next to the target. You should be in position by then. Use our arrival as a distraction."

Brian relied. Roger."

Robert's phone rang. He looked at it. He answered, "Olander."

He listened to Stephen's demand and replied, "It will take me more than a day to get that much cash together."

Stephen was objecting when he heard Cynthia's scream. His heart felt cold, but he held his voice steady. He said, "The money will be ready tomorrow. I swear I will not tell the police anything and I will not harm you or your friends." He hung up.

He changed channels on his headset and said, "They are torturing Cynthia. Pilot, get as much speed out of this bird as you can. And I want a quick landing. I won't mind if you bend the equipment so long as we can fight. Listen up everyone. I want them alive if possible, but take no chances. Your only job is to protect Cynthia."

Brian called, "Chief, we're on the south and west sides of the building There are doors on all sides . She's in a big bay on our side, We can see her through a slit in the blinds. She's moving and looks OK. We're ready to blow two doors on the south side. Land on the north and we'll blow them ten seconds after we hear you land."

"Roger." He passed the plan on to his men.

The pilot brought the copter down fast and hard. This was no "Ease the ship down to a soft landing for the comfort of thepassengers." Hal Anderson had been a pilot in Afghanistan and he treated this as a hot LZ. The skids creaked and flexed as the craft smacked down with a crack on the asphalt. Robert and his men were all out and running to the building when they heard the "Whump" of the det cord blasting the doors open on the far side of the building. Robert left his sniper rifle in the chopper. "Not too useful in a building," he thought as he jumped out. As soon as everyone was out the pilot made a maximum performance climb to a safe overwatch altitude and circled the building.

Robert's team didn't have time to spare to rig the det cord so he ordered Billy, the one with the Breacher shotgun to the front. Billy placed the muzzle of the shotgun against the door knob. The gun had a Breaching adapter that allowed all the force of the shell to literally break the lock's components, while minimizing recoil and fragments. The gun was loaded with "Hatton" shells loaded with a mixture of compressed powders. One of the military items Robert's companies made.

Billy pulled the trigger and the lock was blown through the door in several pieces. The door was flung open and the team stormed into an office. They darted from cover to cover, clearing the rooms they passed. Robert followed his team. The last door opened into the warehouse. Inside they found Brian's team had the kidnappers cuffed, face down on the floor with two men guarding them. Brian and another man were lifting Cynthia off the "Horse."

A wave of relief washed over Robert. She was OK. Her face was tear stained and she had cuts and bruises, but her face lit up with joy when she saw him. She leapt into his arms and they kissed long and hard. When she finally drew back she said, "What took you so long, Master. I've missed you." Her smile turned into laughter and he joined her. They both felt so good inside they couldn't contain it. Finally he set her on her feet and pulled her against him. He motioned Brian over.

"Load them in a chopper and take them to the airfield. Keep them well guarded. Find out who owns this building we've messed up. If its not owned by one of these guys, get it repaired ASAP."

Brian said, "It would be less trouble if we just pushed them out of the copter, say, twenty miles out in the ocean."

"No. I promised them I wouldn't harm them or tell the authorities. Let's talk about this when we get home. Get everyone loaded in the choppers. My driver will be here before you're ready. Cynthia and I will drive home. I'll call you when I get there."

The pain was unbearable. I was being slowly split in half. If I moved the pain doubled. I couldn't even turn my head. I could see Stephen's legs in front of me. A low moan was rasping unbidden from my soul. Coming out of me unbidden. My body was pleading, without words.

I heard something. A loud whoosh like a strong wind. Was it Robert come to save me? Hope flared briefly but faded when the noise disappeared. I saw the legs of the men running past me toward the noise. Two tremendous blasts made me jump and my world dissolved into blackness and pain. When I came to there were more legs, clad in black. Yelling filled my ears without meaning. Then I felt fingers untying my bonds and lifting me off the plank. God, that hurt too. They stood me on my feet. I fell and someone grabbed me. I looked up at my name and there was Robert running to me. I took a few steps and found the strength to leap into his arms. I eagerly sought his lips. They were soft and warm and loving. I clung to him like a leech, sucking warmth and love from him. I felt life returning to me.

When I was recovered enough to think, I pulled away from the kiss. I wanted to show him I was OK and strong so I said, "What took you so long, Master. I've missed you." The look on his face was priceless and so good to see. His worry and fear changed instantly to joy. I couldn't help laughing. I laughed in that loud, uncontrollable, throw-your-head-back kind of way. He sort of gaped at me then he started laughing too. I was still laughing, and when we stopped he said, "I wish I could make you laugh like that more often. You're beautiful all the time, but when you smile like that, my world stops."

He sent everyone else back on the helicopters and Bill picked us up in the car. He had thought to bring my clothes. I wanted to look my best when we got home so I dressed in the car and was once again the "Elegant" slave when we arrived. Everyone had heard about my "Adventure" and was happy to see me back safe. Julie was crying and kissing Brian. When Ms. Johansen moved to take me back to the kennels Robert stopped her.

He said, "Everyone listen. Before Cynthia's kidnapping, She asked to be my slave and I accepted her. She is now my slave. Remember she is only a slave, must obey or be disciplined, and has no authority here. But also remember she is under my protection and I charge all of you to keep her safe. From now on she will stay in my quarters."

An even louder hubbub ensued. Every woman there felt it necessary to kiss and congratulate me. After a half hour or so, Robert raised his voice and said, "Enough. Its been a long day and I want my slave to comfort me. Goodnight. He walked out of the hall and I followed him. One pace behind and one to the left, as a proper woman should.

In Master's room we stripped. He put my hobble back on me and we showered. I wanted to spend the whole night making love, but it had been a really long day. We both fell asleep after one session. Plain vanilla sex in the missionary position. Master was a great lover. I was afraid it would hurt after the "Horse." Master rubbed some tingly cream onto my labia lips and soon I was so aroused I didn't care if it hurt a little. Turns out girl's thingys are built to take a lot of use. Nothing hurt, in fact I came three times before we finished. I fell asleep after he left me empty and didn't move the rest of the night.

I woke to bright sun streaming in the window and filling the room. I was alone in the bed and felt glad to be alive. I heard sounds coming from the bath and called, "Master, do I have to go back to training today?"

The reply came, ""Yes. You have a lot to learn, my gorgeous slave girl. And when you get all the physical things down, you'll still have to learn to be my PA."

"I'm already familiar with some of your more demanding needs, Master. I'm eager to learn them all."

"It may surprise you to learn that I have intellectual needs as well as physical, Ms. Lukens."

I so loved this teasing repartee. "Nothing about you will ever surprise me, Master," I said reprovingly, "But I think I lost the Ms. when I swore I would be your slave forever. Is there a term for a slave girl? How about 'Slut' or 'Slave ' Those would be more appropriate now."

"Hmmm. We never needed one in here. Its obvious which women are slaves or in training and who's free. In a vanilla situation Ms. is still appropriate since you're not married. Then you will address me as 'Sir.'

"Yes, Master."

He came out of the bath, gloriously naked and started dressing. "Take this as an assignment. Talk to the other girls and see if you can find some appropriate titles and bring them to me for review."

"Yes, Master." I slid out of bed and helped him with his clothes. He didn't need my help, but understood I wanted to do it. Besides, a good PA assisted her Master with everything. "May we discuss Stephen now?"

"OK, I'm not sure its appropriate for a bedroom, go ahead."

"Master, he's mean and greedy and hurt me a lot. I hope you won't kill him. I know that's easiest and you don't want him given to the authorities for what he might reveal. Please find some way to let him live. He is my brother."

"Cynthia, I understand. Its why he's alive right now. He thought to hurt you for vengeance and use your pain and the implied threat of worse to coerce me into buying you back. I'm angry with him for stealing my girl, for trying to blackmail me, and for hurting you. He must be punished for his deeds and made so fearful of what else we can do that he never even thinks of trying to get even again. I'm going to meet with Brian after breakfast and we'll make our decision then. I won't harm him or his friends, but I need a lasting solution that gets him out of our lives."

Its really convenient being a slave to Master. I never have to worry about clothing. He took me to breakfast. Normal fare, but excellently prepared. Two places were set on the table. He was going to let me use the furniture! I looked at this and realized I didn't want to. I was not his equal. I had submitted to him and knew where I wanted to be. I knew he was being nice to me because of my ordeal yesterday. I had knowingly, intelligently, put myself below him and I wasn't going to let that damned horse put me back where I started. I wanted to lick his shoes, not wear them. I set my plate on the floor and knelt facing Master. I crossed my hands behind me. I liked being helpless before him. He watched me without comment and held a glass of juice for me to drink when I was ready. The food was good but the feeling of joyful submission rippling through me was wonderful. I heartily recommend it for every female with even a touch of submission in her. The food fueled my body and my submission filled my soul with the rightness of my position.

Master took me to the airfield on the other end of the estate. He met Brian and they decided to let me watch the interview with Stephen over the video link rather than be in the room. I think they were right. Stephen was very angry with me and it would distract him if I was present. I didn't want to see him either after what he'd done and said to me. Master left me in the control room with one of the security men. I could tell he was glad for my company too. I watched his cock stiffen as he tried to watch the screen. His gaze would occasionally find me. I enjoyed his attention and flaunted my breasts at him whenever he looked. You know how girls tease boys with just the right tilt of their heads and an arch look on their faces. I kept my hands crossed behind me and tried to look helpless. He was sweating by the time Master and Brian were in the room with Stephen.

Master said, "Steve, you kidnapped Cynthia, held her for ransom and tortured her. This was extreme even for you. Why?"

Stephen said, "I want a lawyer. I know my rights. I'm not saying another word."

"We're not the police and you have no rights. Brian, what was your idea for Steve and his friends?"

Brian replied, " Load 'em in a chopper and toss them out about twenty miles out over the ocean, from a couple of thousand feet."

Stephen shrunk in his seat, and said. "You promised you wouldn't harm us or turn us over to the cops."

Master said, "Yeah. I did, and I won't. But there are some things I've thought of. I could tattoo 'Slave' on your forehead and sell you to a brothel in Azerbaijan. I'm sure they'd keep you alive and see you had an interesting life."

Brian said, "Steve you've made an enemy with a fertile imagination. I'd start talking if I were you."

Stephen bent his head and said, "OK. My friends and I work for the same firm. We embezzled a lot of money and bet on ourselves in the hunt. We thought we had a sure thing. We were way out in front on points and only needed a fair score to recoup our bet. If we don't replace the funds next week it will be discovered. We were desperate after Cynthia knocked us out of the money."

"And the torture," asked Master?

Stephen's head popped up. He shouted, "She shamed us in front of our friends. She gloated, and she ruined us. We didn't harm her."

Master said, " We'll be back." He and Brian left the room.

I wanted to run in there and smack him silly. I'd never felt such pain before. I wish I could stick him on the horse, or something that hurt him as much.

The security guy said, "Cool down, Cynthia. the chief won't let him off lightly." I was surprised and looked at him. "How...?

"You're about to rip the arms off your chair. Relax."

I looked down at my death grip on the chair arms and felt the pain in my hands. I relaxed them. "Thanks." I looked at him and wondered. "What's your name and how did you know my name?"

"I'm Luke and I was on the raid last night. We were all briefed."

"Oh. "What do the men call girls like me?"

"Girls. Look, we know the girls here are special. You're submissives and the men here are checked out before we get hired. We're OK with bondage and discipline and we all respect the girls. It takes guts to just be yourself and open up to everyone. Like in this case, you are 'The chief's Girl.' Or My boss, 'Brian's Girl.' My girl is Michelle. She's one of the pack. Maybe, in the future..."

"Thanks, Luke. That means a lot to me. I've been concerned you guys might not think much of us. We don't exactly follow the women's rights flag."

"Well, if it matters, neither do we."

Master and Brian entered the control room. He said, "Cynthia, Brian and I have reached a decision. Steve hasn't agreed, but I think he will. I wanted to hear your opinion as the victim. Steve deserves punishment. I don't want to go to the authorities because of the bad publicity for the hunt clubs. You weren't harmed, but hurt, nonetheless. My plan is to have Steve submit to humiliation and shaming, just like Rachel, for a month, then go back to work. I'll loan all of them the money to repay the embezzled funds. They will be banned from any hunts for five years. The loan will be repaid with ten percent interest, all of the interest to go to your retirement fund. If they fail to make a payment or reveal anything to the authorities or the public, then we fall back to Brian's plan. What do you think?"

I liked that he wouldn't die for his sins. I also really like the public shaming part. Master, Will they be shamed just like Rachel?"

"Yes, exactly the same."

I imagined Stephen helpless and at my mercy. And in the pillory. "Master, I have a suggestion. These men are arrogant and treat the girls roughly, so I think they should learn what it means to be a slave girl in the hunt club."

Master smiled and said, "Cynthia, I love the way you think. What specifically do you want to do?"

I reeled off ideas as fast as they occurred to me. He toned a few of them down, but in the end he said, "OK. I think they will be sorry they picked on you and will be anxious to avoid us in the future. I approve, with the caveats I mentioned."

Master and Brian proposed the deal to Stephen and his merry men. They would take a one month leave of absence and submit to punishment at the estate. They would not be hurt and released when the punishment was over. Master would loan them the funds to cover their embezzlement and they would repay it with ten percent interest.

Stephen and his associates accepted. They knew a good deal when they saw one. They had all been expecting a painful death. Shaming and humiliation were bad, but would end and then their lives would be theirs again after only a month. If they knew what I had in mind for them they might have reconsidered the deal.

Master drove me back to the manor and Brian stayed behind to get the miscreants transported.

Chapter 14

Punishment

"Cynthia, I have another assignment for you. I want you to be in charge of their humiliation and shaming. I want them chastised and humble when they leave and I want everyone in the hunt clubs to enjoy their punishment. They have never been particularly enjoyable company. I would enjoy doing this, but I think you will be better at it."

"With pleasure, Master."

Brain joined Master and I in the Pub. He said, "My men have Steve and his crew in a security cell. Now what?"

Master said, "I've given Cynthia the job of their punishment. Cynthia, what's first?"

I asked, "Can you have them taken to Mark, one at a time? I don't want to spoil the surprise too soon."

Brian asked, "Now?"

"Let me talk to Mark for a minute then bring Stephen over, if that's OK, Master?"

"Go."

I went to Mark's shop and explained what I wanted. Mark said, "It'll be a pleasure. I heard what those rascals did to you. Are you going to watch?"

"I wouldn't miss this for the world." I opened my laptop on a table and did a little research. I was amazed at the ready availability of the somewhat specialized things I wanted. I ordered several sets using the men's credit cards, after all, I had permission.

Mark turned back to his bench and started preparing the things I needed.

Brian and two of his men marched a thoroughly miserable Stephen into the shop.

Stephen saw me and asked, "Here to gloat, Cynthia?"

I nodded and said, "You bet. You're going to have the ride of your life. I'm in charge of your next month then you'll never lay eyes on me again, if you're smart. Remember, you agreed to this. Strip him, please."

His guard unlocked his cuffs and stripped him, leaving everything in a pile.

I said, "Mark, he's all yours."

Mark said, "stand on this," pointing to a block on the floor between two arms of an "X" shaped table.

Stephen stood on it, facing away from the table. Mark lay him back on the center and strapped his arms and legs to the arms of the "X". The arms were short and Stephen's hands and feet hung off the ends. Another strap went over Stephen's waist and I saw his balls and dick hung off the edge too. Mark measured him in several places and went to a cabinet. He came back to Stephen holding a four foot piece of chain and a round metal ring, hinged and open. He threaded the end of the chain on the ring and put it around his penis, above his balls.

Stephen yelled, "Hey, stop that."

Mark slapped his balls, hard and said, "Silence, slave."

Stephen yelped and shut up.

Mark used a hydraulic tool and riveted the ring shut. I always thought Stephen should be kept on a leash.

Mark put steel bands on Stephen's wrists and riveted them shut. Another trip to the cabinet produced a pair of shackles. Mark riveted one shackle on Stephen's right ankle. He released his left ankle, drug it across and riveted the remaining shackle on it. Last came a steel collar, with a trailing length of chain, also riveted shut. Mark unstrapped him from the table and, yanking on his penis leash said, "Up you dog."

Stephen stood and Mark yanked first one hand then the other high on his back and locked his bracelets to the dangling chain. Stephen groaned and Mark said, "Your tendons will stretch and feel better tomorrow. We'll keep adjusting them until your hands are locked to your collar."

Mark fitted a black leather strap around Stephen's folded arms and pulled it tight, eliciting another groan from Stephen. Mark laughed and said, "This will help your tendons stretch faster and make you look tidier." He handed Stephen's leash to me and said, I'm done."

I took his penis leash and dragged him close. I saw that Mark had put a nametag on his collar that read, "Suzy." I had to look up at him and this wasn't right, so I said, "Kneel, slave," and used my foot to push his leash to the floor. He dropped to his knees with a groan.

I told him, "Your name here is 'Suzy' and if you fail to respond to it, you'll be punished. Whenever you hear an order, you will acknowledge it verbally. You will address every woman as 'Mistress' and every man as 'Master.' Is that clear?"

He looked up at me in pain as I had continued my foot's pressure on his balls. He croaked, "Yes, Mistress."

Damn, I wanted to have an excuse to punish him. Instead I said, "Good"

I stuffed the large black ball gag in his mouth and strapped it tight. "Stand up and follow me." I took my foot off his leash.

I said, "Brian, Master, will you bring the next one to Mark?"

Brian smiled and said, "It will be my pleasure, Cynthia." He and his men left.

I tugged on Stephen's leash and he jumped to follow me. This was almost as good as a nose leash and boy was it satisfying. I led him to Suzanne's work station, enjoying him by taking a winding path and yanking on his leash. His groans and squeals were gratifying.

I reluctantly stopped in front to Suzanne and said, "Suzy, this is one of the men who kidnapped me and tortured me. He needs a pair of nipple rings and a nose ring with a leash. Would you hang bells and a chain between the nipple rings, too? "

She smiled and said, "Such a brave man doesn't need anesthetic, does he? Sit him in my chair."

I grabbed his semi-rigid penis with a firm grip, steered him to the chair, and pushed him down. Suzanne strapped him down, rubbed and pinched his nipples to stiffness, brushed some disinfectant on his nipples and skewered each of them. He yelled but the gag muffled most of the noise. Her table had items for the men laid out in groups for each one. There were bells on two inch chains, rings in individual boxes, and twelve inch lengths of gold chain. She picked up a half ring and replaced a needle with it. She threaded one end of the chain and a bell on the other half and mated it to the one sticking through his nipple. A pair of sturdy pliers with jaws to fit three fourths of the way around the ring was used to squeeze the ring closed.

She said, "These lock in place. They don't open so they'll have to be cut out. It'll take a diamond saw."

I nodded. "I know." One day she would put them on me. The difference between Stephen and me was that I wanted them.

She did his other nipple the same way. The chain dangling between his nipples was eye-catching, and the bells swayed and dinged with every breath or movement. I hoped he'd hate them as much as I liked them.

I took a bell in each hand and tugged, gently, Stephen's eyes widened and he yelped. I said, "All the slave girls here get these. You'll feel right at home."

"OK," Suzanne said, and brushed some of the orange liquid inside his nose with a q-tip. She stuck a piercing gun's arms in his nostrils and squeezed the handles. There was a snapping sound and Stephen jerked like he'd been shot. He screamed through his gag. A sound like a wounded deer. His forehead furrowed in pain. She pulled the thing away from his face. I saw his blood on it and smiled. He strained at his bonds, but couldn't move. She brushed some more stuff in his nose. I watched her load the grommet halves on the ends of the installer. She inserted both ends into his nose and put the center prong in the hole. When she was satisfied with the location, she pulled the trigger. The ends squeezed together and sealed the two halves of the grommet together around the hole. Stephen winced at every movement. He must have felt the squeeze on his septum since he stared cross-eyed at his nose after she pulled the grommet installer out.

She inserted another gold half ring, threaded the end link of a light chain on one half, and squeezed it together with the large pliers. Another click. I smiled benignly at him. I thought he looked quite appropriately outfitted with his nipple rings and bells; his big nose ring, and a four foot length of light chain dangling from his nose.

As a final touch, Suzanne pierced his ears and gave him another set of permanent gold earrings with bells.

Suzanne released the strap holding his head. He shook his head and I saw the heavy ring and the end of the chain swing back and forth like the clapper in a bell. All his bells sang with delight when he moved. I couldn't wait to watch him see himself. I asked, " Suzanne, do you have a mirror?

She handed me one from her table and I let Stephen see his face. His expression was worth waiting for. Surprise, humiliation, shame, disgust, horror, fear, and dread all slid across his features, clearly visible despite his gag.

"Suzy, your humiliation hasn't even begun. I'm going to enjoy this job."

I turned to Suzanne, "There are three more coming. Let's get him out of the chair and secured somewhere so the next ones will be surprised too."

She unstrapped him and I used his new nose leash to stand him up and followed Suzanne to a storage room with handy rings set in the wall every two feet at waist height. I felt such awesome power in me. I had total and complete control of "Suzy." All the mean things he had done to me when I was growing up. His dismissal of me as a "Whore" when I needed his help. All of it came surging through me and I wanted to whip him. I locked his penis leash to the wall ring, turned him to face the wall, pulled his nose leash between his legs, and said, "Kneel, slave."

He knelt and I told him, "Spread your legs as wide as you can." He complied.

"Bend your head down and touch your forehead to he floor." He complied.

"Stick your ass high in the air." He complied.

"This is punishment position. Remember it."

He said, "Yes, Mistress."

 I pulled his nose leash tight and locked it to his ankle chain. What a wonderful target. No wonder the masters made us learn it.

His ankle chain was resting on the floor. "I told you to spread your legs as far apart as possible. You disobeyed me."

He moved his feet an inch further apart. Good. I opened my whip and flicked it across his ass. He gasped. I hit him harder and said, "Twenty strokes for disobedience. Count them, thank me. Beg for another. Do it right and you'll get twenty. Screw up and I start over."

I hit him hard across the middle of his ass. He yelped and said, One, Mistress.   Thank you. Please may I have another?"

God, this felt so good. I was getting aroused. I had heard girls got aroused whipping other girls. Never heard that about whipping guys. Maybe because he was helpless and I was going to turn him into a girl? I didn't really care. Suzy was an asshole and I enjoyed beating her.

I slashed the whip across his ass again, just below the first one. He screamed like a little girl. There was no hero or guts inside this loser, She said, "Two, Thank you, Mistress. Please may I have another?"

At five he forgot to say "Thank you." I told him, "You didn't thank me. You're back to 'One' now. Count properly or I start over."

When I got to fifteen his ass was bright red and he had been crying for a few minutes. I was having a hard time stopping. I loved this. I loved hearing him cry. I loved his red ass. I remembered all the times he had used his strong body to humiliate me. The next stroke I gave underhanded, straight up between his legs. The thong hit right on the tip of his penis with a sharp crack. He jumped, flinging his chained body into the air a few inches. His scream was piercing and music to my ears. He sounded just like a little girl. I asked, "Are you going to count, Suzy, or should I start over?"

Suzy sobbed and said, "S...Sixteen, Mistress. Please can I have another?"

I aimed to the side of his penis and laid the thong across one of his balls. He screamed magnificently. I allowed the count now to be slow. It took a little while for Suzy to regain her composure after each pain blast.

I figured twenty was enough for now. I said, "Don't go anywhere, Suzy. We'll bring your friends to join you when they're ready. Then we'll all go meet the girls. They will enjoy having you as their sex toys. It'll be such a change for them. Don't move or you'll be punished."

I left her there, whimpering and sobbing. "Vengeance is wonderful," I thought.

I soon had all four of my former tormentors lined up on their knees facing the wall. They all looked terrified. I read their name tags out loud, "Remember, you are Suzy, Lily, Tanya, and Rose while you're here. You're going to learn what it is to be a slave girl. You might come to like it. Be sure and let me know. I'm in charge of your punishment for the next month. You won't be harmed. You will obey the same rules as all the girls. I've told them to you already. Are you clear on them?"

Rose said, "Yes, Mistress."

Suzy said, "Yes, Mistress"

Lily and Tanya just nodded.

I said, "Some of you are slow learners." I gave Tanya, and Lily two strokes of the whip on their asses. I said, One more time, "Are your rules clear?"

This time all four said, "Yes, Mistress."

"Good. Stand up and face left."

They all stood and said, "Yes, Mistress." Suzy was a little slow. I let it pass, figuring it wasn't her choice.

I unlocked the last man's cock leash from the wall ring, pulled it between the third one's legs and locked it to his cock ring. I repeated this for all of them and left Stephen's chain laying on the floor. I went back to the last man and unlocked his nose leash from the wall ring and locked it to the back of the third one's collar. I repeated this for all of them. I took both of Stephen's leashes in my hand and led the coffle to the kennel area. I locked the coffle to a ring and had them kneel while I looked for Ms. Johansen.

I found her and had her assign a kennel to each of them. She told me the pillory was ready and the girls were waiting in the yard. I took my charges out to meet the girls.

I was greeted with cheers and applause as I marched my captives out. I motioned for quiet and announced, "These slaves are to be humiliated and shamed for a month. They are experienced hunters and some of you were caught by them, undoubtedly. Each of them will spend an hour today in the pillory. The rest of the day they are available for your pleasure for two hours, each. They will eat with us and be kenneled at night. First use after the pillory goes to the girl with the best score. Rachel is scorekeeper. Tonight we are going to transform them into slave girls, as much as we can without harming them," I held up Suzy's leashes, "this one is Suzy. My brother and the ringleader of the group. He'll be first on the pillory."

A cheer went up. I unlocked him from the coffle and handed his leashes to Sylvia and Nylla. They put him on the pillory and made sure the spiked balls were well positioned to hit him on his cock and nipples. They removed his gag so he could scream loudly. Ms. Johansen formed the girls into a line and the first girl stepped to the rail. The first ball hit the lower ball squarely and the girl's cheers nearly drowned out Stephen's yelp of pain.

I tethered the other three to a pillar so they could watch.

When the hour was up, the winner, Anna, took "Suzy" to the hose and washed the colored mud off him. I took

"Rose" off the coffle and handed her leashes to Ms. Johansen. I watched Suzy being cleaned. She had a nice collection of scrapes and bruises on her groin and chest. She didn't look happy. I handed Anna my whip and said, she doesn't know the positions yet. Maybe you'd like to instruct her?"

She smiled prettily and said, "I would be delighted. Its about time some of these high and mighty hunters learn what we girls have to do." She led Suzy to a pole and locked his cock leash to it. Holding her nose leash in one hand and the whip in her other, She said, "Kneel, Slave."

Crack. "Spread your knees wide."

Crack, "Wider, dog."

She was smiling and I was glad she was being strong with Suzy. I wanted them thoroughly obedient by the time the month was over.

After the last one was off the pillory, I walked around the yard to see what the girls were up to. Margery had Suzy now kneeling and eating her out. I bet she's never done that before. Her back and ass were covered with red stripes. Margery was about to orgasm so I guess she'd learned to do it right.

Sandra had Lily laying on the ground and she was sitting on her cock riding her strongly. She had her cock leash in one hand and her nose leash in her other, screaming, "Hold it in slave. Don't you dare come without permission." Go girl.

Several girls were playing with the other Tanya and Rose. Each of their leashes were held by a different girl. Lily was kneeling in punishment position, her head on the ground and her ass high in the air. A girl was standing on the nose leash and another had hold of the cock leash pulling it back between her legs and up. The Tanya was working on Lily's bottom hole. Nancy was holding Tanya's cock leash over the back of the recipient, making sure she couldn't pull out. Tanya's nose leash was locked to Lily's collar and Shauna was encouraging her to more vigorous efforts with a riding crop.

I walked over to them and said, "Nice group effort. Do you have other plans?"

Nancy said, "When the Tanya comes, we'll switch positions. Not many straight guys knows what a good ass reaming feels like."

I said, with glee, "Don't forget to have the Lily clean Yanya's dick when she's done."

Shauna giggled and said, "Right. Cleanliness is next to Godliness."

I estimated there were at least two more hours of fun for the girls before dinner. I was certain these pukes would never forget their punishment.

After dinner I selected four girls to help with the men. I secured them over the enema drains and had the girls clean them off inside and out. From their cries, I don't think any of them had ever had an enema. No matter. They would get familiar with them.

My goal was to make them look and feel as close to a slave girl as possible. First was appearance. I needed to remove their body hair, and keep it off, at least while I had them. Afterwards was up to them. First I had the girls shave them. I had talked to the nurses and had a hair growth prevention plan in several steps, shave their faces, laser hair removal, vaniqa cream to prevent re-growth, a pill to decrease androgen production in their bodies, and finally an estrogen injection. At the end of their first treatment they were clean and their skin was soft. I would give them another laser treatment at the end of their month and continue the rest of the regime every day. Suzanne had selected some wigs for them and gave their lips a botox treatment.

I had the girls make up their faces in a sexy way. I insisted on bright red lipstick. The girls had a great time. The men were like life size dolls. The estate had quite an extensive wardrobe selection for the girls. They were naked most of the time, but costumes and clothing was allowed for special occasions. I put corsets and high heels on them next. I had the girls lace the corsets as tight as they could. The heels I selected were very high, even for me, and one size too small. I had found open toed ones so their nail polish would show. Girls sacrificed comfort for beauty all the time, right? I filled their mouths with black ball gags and strapped them tight. I wanted nothing but moans from them.

We took the "Girls" into the rec room and I assigned a pair of slaves to teach each "Girl" how to walk in her heels. One girl led her around by her nose leash and the other followed with a small whip, for encouragement. Once a "Girl" learned to walk smoothly in her heels, she was taught how to walk sexily, with the proper sway of her hips. The rest of the slaves gathered around to watch. They offered cat calls, impossible suggestions and cheers. The "Girls" had learned to blush quite well.

After all of them learned to do a suitably sexy walk, I fastened thirty pound weights to the end of their penis leashes and had them walk around the room with a whip wielding follower to keep them moving. It took another half hour before they were all walking sexy and dragging their weight. I was tempted to increase the weight, but the girls were getting horny so I let them play more sex games with the "Girls." By lights out the new "Girls" were exhausted and had had a chance to be used by every slave girl . They were forced to use each other's body more than once, too. By now they should be feeling just like the girls who had used them.

Pillory sessions were held every day. I invited the rest of the staff to help with the pillory punishment when the girls were off working. This was a whole new ballgame. I had to caution some of the stronger men that Master didn't want them injured.

Every morning they received a "Beauty" treatment to impede hair growth and soften their skin. The girls loved doing the "Girls" makeup every morning. They painted their nails and encouraged them to not smudge them by the simple expedient of the whip.

I suggested to Master that we could leave them a more lasting experience by having Suzanne tattoo the makeup colors on their faces, but he rejected it. I had photos taken of them every morning to record how they were changing.

I had them put on the roster for exercise and work parties. When they weren't being used they were put in the rec room or in the yard to be seen and used. The girls were sated after the first two days. Some of the girls just liked to lead them around by their cocks or noses. I asked some of them what they liked about that and always got a vague answer. I wondered they wanted the same treatment and weren't getting it. I mentioned it to Mr. Alistair and he said he'd see if they liked that.

At night the "Girls" slept in their kennels. Unlike the other slave girls I instructed Mr. Alistair to fasten their hands as high on their backs as possible and put the leather strap around their arms for sleep. The first two nights they didn't sleep well, but after they got use to the strain there was no problem. I kept their arms rigidly restrained unless I needed them for a task. It was pure aesthetics. I wanted to have their arms locked to the backs of their collars in perfect "Reverse prayer" position. I couldn't think of a more helpless position for them. A month of little use and the strained position, would shrink their arms and aid my feminization goal.

Later in the first week I decided on a new type of humiliation for my slaves. I kept the pillory in the morning and trained them as human ponies in the afternoon and evening. Master had shown me his stable and tack for pony girls. He told me he never really used it since the hunt became an instant success. I thought it would be a great new humiliation for the men to be forced to be livestock totally controlled by the pack girls. I had Sylvia, Rachel, and Nylla help me introduce the helpless men to their new game. I had learned that the men were most docile when I fastened their cock chain to their ankle chain. If I had them stand with their feet shoulder width apart and fastened the cock chain so it held the ankle chain in an inverted "V", then any sudden movement yanked on their cocks. We each led one of them to the stables by their leashes and fastened them to wall rings while we looked over the tack. Nylla had been an avid equestrienne in her youth and started suggesting suitable tack.

I could see the startled and horrified expressions on the helpless slaves as Nylla talked about the many items associated with a stable. Bits of black rubber and gleaming steel. Harnesses, bridles, reins and blinkers of black leather. Leading reins and trace chains hung from the walls and rafters. As Suzy and the others stared around them in disbelief, they realized that all of the equipment was much too small for a horse.

I knew I didn't have enough time for proper pony school so I just focused on the basics. I harnessed Suzy and took an enormous amount of joy watching her expression as I turned her into a human pony. She knew exactly what I was feeling and shrank from my terrible power. I put a wide belt around her waist and cinched it tight. It would have to bear the strain of the cart and rider. I picked up a bridle made entirely of black leather straps and showed it to Suzy. She shook her head and said, "Mistress, this is unfair. We agreed to punishment, but this was not what Robert or we meant."

I smiled and said, "I think this is a fitting punishment and you didn't limit what you agreed to." I picked up my crop and struck his cock four times, Forehand, backhand, forehand, backhand. I wasn't hitting unusually hard, bur he screamed and stamped his feet. When he stopped moaning I asked, "Are you going to give me any more trouble?"

"No, Mistress."

"Beg me to whip your cock hard whenever I want."

His eyes widened in surprise and fear. "M..Mistress, please hit my cock hard whenever you want. I beg you."

"Good, this won't hurt unless you are stubborn. Then your cock will suffer. Understand?"

He said, "Yes, Mistress." and held still.

He had learned.

I dropped it over his head and tightened all the straps. When I had finished I grabbed a couple of straps and jiggled it. I tightened one strap then it was snug.

I chose a bit for him. A thick steel bar, curved to fit in his mouth over his tongue, preventing speech. The underside was deeply scored so if the reins were pulled it would press the tiny points down into his tongue. There were plastic cylinders to protect his teeth while letting it rotate freely when he bit down. The bridle and reins attached to rings on the ends of the bit. His driver's slightest tug on the reins would cause instant pain in the most sensitive nerves of his body.

I held it in front of his face and explained the finer points of the design. He groaned and gazed imploringly at me, terrified of the thought of having it clamped in his mouth. I laughed, softly and ordered, "Open."

He stared at me for a moment. I lifted the crop and he opened his mouth. I slid it in and fastened it to the bridle. I tightened the chin strap forcing his teeth closed on the plastic guards. I waggled the rein rings to make sure it rotated freely. I laughed at his expression. I was exhilarated at my total control over the "Girls." They feared me and obeyed my every command. I was their Mistress and I loved it. They knew I got great pleasure from whipping them. I wondered about myself. I don't think I was sadistic before they came into my power. I had always heard the "Absolute power corrupts absolutely." Would I feel this way about the pack girls after these "Girls" were gone? I hoped not. I would not be proud of myself then. My rationalization was that these assholes soundly deserved what they got.

Master had some colorful tall plumed bridles with peacock feathers in his tack room. There was a vase or stand with a dozen very long ostrich feathers dyed different colors. Interested, I pulled one out. Its end was "J" shaped ending in a large rubber butt plug. How interesting. I took Stephen to a stout metal bar at about waist height and bent him over it. I clipped his nose leash to his ankle chain to keep him in place. I lubed his ass and slid the plug in. When I stood him up the feather waved a couple of feet over his head. I found a small strap and secured the middle of the feather to his arm strap. I had Sylvia lead him around the room. He was magnificent. I took a picture and showed it to him. He looked pained but couldn't say anything. We put these on the rest of them and harnessed each one to a cart.

I put pack girls on the carts as their drivers. I had them take the carts around the track several times until the ponies learned to follow the reins. Their bridles came with blinders and I adjusted them to be fairly restrictive. To start I clipped their cock and nose leashes to their collars to keep them out of the way. One of the ponies got a bit frisky and didn't obey the reins at first. Each of the carts had a carriage whip, but he didn't even respond to that. I stopped his cart, whipped his ass five good hard strokes with a cane, I tied a line to his cock leash and tied the other end to the cart rail. If he acted up again, the driver would give his cock a good, hard yank. The threat was enough and he obeyed the reins after that. After the first day of training, I had all the girls take turns driving the carts. The last day before their sentence was done I staged cart races. The girls had a great time and the slaves, not so much.

After dinner Master always had me tell him how the punishment was going and show him any interesting photos. He was particularly interested in the pony training. He told me he had thought of doing pony training for the girls and its why he had a fully equipped but unused stable and all the tack. He'd never followed through because the hunt club idea was so well received and pony girls just didn't have the same level of interest. He thought it was because the hunt allowed everyone who wanted to play a role: hunter, prey, or observer, and it had a high level of excitement.

He often visited the training to further cow the prisoners and to offer any advice. He told me about overcheck reins and how it keeps the pony's head erect. He showed me the ones in the tack room. They were perfect. They would make the ponies hold their heads high and make them even more responsive to the reins. I immediately fitted them all with one. It worked miracles on their appearance. The drivers thought it made them more obedient too.

About the middle of the second week I noticed appreciable bosom development. By the end of the third week they had moderate but firm breasts. I thought by the end of the month they would have great racks.

I arranged a party for the last weekend to show them off to all their friends and acquaintances from the hunt clubs. Master agreed it would be appropriate for their deeds and punishments to be known to many people. It would further deepen their humiliation and shame. It would also deter anyone else who might have hostile thoughts toward Robert.

I made sure many photos were taken of their activities, just for the records. They were all put on a heavily encrypted thumb drive. Master took it for safekeeping. The captives were forced to have sex in every way possible with themselves and the girls.

The party began at noon. I planned to put one of the miscreants in the pillory for an hour each starting around two. Of course I would put Suzy there first. I had four posts erected on the patio and fastened them there with short chains to their collars so they couldn't sit down. I fitted them with black ball gags.

I hung a whip, a riding crop, and a medium cane on each post and put a sign on the post detailing the man's name, occupation, employer, address, team results for four years, what he had done, and his punishment. It invited passersby to chastise him with the provided instruments.

Master stopped by before the guests arrived and we looked at the "Girls." Master said, "Cynthia, I've watched their progress with amazement. Hide their penis and they look like females. Why don't you put tiny skirts on them and hide their members for a grand unveiling when all the guests are here?"

It was a great idea. I sent girls off to find suitable skirts, blindfolds, and sheets. I draped the sheets over the signs, put the skirts and blindfolds on the "Girls" just in time. The first guests arrived and I explained these "Girls" had been bad and were being punished. A lot of fingers played with their now sizeable breasts and nose rings and were rewarded with moans and gasps.

When everyone had arrived, Master came up in front of the four posts and got everyone's attention. He announced in a large voice, "Ladies and Gentlemen. These four women committed crimes against Cynthia and I for which they would have faced life in prison. That would have brought national attention onto our clubs. They agreed to submit themselves to our punishment and humiliation for one month, instead. We promised not to cause them physical harm or death. But, as you will see, their experience has changed them. Cynthia. please reveal their faces and their information."

I walked to each of them, Suzy, Lily, Tanya, and Rose and removed the blindfolds, then I stripped the sheets off the signs. Master and I walked to the sidelines. The throng of club members closed around the hapless "Girls" and peals of laughter and chatter arose. Many men slapped the "Girls" breasts to see if they were real. The cries of female pain assured them that the breasts were indeed real. The slapping of breasts continued far after their authenticity was proven.

Mr. Reynolds came up to Master and I and congratulated us, "Robert, Cynthia, I love how you took care of Stephen and his team. They are thoroughly disgraced and I'm sure they won't bother us again. And they're alive and unharmed. I don't know how they'll go back to work like that, but its a fitting consequence to their actions."

Master said, "Thank you, Jonathan. Its all Cynthia's work. Brian almost had me convinced to drop them out of a copter twenty miles offshore. I don't think those four will ever see women the same again."

I excused myself when they started talking about hunts. I took the skirts off to reveal their male members and put Suzy in the pillory. The pillory was quite a hit and all the guests tried their hands at throwing the shot.

There was usually a crowd around each chained miscreant when I looked. Once I looked at Suzy's post when and saw people were walking away from it. I sauntered over and he looked at me. He said, "Congratulations. You have done well in your assignment. I've been so thoroughly humiliated. I will try my best to never see any of these people again. I'm thinking of joining a monastery in Tibet. I don't think they will have heard of me there."

I replied, "Thank you. I hope you appreciate that security took everyone's cell phones and are jamming the frequencies they use just in case. We're trying to keep you off Instagram and Facebook."

"Thank you for that, Cynthia. For what its worth, I am sorry. I was desperate, but I didn't have to be such an ass."

"Good. How do you like being a sex toy?"

"Well," he said, " I can't stand being so helpless and that takes much of the joy out of sex. On the other hand, I've learned a lot of my old prejudices were unfounded. Let's say my horizons have expanded."

"A lot of the joy from sex for girls comes from the helplessness. Just the way nature designed men and women to ensure the race continues, I guess. Anyway, now you know what it feels like for us."

"Indeed I do. Once I get out of this, I will definitely treat women differently. I'll still want them helpless, but I'll make sure they're comfortable."

I took a cane off the post and said, turn around Stephen. I haven't gotten even yet."

He said, "Of course," and turned to face the post. I saw a collection of red stripes on his back and ass.

I hit his ass five times, as hard as I could. He jumped at each one and yelped. I watched the impact. The skin made waves and fled from the cane, leaving a bright scarlet stripe shading through red to pink. I spaced them out so he had five parallel stripes about an inch apart. She jumped and moaned quite nicely. I rather liked the way they looked on her and wondered about other remembrances I could leave her. Tattoos, or brands. Something lasting and memorable. I said, "I'm done. We're even. Turn around." I hung the cane back on the post and turned to leave.

He said, "Cynthia, I'm still your brother, call me after this is done, please."

I walked away. It was time for the ladies. I had Ms. Johansen take Lily off the pillory and clean her up.

Sylvia and Rachel helped me take the three others off their posts and set them up for the ladies. We took all four to an area of the patio with floor rings and had them kneel with a ring behind them. We locked their cock leashes to the rings leaving them only a foot of slack so they couldn't get up. We moved a wicker chair in front of each of them. I positioned a girl with a whip behind each one for encouragement. Then I announced that the men should retire to the lounge where the pack girls would entertain them. I asked the ladies to stay and have the slaves entertain them.. Given the association of both men and women guests with the hunt clubs, I didn't think anyone would abstain. I was right. The slaves had a steady stream of women guests who hadn't had an orgasm in ages.

When a slave was available the girl would wipe his face and hand his nose leash to the next customer. She would sit in the chair at a comfortable position and pull his face to her pussy. She would instruct him if needed and wave to the girl with the whip if he needed encouragement. The women would orgasm in a couple of minutes and she'd get up. There was a line behind each chair for a couple of hours. Refreshments of an alcoholic nature were available to the guests. Water for the slaves and staff.

Most of the women went through the chairs three or four times. Some ladies made a point of sampling each of the men. I was approached and thanked for arranging such an interesting and fun party. Several women asked if they could borrow my slaves for their next party. I explained these would only be released soon. But she should ask Master if her party would occur before their time was up.

People started leaving around midnight. After the party I gave the "Girls" a final present. Sylvia and I took them back to see Suzanne. I had her put a tattoo on their right ass cheeks. A black horseshoe, turned up to hold their good fortune, with their local names, Suzy, Lily, Tanya, and Rose, in red inside the horseshoe. I took some more pictures. Sylvia, Suzanne, and I thought they were lovely. Again, the slaves, not so much.

After everyone was gone, Master took me up to bed. I was exhausted too. I would have thought he'd be tired, but he managed to fire me up and I slept the sleep of the well fucked slave girl that night.

The morning of their release came way too soon, but a promise had been made.

After breakfast I put the "Girls" in the bath area and had them cleaned, inside and out. I had the girls do their makeup. Their hair had grown long enough it could be styled properly. It was short, but we gave them Pixie cuts and iridescent dye jobs. They really were lovely girls now. We used the smallest corsets now that their waists had shrunken so nicely. As another surprise for them I replaced the cords in the corset with a woven stainless steel cable and when we pulled it tight I used a crimping tool to lock the wires together in a tidy little clamp. The cable would have to be cut to remove the corsets now. Of course I didn't tell the "Girls" about this. Wearing just their corsets, heels and chains, I put them in coffle and led them back to Mark, carrying their clothes.

I wanted to leave their rings in too, but Master told me to take the nose and cock rings off. He said it was OK to leave the nipple rings. "They might like them," he said.

Brian sent some security guys over to make sure they behaved.

A couple of security men watched them as Mark removed their restraints and ring. Once they were free of everything but the nipple rings, I dressed them in the clothes I had chosen. A tiny leather skirt, and a tight, translucent white blouse that highlighted their ample breasts and nipple rings. They looked like cheap hookers. I put a ten dollar bill and a dollar in quarters in the skirt pocket along with their driver's license. They didn't look like those picture anymore.

Each of them had lost more than twenty pounds on their diet and exercise regime. They all looked like tall, healthy, slim young women now. Their arms were perfect. My strict binding regime had shrunk them to feminine proportion. Their hands were a little too big, but they were on the small side to start with. The security men cuffed their hands behind them and took them outside to a large white van. They were going to be un-cuffed and released one at a time within a couple of blocks of their homes. I told them, "Its been fun girls. Your hormone treatments will wear off in a month and your female secondary sexual characteristics should recede after that. If you want to keep them, here's the contact data for a sex change specialist. You're halfway there." I stuffed a business card in each of their halters and the security men loaded them into the van.

Master told me later that they were all very diligent in repaying his loan. It looked like we wouldn't see them again. I was sure the girls would miss them. For just that month there was someone who had to obey them. I sometimes wonder what they told people at work when they showed up with their jewelry, enlarged mammaries and hair. I suppose a wig and a strap around their breasts and loose clothes would do, but how would they explain them and their tattoos to a girlfriend?

I learned that Master went to exercise the same time I did. I never knew, but I guess it should have been obvious from his physique. He had a complete gym he let his executives use. He also had a Krav Maga instructor come in twice a week for a session with him and the security staff. He also had a fitness trainer come in once a week. Having money and people to arrange things for you is real luxury.

I finished my training and lived with Master full time. I loved the pack girls and visited with them in my spare time. Master insisted I go to their daily exercise class. I liked it. Truth be told, I envied them. I had become enmeshed in Master's business life and it wasn't fun like playing with the girls and gardening. I missed the camaraderie and the excitement of the hunt. After I had learned enough to be a real aide to Master I would stare out the window at the pack yard and watch them frolicking and eating in their paws and boots. I often wanted to shuck my job and join them. Master watched me all the time and seemed to know my thoughts. He kept giving me new things to do and learn, but what was interesting and exciting for him, was work for me. Don't get me wrong. I was surprisingly good at his tasks and he praised me all the time. I loved serving him and felt that wonderful joy whenever I performed well for him.

Now that I was an "Upstairs" slave full time I got to wear shoes. Rather, I had to wear shoes and the only ones I had were several pairs of "Fuck Me" five inch heels. They were tall enough that if I stood in display position my ankle chain cleared the floor. They were uncomfortable for the first few weeks but got better over time.

He was proud of me and I was present for all his meetings. It was clear that the people who came to his meetings were delighted he had a slave girl, even the women. I would stand in display position while he greeted his guests and invite them to handle me. The men always started with my breasts and the women with my shaved pussy. The first thing they did was see if I was wet, and I always was. I was truly an exhibitionist and I became very aroused when Master displayed my naked body to strangers. They were too gentle with me. I wanted my nipples pinched and pulled, but they just touched. Master knew this and wore a sly grin when the strangers touched me. Girls were tougher stuff than they realized. Every now and then a knowledgeable master would come to a meeting and he would make me gasp and squirm in joyful anticipation. They never got me off and I would be uncomfortably aware of my need while kneeling by Master.

I hadn't realized it when I prepared my resume, but what made him flag me for an interview was my eidetic memory. I could recall everything I heard or saw. He had hoped I would otherwise be suitable for this unusual environment. Lucky for both of us I turned out to have a wide submissive streak in me. In most meetings he would show me to the others and explain I was his slave. I certainly looked the part with my bands and ankle chains. I would have my hands locked behind me and kneel beside him for the meeting. I was also responsible for refreshments. I became adept at making and serving drinks with my hands locked behind me. After the meeting I would retire to my tiny office and speak into a microphone describing who was there and what was said or done. The computer would convert it to text and send a copy to Master's computer. It was rare that I would have my hands free at work.

Master had more tricks up his sleeve. One night I told him I missed being a pack girl and explained as best I could. He said he understood and He would help. I slept well that night wondering how he planned to help. The next morning after breakfast we visited Suzanne and Master told her to put nipple rings and a nose ring on me. As soon as he told Suzanne what he wanted, I almost fainted. I had wanted nipple rings like Julie's for a long time but had not considered a nose ring. Rachel had one. I had them put on the captives as a way to control guys so much bigger than me. Now I was getting one too. I remember thinking they were very erotic. I guess I'm going to find out. A chilling thought occurred to me. Oh shit. I asked, "Master, are you going to put a leash on my nose ring?"

I clamped my mouth shut. I had spoken without permission. I looked at him, afraid to apologize.

He looked at me as a Master. He made decisions, not me. He said, "Open your mouth."

I obeyed and he took a black ball gag off Suzanne's table and strapped it in my mouth.. No talking without permission."

I nodded "Yes."

He turned back to Suzanne and said, "and hang a large bell on each nipple ring." I had not seen any bells before on girls. He saw my concerned expression and said, "Breaking the rules may earn a slave girl punishment. They will look wonderful on you. Don't worry. I will like them on you too. Besides, you will want them for your next training."

I couldn't avoid it, so I was obedient as Suzanne strapped me into her chair. I watched as she cleaned, coated, pierced, ringed, and belled my nipples. I wondered for what new training I would need bells on my nipples? The bells weren't threaded directly on the rings. They dangled on two inch chains below the rings. There was no pain beyond the pricks in my nipples. Very slight compared to the pinching I loved. I think I got a little aroused.

"They look good on you, Cynthia. Your nose ring will be even better," Suzanne said, and brushed some of the orange liquid inside my nose with a q-tip. My nose got numb and she stuck a big metal thing in my face. Big parts stuck in my nose, then there was a snap sound and pain erupted in my head. It was much worse than my nipples. I thought I had been shot. I screamed into my gag and she pulled the thing away from my face. I couldn't move. She brushed some more stuff in my nose that stung. She stuck something else up my nose and moved it around. Everything she did hurt. Then I felt the grommet squeezing the middle of my nose. I felt a click and she took the things out of my nose. I still felt the pressure. She inserted another gold ring, threaded the end link of a light chain on one half, and squeezed it together with large pliers. Another click. Then I was left alone with my pain, another heavy ring, and a four foot length of light chain dangling from my nose. He did have a leash put on me. Damn.

I expected her to let me up, but she didn't. She approached me with the piercing gun again and gave me some large gold earrings. The same ones as in my nipples. They didn't hurt much, more like a prick. She didn't put bells on these.

She released the strap holding my head. I shook my head and felt the heavy ring and the end of the chain swing back and forth like the clapper in a bell. I wanted to see myself so much.

Suzanne said, "Just a minute Honey. Let me get these straps lose and you can look in the mirror on the wall." She took all the straps off me and I sat up. I felt all the new metal moving in sensitive areas.

Master walked up and said, "You look gorgeous. You were meant to wear chains." He took the gag out of my mouth.

Thank God, I was beginning to drool. I smiled, "Thank you, Master. I feel like I was assaulted by a hardware demon."

I stood, he took hold of my upper arm and let the chain leash dangle. He steered me toward the wall. I was grateful for his help. Then I saw my reflection in the mirror. I knew what I looked like. but the girl in the mirror was gorgeous. Her rings shone in the light. Her breasts were high and firm with erect rosy nipples and pierced by those huge gold rings. She was the most sexy and erotic creature I had ever imagined. She wore her chains with distinction. Their graceful lines enhanced rather than shamed. I watched the creature in the reflection smile. I realized I was smiling. I could have stood there the rest of the day, but I was also impatient to be done.

I turned to Suzanne, "Suzanne, thank you for giving me these rings. They are beautiful."

"Master, what now?"

He took the dangling end of my leash. "What do you think of your new leash?"

"Master, you don't need it. I will obey you without question."

"It was very useful for controlling Rachel and the penitents. I wanted to see how it looked on you."

Using a little reverse psychology, I said, "It is eye catching, Master."

He smiled, "So you like the way it looks?"

Caught me. "Not really, Master. Its kind of a nuisance and it really doesn't enhance the way the rings do."

OK, Cynthia. I won't tease you any more, but remember how easy it is to put it back. Be good. Suzanne, would you remove the leash, please"

Thank you, Master.

Suzanne brought a large set of bolt cutters and snipped the leash off my ring.

I turned to the mirror again, smiled, and said, "That's a load off my nose."

Master chuckled and put a removable leash on my nose ring and led me away."

I was more conscious of the bells than the rings as we walked back to his office. I was a cacophony of sound. Every step started with the clinking of my ankle chain being pulled, punctuated with the sharp click of my heels on the hard floor, and ending with the dinging of my nipple bells flinging themselves against my ribs and breasts. I made loud and unusual sounds, like a peg leg vendor pushing an ice cream cart. Everyone we passed gawked at me long before we were close. I held one in each hand to quiet them. Master stopped me, said, "None of that," and locked my hands behind me.

Master took me to the Pub that night and allowed me one drink. It came with a straw. The servers were used to girls whose hands were locked away. He chose a booth and pulled me up against him.

Many of the girls came over to me and congratulated me on my new rings. They seemed genuinely envious. After a couple of these visits I was happy I had them and started gushing right back how much I like them and what a perceptive owner Master was. Master was also congratulated by men in the Pub who came over and told him how good I looked. He took the praise with grace, allowing it was such an obvious improvement he really didn't deserve any credit for noticing the obvious. Many of the men and a few women allowed all the girls would look good with a nose ring. I remembered how obedient they made the four men and decided I didn't need to be any more obedient than I was now. I tried to make it sound dull and not worthy of further consideration. Even while I was speaking, I saw Master watching me knowingly.

When we were alone he said, "You really wanted a complete set like Julie, didn't you?"

Tears started leaking out of my eyes and I cuddled closer to him. He knew me better than I knew myself. My voice quivered, "Yes, Master. Julie's are beyond beautiful. She's like a goddess of submission. I don't know if I would look like that with the rings. I'm afraid I'd look silly, with the labia rings, too."

"Cynthia, don't be afraid. Its my decision, not yours. You will be magnificent when I put them in you. But I won't yet. I will let you get used to these. Done properly, it's a progression to match your appearance with your soul. Just watch. I will do it right and you will feel perfect at every step.

He had a meeting a few days later. I was glad my piercings had time to heal. My rings were an instant hit. Even the two women played with them before feeling my pussy. Master was correct in his timing. I loved being fondled and appreciated by strangers. I felt more valued than ever in my life. I wanted him to take me out in public, wearing nothing but my rings and chains. I think I am ready for that now. Women weren't born with clothes. This was me, pure and naked to the world.

Chapter 15

Mistress of the pack

One morning after breakfast Master took me down to the kennel's exercise room. Ms. Johansen, Sylvia, Julie, and an unknown woman were waiting. The stranger was dressed in a flowing long skirt and a halter top, both adorned with strings of coins and small bells. Ms Johansen was wearing a bikini. Sylvia, Julie, and I were naked and our feet were chained. Master said, "I've hired Joline to teach you belly dance. She has whip rights over all of you, so obey her."

We all said, "Yes, Master." He left us. I was a little shocked. I never knew Ms Johansen was a slave too. I always treated her like a free woman because everyone else did. He left.

Ms. Johansen now wore chains on her wrists and ankles too. They were cuff- style that could be easily unlocked and removed. They had two feet of chain between the cuffs, She put a similar length of chain on Sylvia, Julie and I.

I went to dance training every day for a month. Master would send the off duty security and gardening men to watch us. He said that only a man could fully appreciate the beauty of this kind of dance. I expect he was correct. We got few strings of coins tied around our waist and draped around our neck. I don't expect a woman would appreciate the trim bodies showing off our extraordinary pectoral control as much as men. The sexual keys are different.

The exercise room was lined with mirrors so we could see all the instructors actions. I enjoyed the dancing. I was surprised that my chains did not hinder me at all. Almost all the action in my hips and torso. I learned that all the floor motion used tiny steps that didn't come close to my hobble's full length. I learned to control my hips, breasts, stomach and shoulders as much as I did my arms.

Considering how much my chains limited me, I felt sensuous and attractive and in control as I danced. I cast furtive glances at my audience as I moved. I noticed how they smiled at the girls in motion and watched as their cocks swelled their pants.

One of the most enjoyed exercises was that used for strengthening the pectorals. We were required to learn to lift our breasts and shift them from side to side. We had to learn to twirl our nipple rings in a circle. The trainers clapped and cheered when one of the girls succeeded. Of course, theses exercises caused all the slave girls to become aroused.

I loved performing in front of the men. I wanted them. I became very aroused as I danced for them. I imagined they were my masters and were going to take me fully when the dance ended. But it always ended in frustration. I knew this is the life of a slave girl and I acknowledged that I was a slave girl. I wanted my Master to take me after every dance. I was so aroused I would have come in an instant.

When the trainer said we were good enough and only needed practice, Master paid her well and ended the training. He had us perform in the pub four evenings a week. I loved dancing to an audience. The other girls asked me to see if Master would train them too. He agreed and now The other trained girls and I give a dance workshop to the other girls twice a week. All of the girls are athletic and conditioned so they pick it up quickly.

Master knows how to run a tight ship. He listened to my whining and moping and determined I need a larger variety of things to do. Now I'm busy with personal jobs while being his PA full time. And of course, my ongoing lessons in sexual stamina from the Master. Sometimes,. as I'm about to fall asleep, I reflect on how lucky I was to lose the job with Ralph. So lucky...

Master is going to take me on a hunt. In two days I'm going to be chasing down fleeing girls on my horse. I'm going to feel the thrill of the hunt from the other side. I can't wait. I used to ride all the time when I lived at home. I was a 4Her and even competed in some barrel racing when I was a teenager. I haven't been on a horse in years, so Master has arranged a riding lesson this afternoon. He's even gotten me some hunter's clothes. I dread having to wear those heavy things. I'm quite happy going without, but he said it wouldn't be right to so confuse the dogs.

We traveled by car to the hunt club. Our horses and dogs were waiting for us. Master let me have one glass of wine in the pre-hunt party. I watched as the girls were lined up for the dogs to sniff. Here their hands were tied over their heads to projections from a wall and they spread their legs for the dogs. I saw the girls were as excited as the dogs. A couple of them lost bladder control and peed on the ground. No one paid any attention. The hunters were walking up and down in front of the girls, trying to choose their favorite if they were lucky. I joined them and decided my choice was beautiful, redhead with piercing green eyes and a please fuck me look on her face. I asked her how many hunts she had been in and she said, "Ten, Mistress."

"What's your name?"

"Aileen, Mistress."

"Do you like being chased?"

"Forgive me, Mistress, but doesn't every woman want that?"

I decided she was right and I hoped I'd be lucky enough to capture her. I walked on.

The dogs were brought out and were frantic to smell their quarry. I told Master I would like to catch Aileen and pointed her out.. He talked to the dog handler and made sure our dogs smelled her last, and well.

The pack master came by and freed the girl's hands. They stood in display until he said, "Girls, give good sport. Run." They took off for the woods and vanished from sight. In a little while he announced "Dogs away in three minutes. Take your horse."

We all mounted up and got ready to ride. The horses sensed the excitement and acted skitterish. The dogs barked impatiently but were reasonably well behaved. The leader of the hunt was resplendent in his scarlet coat and white pants. All the rest of us wore black and had team colored armbands. Master had a team of four. Myself, Master, Brian and a security man named John. Our armbands were green over red. The pack master announced, "Loose the hounds." In a flash the dogs were away, bounding over the pasture. I sent my horse racing after Master.

As soon as our dogs entered the woods they veered off to the left, upwind. Aileen definitely had not gotten the memo on which way to run. We followed the dogs through light brush and around clumps of trees. They crossed a small stream without hesitation. I saw a team off to our right watching their dogs circle a tree. A girl must have climbed it.

Our dogs baying increased in tempo and volume. They must have eyes on a girl. My heart was pounding too. This was just as exciting as being hunted and a lot less tiring. The dogs baying changed to an excited barking. They caught her. I rode up and saw Master leap off his horse and kneel beside the whirling cluster of dogs. Brian tossed a handful of chocolate on the ground and the dogs ran to them. Master locked the girl's hands behind her and turned her onto her back. It was Aileen. My heart leaped with our success. We all dismounted and went to enjoy our prize. Master felt her pussy and said, "She's wet and ready."

Aileen looked at me and said, "See what I mean, Mistress." Master took her first without foreplay. He orgasmed quickly but she didn't reach the edge yet. Master stepped aside quickly for Brian who also came quickly, depriving Aileen of release. John took her next and she orgasmed along with him. My turn, I pulled down my pants, squatted over her, and put my pussy on her mouth. "Eat me, Aileen."

She started doing a good job and I was soon flying toward release. I leaned back and used my fingers to renew her arousal. I came in a gush and coated her face liberally with my love juices. She tried hard to lick me clean., but there were so many places she couldn't reach. I kept up my manual stimulation and she orgasmed again. I stood up, wiped my pussy on her hair and pulled on my discarded pants.

She smiled up at me and said, "Its nice having a lady hunter. Thank you, Mistress."

I responded with my own smile and said, "My pleasure, indeed, Aileen."

John pulled her to her feet and put a long leash on her collar. We walked back to the manor with Aileen following us and smiling broadly. She would be ours tonight at the party and afterwards. John handed her over to the pack master and sent him the capture photo he had taken when she was cuffed. The time stamp would be used to determine our team's score.

We went to our rooms and cleaned up and changed clothes. Master allowed me only a short diaphanous skirt. He wanted to show off my new rings and bells. I saw several guests with bare breasts. I was the only one with a collar, nipple ornaments and chained ankles. They were a great conversation starter at the party. Again, I had to nurse my one drink. Everyone's first comment was something like, "Those are beautiful. Are they real or costume."

When I said, "Real, Mistress/Master." The second question was always, "You're a slave?"

Master explained that I was his personal slave. They would then discuss the legality of a slave being allowed to be a hunter. He always won the discussion by quoting the club bylaws, which he wrote. I was the only slave who was a guest. Master told me in private the ladies there were envious of my breasts. I agreed they were some of my better assets. Our captures were delivered en mass to the party and Master took custody of Aileen. She was spotless and shining. She was leashed and her hands locked behind her. Master handed the leash to Brian and said, I have my own slave to play with. You two go play with Aileen. She looked at me in surprise.

I said, "Yes, Aileen, I'm a slave too. I enjoyed our time and maybe we can do it again sometime."

She said, "I will remember you as my Mistress who was a slave. I hope we can play again."

Brian and John went upstairs. Master put a leash on my nipple ring and said, "Let's go play too."

We were driving home the next day and Master had me describe my feelings on the hunt. I tried to convey my sense of excitement and couldn't find the right words to make it clear. He said he understood fully. He had the same difficulty describing it to other non-hunters. We talked about the hunt and difference between the two I knew of. In the end he asked about Aileen.

I told him of the spark I felt when we touched. It was like when he touched me or loved me or punished me. It felt so right. It wasn't love, or even sex. It was a sense of belonging. I waxed poetic and tried to make it clear she was no threat to the intense feelings I had for him. He listened to my ramblings with a smile and told me he understood. He said she was very pretty but he didn't see the spark in her that he saw in me.

"Thank you, Master. I think she's special but not like us."

Several weeks passed and one morning we were eating breakfast when Master changed my life again. He said, simply, "Cynthia, I have a new assignment for you. I've promoted Alistair and sending him to run an operation in Switzerland. I want you to replace him. You start after breakfast."

I was startled, to say the least. "Master, I ask this with all possible respect, are you out of your mind. I'm a PA, a slave. I follow orders. I don't make decisions. I'm unqualified to run a pack."

"Cynthia, I've watched you take all sorts of situations in stride. I have confidence in you instincts. I can't exactly advertise for a girl pack manager can I? Alistair was an accountant when I gave him the pack master job. He's done well. Besides, your duty is what?"

"Obedience, Master." Oh Boy. I knew where this was going.

"I've just ordered you to be my pack master. What is your response?"

"Yes, Master."

"Here's how I want this to work. If it doesn't tell me what you need. First you are in charge. Ms. Johansen and another assistant work for you. You'll stay as my PA most of the time. Once a day you'll go to the kennel and make any decisions needed. Ms. Johansen knows the routine stuff. Your job is the big picture changes. I'm going to give you another assistant. You choose who you want from the girls."

Go down there after you finish and talk to Alistair. He doesn't leave until Thursday. Decide on who you want for your second assistant."

Yes, Master. May I ask why I will need a second assistant?"

"In a few weeks I'm going to give you an additional duty. You'll need the help. Don't worry. You're qualified."

Great. I don't get paid any more for additional duties I realized. Of course it wasn't about the money after the first week.

I went to the kennels and told them what Master wanted. Both Mr. Alistair and Ms. Johansen agreed it could work. I asked who they thought would be a good assistant. They decided on Nylla. Surprised me, but they knew the girls best.

It worked out fine and I taught the girls what I knew about tracking dogs and the effects of wind. They huddled immediately to discuss future tactics. My work was done there.

Master's additional assignment was pony girls. He had liked how I had set up and run the pony training for the captives and wanted to try pony girls again. He had the idea that if I made an impressive enough show, he could start a pony girl competition in dressage and racing to broaden the club's repertoires. I liked the idea too. I thought the girls would like a variety and it would fill what were now empty hours. We had the girls, the equipment, and the space. Why not?

I brought all the girls down to the stable it the morning and got them all dressed in their tack. Ms. Johansen and I fitted the bits since the proper size and rigging were important to comfort. I started them on the high step, something I never bothered with the men. I was thinking dressage for the girls. I saw the rack of pony boots, strange heelless boots with wide hoofs under their toes. Like high heels with no heels. I had them don these before I locked their hands behind them and put a lunge rein on their bits. I clipped the other ends of their reins to a post in the yard and had them stand in a circle around it, lunges taut.

I stationed Ms. Johansen on the far side of the circle. Both of us had long whips. I told them how I wanted them to walk. "Girls, walk slow. Lift your legs until your knees are as high as your waist before moving forward. Its a hesitation step with your feet held high. Ms. Johansen and I will correct you as you pass by us. Stay evenly spaced like you are now. Always start with your left foot. Everyone lift your left foot and hold it. Nylla, Suzy, Jeanne raise your knee higher. OK, good step forward one step and raise your other knee."

I had them practice for ten steps. Everyone was even so I said, "Looks good girls. Now walk slowly around the circle. Go."

I watched them parade in a circle. Twenty naked young women, their hands locked behind them and pony boots on their feet. Their boobs bobbing up and down as they stepped in unison. They looked like the Crazy Horse dancers, but there was a difference. They were mine and helpless. I could do anything I wanted. I could pull one out and make her eat me. I could whip any of their asses as they paraded past me. I owned them. Yet I envied them too. They were so hot in their gear. I knew I would look just like them if I were in the line. They had nothing to do but obey my orders. I had to decide what to order them to do to meet my orders. I had no training in this and was afraid I would do it wrong. It would be so much more comfortable to be one of them. I was anxious for the day to end so I could enjoy being helpless again in Master's control.

They did well. Ms. Johansen and I didn't have to use the whips at all. I let them walk for twenty or so times around. They were perfect. I was proud of all of them. Next I rearranged them into ten pairs of two girls. The inner girl I left the long rein on. I moved the other girls to the outside and used a four foot line to join their bits. I wanted them to learn to coordinate. I started them walking and after they got used to the routine, sped them up. The inner girl had to take shorter steps or the outer girl longer. I just told them to stay in line. I had to use the whip a couple of times to get them all together. I increased their sped twice and they did well. I decided that was enough for now so we took the reins off them and let them wander loose in the yard to cool off. I told them to practice high steps on the grass too. I was curious to see how they would act in their tack and bitted. This was a new condition for them. I saw a lot more touching and rubbing as greetings than when they were in puppy gear. I tossed a couple of volley balls out in the yard and a few started kicking them around.

All the girls were fit and well exercised so they formed up into four teams of five girls each and played two games of a sort of soccer. They ran and kicked the balls quite energetically. Again I envied them. I was in charge and couldn't play. After they tired of it I collected them and unlocked their hands. I had them wipe down their tack and put it away. I told them it was ok to talk now and asked for questions.

They were excited and the consensus was they liked the pony girl experience. They wanted to know if they were going to be able to pull carts and race like the men did. I said, "Of course. Racing is part of our plan. You will also compete in dressage, be show ponies. Master says if we do well, we may be able to compete with the other hunt clubs, too." They were seemingly happy at the thought of more different things to do.

Chapter 16

Graduation

We were still living in the guest wing of Robert Olander's estate. My year here was almost up and I wanted to go home. My Master, Allen, spent half his time here and the other half in our home fifty miles away. My sister Ruth stayed here and trained me to be a better slave at home. I think she still loved me but it was the love for a pet, not a sister. I had to obey her not just because I was the slave, but also because I was always kept chained and she had a whip. My respect for her was largely fear. Well deserved fear. She scalded my ass for the slightest fault. I heard Allen call, "Rachel, come."

I hurried into the living room. I wasn't fast. I was in puppy mode this afternoon. My arms and legs were folded and bound with bondage tape. Wide black, elastic tape that stuck to itself, not skin. Ruth had wrapped several turns around all my limbs. I had to "Walk on my elbows and knees. I wasn't good at this, though she had put me in this condition every day for the past two weeks. I had to be extra careful because my nipple rings dragged on the floor and my nose leash was trailing under me. If I put an elbow or knee on it the pain would be great. I crawled to Allen as fast as I could and barked a greeting. I rolled over on my back in hopes of a good breast fondle. Human speech was forbidden to me in puppy mode so I had a whiffle ball gag strapped in my mouth.

My Master said, "Has my little Rachel been a good puppy today?"

I wagged my stiff tail and barked once, meaning "Yes." It was two barks for "No."

Ruth said, "Yes, she was pretty good. She did track a few grains of kitty litter onto the bathroom floor, but it was an accident and she didn't see it."

Shoot, I didn't know. I was careful. The penalty for getting litter on the floor was that I had to put it back in the box. Which meant I had to dip a breast into the toilet, collect the litter on my wet breast and then scrape it off on the edge of the litter box. Possibly even more degrading than having to use a litter box to pee.

Master said, "Good. She's learning to be a good puppy. I can take her home in a week or two. All the alterations are finished. So I need to have a couple of changes to her rig. Untie her arms and legs and get her ready to walk. I'll be back in a few minutes."

Ruth said, "OK. I'll get her ready."

Master left and I heard the front door open and close.

Ruth said, "Hold still and I'll remove the tape." She peeled the tape off one leg, then the other. It hurt to try and straighten them out. She said, Don't move and I'll massage them after I remove the rest of the tape."

She pulled on leg out a little and ,massaged my stiff muscles until I could reach full extension. Then she did the other leg. She locked my hobble chain onto my ankles. After I could straighten my arms she rolled me over, pulled them behind me, and locked my wrist cuffs together. She helped me into a kneeling position. I adjusted my posture and she took my nose leash and said, "OK. Stand up."

I was wobbly and ungraceful, but I did manage it. She took the gag out of my mouth. She led me around the room until I could walk normally then she clipped my leash to a wall ring and said, "Stand there until your Master returns."

I said, "Yes, Mistress."

Master returned in a few minutes carrying a box. He took my leash off the ring and said, "Heel."

I moved to his left side and knelt, waiting his movement or another order. I watched him closely, ready to jump to my feet at the slightest change in his center of mass or leg movement.

He said, Ruth, We'll be gone maybe an hour. You're done today. See you in the morning."

Ruth said, "Bye."

Master started for the door and I leapt to my feet and took up position behind him and to his left. He went to the shop and entered. He stopped close to Mark and I knelt beside him. Master greeted Mark and said, "I'm about ready to take Rachel home. I would like to get her nipple covers and chastity belt ready. I have the CB Robert recommended."

He handed the box to Mark. Nipple covers? Chastity belt? WTF. Why does he want me chaste? He never has before.

Mark opened the box and pulled out the belt. He looked it over and said, "Yes this is a good one. Made in Denmark and it seems to be the most comfortable steel one for long term wear. Do you want me to fit it to her now?"

Master said, "Yes, if you can that would be great. I'll have her wear it and see if it needs adjusting before we leave."

Do you want to wait while I fit her or should I call you?"

"I want to watch. I may have to make adjustments at home if she changes her weight."

Mark said, "All right. Pull up a stool She has to stand at first. I can let her sit later."

Master said, She won't be sitting much. A lot of time kneeling, standing, running, walking and laying on her back."

Mark said, "That's normal for our girls. You plan to enforce the 'No furniture' rule at home?"

"Of course. And every restaurant, public meeting, and visits to other people. No furniture will be her constant rule."

I quailed inside, but it was what I had done for the past year. I could do it. I would have to do it if I wanted to stay with Allen. I wanted that more than anything else.

Mark spent almost an hour adjusting it and making me get into different positions. I have to admit, it was not uncomfortable after he adjusted it. I had never thought about it, but there were lot of adjustments available to tailor it to any normal woman.

Finally, Mark said, "I'm done and everything is set. I'll fit the nipple covers now."

He turned me to face his bench. He picked up a gold cone about an inch and a half in diameter. It was wider than my nipple rings. He held it in front of my right breast and rotated it. I saw there were two slots in it. He sli one of the slots onto me ring an rotated it again and slid the other slot onto the other side of the ring. He held my ring level and pushed it toward my breast. I felt it touch my nipple. He moved something I couldn't see and the slots closed up and I heard a click. He put another one on my left breast.

When he was done my rings lay down in front of my breast like before he started and my nipples and aureoles were completely covered by the golden shields.

Mark turned me to face my Master and said, "What do you think?"

Master beamed at him and said, "They're perfect and look good too. You're a genius, Mark, and quite a craftsman."

I looked down at them and thought they were pretty, but I didn't know why I had them.

Master asked, "How do I take them off?"

Mark lifted my breast and showed Master the bottom of the shield. He said, "See this slot. You insert this key," he held up a small key and showed it to Master, "like this," he inserted the key, "and turn it," the slots opened, "the retainer will open and you can remove it. Installation is just the reverse."

Master said, "Wonderful. Great job."

Mark asked, "Is there anything else I can do for you?"

Master said, "There is one more thing I'd like if you can do it easily. I saw Cynthia a couple of days ago and she had some enticing bells on her nipple rings. Can you put some on Rachel?"

Bells. Oh no. I already sound like a wreck in a hardware store when I walk. Why does he want more? Should I say something? No. He'd just ask for bigger ones. I closed my mouth which I noticed had fallen open.

Marl said, "Sure. That's easy. Bring her to the bench."

In ten minutes I had two big bells hanging from two inch chains off my nipple rings. Oh joy unbounded. I had been belled, just like the proverbial cat.

Master thanked Mark and led me back to his rooms. All the extra metal on my nips was quite noticeable. The cover didn't deaden the sway and arousal created by the bell and chain. Just walking made me hot.

Ruth had gone. Master unlocked my hands and had me put up his coat and tie then make him a drink. I was not allowed any alcohol, of course. I knelt beside his chair and he watched the evening news. I watched him. The news didn't interest me at all. I was interested in learning how to please my husband of six years. I had been lax before and it was why I was here, naked and chained and trying my best to be his only love.

When the news show was over he stood up and picked up my leash. "Stand," he ordered. I sprang up and followed him into the bedroom. He undressed and I hung up his clothes and tossed the soiled ones in a hamper. We showered and washed each other's back. I realized I was still wearing the chastity belt. Unless he opened it I wasn't going to orgasm tonight.

I soaped and caressed his cock, hoping he would get my unsubtle hint. He did. But it didn't turn out the way I wanted.

When we were dry he said, "Kneel."

I snapped to kneeling display. He said, "Service me."

I opened my mouth and licked and sucked him hard. I felt him swell inside me. Just when I thought he would come, he pulled out and snapped, "Punishment position."

I put my head and hands on the floor and raised my ass high. He slathered my bottom hole with lube. I felt his rigid cock probing the hole. With a surge of power he spread my sphincter wide, powered in, and reamed me out with vigor. I felt my belly heating with arousal. I controlled my muscles as I had been taught, relaxing for the in stroke and tensing for the out ward run. I remembered my mantra, "Welcome him in, then keep him in." Soon I felt his hot spend fill me and he withdrew. I hadn't come but I was close to an orgasm. He was satisfied. I ached with need. I was hollow inside and I needed a man in me. It didn't happen. I whimpered and he just said, Its not my job to pleasure you. Its yours to pleasure me and you were fine. If you are very, very good, I may let you orgasm on your birthday."

My birthday wasn't for six months.

"Yes, Master. Thank you, Master." Six months. Oh My God. How can I last. My insides were churning, demanding release.

He ordered me clean up and use the litter box. I approached the litter box nervously. I had never worn a chastity belt before. I squatted and peeing was normal, but it was strange to hear the urine dripping out of the belt. I couldn't touch my pussy. The belt was rigid and tight and I couldn't even slip a finger inside to wipe. I looked at Master.

He smiled and said, "You're not the first girl to have to wear one." He handed me a spray bottle with a clear liquid. He said, "Its a mild vinegar solution. Spray it in the slot and let it drain for a minute."

The spray felt cold and strange on my heated pussy. I waited until the dripping died away. I set the bottle next to the litter box and stood up. He took me to bed. He locked my hands behind me and I lay down. Of course my ankles were still chained. That had never come off in the past year. He locked the end of my leash to the headboard ring and I rolled onto my side, facing away from his side. He lay the covers over me and lay down beside me. He faced me and cupped my breast in his big hand. He said, "Your new nipple covers feel different. I'll take them off at night if they bother you."

I thought about it. They weren't bothering me. I could feel their weight, but I think the new balls were worse. I replied, "Master, they don't bother me, but why do you want me to wear them. Don't you like my nipples?"

He laughed and said, 'Rachel, I love your nipples. This is a legal thing. I am going to parade you in public every chance I get. The decency laws require your nipples and pussy to be covered in public. That's why bikinis are shaped the way they are. Consider these delightful new trinkets of yours to be your bikini."

Oh no. He's still planning to parade me around in public. Naked and chained. I've got to persuade him not to do this to me. "Master, .."

He interrupted me, "Rachel, I know you hate this, but its my dream and you're my slave. Would you rather I took Ruth out as my slavegirl?"

Ruth? What? How? NOT RUTH. "Master, I'm your slave, not Ruth. I hate the idea of being seen in public like this. I'm going to die of humiliation. But If you have to have a slave girl on your arm. Its going to be me."

"That's what I thought. You're done here on Saturday. On Thursday, Robert and I are going to take our slaves out to dinner at a nice restaurant. You and Cynthia are going as our slaves. You should be prepared for a thrilling ride. Now go to sleep."

Thursday was two days from now. Shit. I hope no one I know is there.

Master said, "I sometimes see the women who were here for your inauguration. They always ask when you're coming home. I've invited them and their significant others for dinner. This will be your graduation party."

Shit. I might as well die now and get it over with.

He went on, "Well, I've just told you I'm giving you a party. What do you say?" He pinched my ass.

I squealed and said, sarcastically, "Thank you, my thoughtful Master."

Thursday afternoon came. I was in puppy mode, running around the room on my elbows and knees again when Ruth said, "Its time to get you ready for your party. Come here."

I crawled to her and she started unwinding the bondage tape from my limbs. She said, I'm anxious to see how you react. Its been a year since these women first learned you were a slave." She took the ball gag out of my mouth and asked, "How do you feel about the party?

Mistress, I'm terrified. I'll be naked and chained in front of all the women I know. I'm going to be mortified."

"Well, Rachel, you'll be a slave girl in front of a gaggle of free women. What will you do?"

"Mistress, I'll smile and do what ever they and Master tells me to."

"Will you have any choice?"

"No, Mistress."

"So nothing that you do is your fault."

"No, Mistress."

"So, we know what you will do. How will you feel?"

I stretched out my arms and legs while Mistress rubbed feeling back into them. I said, "Mistress, I will be embarrassed to be naked in front of these women. I used to be one of them. They will look down on me and laugh at me."

"As a slave you must expect free women to look down on you. You are lower than all of them. But you are still going to smile and obey, so what do you care what they think? Just imagine them naked too and be glad you have a Master while all they have are husbands. Remember, you have been found beautiful enough to collar. You have a Master that cares for you. Your life is exciting and full of joy while they have traded their joy for conformity. You are the freest one there since their feelings are ruled by others."

"Thank you, Mistress. I will try to ignore them."

She rolled me on my belly and locked my hands together. "And the others who will see you. They will be shocked by your nudity and chains. They will never have seen a slave girl before. What of them?"

"Mistress, I will smile and be proud that I have been found beautiful enough to collar. I will feel joy at their surprise and envy. I will feel superior at their disdain. I have a Master."

"Excellent." Mistress led me into the shower and cleaned me. She fastened my leash to the make up table and freed my hands. I brushed my hair until it shone with vitality. I did my makeup. She looked at me and changed it a little so I had more exotic eyes. I used a square of cloth and some cream and polished my hardware until it shone. I painted my nails while Mistress went to get dressed.

Mistress wore a dark blue dress and matching heels. A gold chain was hung around her neck. She locked my hands behind me and I slipped into my heels. She led me into the living room.. Master was there and he positively beamed. We were ready to fulfill his dream. He was going to take me in public as his helpless slave girl. I found the excitement flowing in my body too. I was going to be displayed by my Master as a living testament to his power and my submission. I realized I was looking forward to seeing other people's expressions. After all, they really meant nothing to me. Master stopped us in front of the mirror and I saw the tableau as others would.

Master was big, strong, athletic, commanding and proud. Ruth was smaller than me and looked expensively dressed and confident. She held my leash. I was medium height, slim waist, and above all naked, That was the first thing I thought of. Then my chains came into focus, A golden collar on my neck. Golden leg irons hobbled me above my black heels, so incongruous. I had large gold rings in my nipples which were covered by the gold metal shields, Bells hung from my nipple rings and my chastity belt gleamed in the light. I was the epitome of sex slaves, locked up for only my Master's use. And I was smiling broadly. It was true. I was happy and looking forward to showing my former associates how I had shed my depression and found joy. I was sure they wouldn't believe me, but I might raise a few doubts.

Master led us into the hall and to Master Robert's quarters. He was there with Cynthia. She was taller than I and just as naked. Her hands and feet were chained like mine. I was surprised to see she wore the same nipple covers as me. Her nipples were ringed and belled like mine. The only differences I noticed were that she did not have a leash dangling from her nose ring and she wore a short, white, frilly mini-skirt instead of a chastity belt.

Master Robert looked at us as we entered. He said, "Good evening Allen, Ruth. Rachel, you look spectacular."

I said, Thank you, Master."

He clipped a short chain leash on Cynthia's nose ring, handed it to Ruth and said, "Let's go."

Master Robert's driver held the door for us. Ruth got in first and led Cynthia and I into the car. She put Cynthia in the rear seat and me in the rear facing front seat, both of us on the far side. Ruth sat on the jump seat on the far side. Master Robert sat beside Cynthia and Master sat beside me. Ruth hung on to our leashes. I guess it doesn't matter, but I really wanted Master to hold my leash. If I was going to be controlled, I wanted him to do it.

Cynthia cuddled up against her Master and he out his arm around her. She looked like a contented cat. I emulated her. I wanted to feel that good too. I cuddled close to Master and nudged his arm until he put it around me. Cynthia and I spent most of the ride looking at each other. I saw that she was nuzzling her Master for more attention. I heard her do a great imitation purr and he responded by fondling her breast. Sometimes she screwed up her face and mouthed a word to me. Usually it was some encouragement for me to beg more. She didn't understand. I had only had two orgasms since he locked me in this damned chastity belt. One on my birthday and one on his birthday. I was more needy than a mink in heat.

The Masters talked of politics and elections, of the business climate and other things I didn't have any interest in. I looked at Ruth. She spent much of the time looking out the windows and occasionally at me. When she looked at me she smiled sardonically and whispered, "You are beautiful." I was grateful for the encouragement, but I didn't need it anymore. She had made the logic of the situation clear to me already. When Ruth looked away I watched Cynthia and envied her orgasms.

The car stopped and my fate was upon me. I hoped to do my Master proud. The men alighted, then Ruth, She led me out next, then Cynthia. The evening was warm and humid. Master took my leash from Ruth and Master Robert took Cynthia's. They led us to the door of the restaurant and Ruth followed us. A couple came out of the door as we approached. Her face grew shocked when she saw Cynthia and I. Her hand flew to her mouth. The man looked delighted. We were a wonderful end to his meal. They stopped and stepped back as we approached. Master Robert said, "Good evening," in a cheery voice. They just stood there with their mouths open as Cynthia and I were led past them.

I heard Ruth say, "Close your mouth. There are flies around."

We entered the vestibule and Master Robert informed the hostess of his reservation. She found it and waved a waitress over and told her we were in the private room. Both the hostess and waitress looked us over with nothing more than studied interest. The waitress said, "Follow me , please. She led us through the middle of the crowded room. We must have passed twenty tables, all full with twice as many filling the room. We creasted a wall of silence across the room. There was a general miasma of conversatio filling the room when we entered. Nothing changed as the hostess entered. A few people looked up at MAster Robert. but there was no noticeable change in volume. When Cynthia entered the sound level started falling. It got lower the further she got in the room and when I followed Master into the room it grew quieter still. By the time I was halfway across the room the conversation hd stopped. The only sound was the rustling of cloth as everyone in the room turned in their seats or stood up to watch Cynthia and I . As I walked out of the room It exploded in sound, "Did you see that." Holy shit." My God, they were naked.' "She was chained." "He was leading her on a leash." "She had a ring in her nose and he was leading her by it." "Who were they?" And a plaintive, "Where can I get one of those?"

The hostess opened the door to the private dining room and held the door for us. Inside was a long table with five reserved placards on the far end. The rest of the table was filled with my erstwhile friends and their men. Master Robert led Cynthia to the head of the table and seated her beside him.

Master pulled me around in front of him, facing the table and said, "Thank you for coming to Rachel's graduation party. You all know she is my slave and she has completed a year long training program. I will take her home in a few days and you will see her more often. You can see I have decided she does not need clothing. I intend her to be naked from now on, with some accommodation to the weather. She will continue to wear ankle chains and a leash. I want her to remain as you see her now in all public venues. I think she is beautiful and I want to see as much of her as I can. I hope you approve of what you see, but I won't change it if you dislike it. Since she is a slave girl she must obey your every command, unless it conflicts with one of mine. I am going to hand her leash to Mildred here. They can talk for a while. " He handed my leash to Mildred, an old and dear friend. I think.

He walked to the head of the table and said, "Pass her around and enjoy her. I want her back when the food arrives. She will be available after dinner is over, too."

Mildred and her husband, Fred, stood up and turned their chairs around. They sat back down and Mildred said, "Kneel, Rachel."

I knelt and said, "Yes, Mistress."

Mildred asked, "Why did you do this?"

I lied, "Mistress, I have always dreamed of being kept in bondage. Of having to obey Allen , completely. This opportunity came along and I jumped at it."

"But," she said, "you are helpless and naked. Did you expect this treatment? Are you happy this way?"

"Mistress, I expected nudity. Slave girls don't need clothes. I'm available all the time this way. I didn't expect the chains. After all, I volunteered. I won't run away. And yes, I'm very happy."

"Do you mean he has sex with you when he wants?"

"Mistress, I am used for his pleasure whenever he wants. You see I am locked in a chastity belt so I won't orgasm too much. Master wants to keep me needy and attentive."

Fred said, "And you are happy this way?"

"Ecstatic, Master. This is my dream. I have no responsibilities save pleasing my Master and he takes good care of me."

Fred said to Mildred, "Shall I book you into this training program now?"

Mildred asked, "Would you want me to be like this?"

"Mildred, I've never seen a happier woman in my entire life. How many shrinks have you seen for depression? I may just take you and put you in the program just to fix you. And I wouldn't mind one bit having you chained to my bed."

She looked at him appraisingly, "I wouldn't mind being chained to your bed for a little while, Fred. But I'm not in good enough shape to go naked like Rachel."

"Rachel," Fred asked, "Were you this fine before the training program?"

"No Master. They worked me a lot. I lost over fifty pounds in the program. There is a lot of exercise."

Fred looked Mildred up and down, smiled, and said, "Fifty pounds, huh?"

Mildred smiled at Fred and said, "After dinner, take me home and try some games. Maybe I'll consider it if you're vigorous enough."

He said, "Why wait. I'm not that hungry. Maybe Allen will loan me some gear."

"Mildred smiled, "Not yet you horny old goat. I want to eat first. I'm going to need my strength."

Mildred said, "Stand up, Rachel."

I stood and she handed my leash to Jane and said, "Be careful. She'll talk you into being Roger's slave it you're not careful."

I was handed around the table. The waitress brought drinks and took orders and I was taken back to Allen when the food came. He asked, "How was it?"

I said, Master, everyone was friendly. I was invited to come to their houses by many people. I think some just want me to clean for them, but most want sex, not talk. I told them they had to ask you. But I actually enjoyed talking to my old friends. It didn't bother me as much as I had feared, being a slave now, I mean."

"That's good, since you're a slave from now on. After we get home I'm going to take you around to the stores we use and the theatres and restaurants. I want to show you off everywhere you used to go. You will continue to shop and go out just as you did previously, but only when I permit. As I said before, you will be a in public. Your nipple covers and chastity belt make you legal, but I imagine you will be quite the spectacle until everyone becomes accustomed to you."

I quailed internally at the thought of going in a grocery store looking like I did now. I guess I'd get used to it since I had no choice. I knew not everyone would be nice. I was afraid the young men would be rough and physical with me. I still had two holes open for use. I wondered if Master would mind? I decided not to ask. But hate the thought or not, my belly pulsed with heat. I was excited by the thought of being taken by a stranger. The joy of submission was strong in me.

I said, "Thank you, Master." Was it a Freudian slip? Did I really want to be so exhibited?

The food was great even though Cynthia and I were only allowed tiny portions.

The most wonderful thing happened after we got back to Master's rooms. He put me in standing display in the bedroom and said, "Its time for your graduation present, Rachel." He took off my chastity belt. The cool air rushing over my heated loins was breathtaking.

Chapter 17

Taken

After Rachel went home the pack was short staffed so
Master decided I needed to run in the next hunt while he
had Julie hunt for some new girls. I was doubtful he could
find some easily. He explained that finding a new girl was
not hard. That there were many unhappy young women
who had dreams of Prince Charming that lunged after this
opportunity once we had gotten past the societal barriers.
He did that by taking advantage of their need for security

and sexual freedom. He said his generous salaries usually took care of the security concerns and talking to the girls already here was all the sales pitch needed. I guess he's right. Julie and Sylvia's sincerity and happiness would be hard to fake.

He had me start exercising with the girls and put Ms. Johansen in charge of the pack when I was training. She was just as hard on me as on the other girls. In a few weeks I was in top form again and I started drilling the girls on evading the dogs. Of course Master knew all my tricks and I wondered what he was telling the hunters.

A week before the hunt he informed me that he was going to be a hunter. I was surprised and asked if he had a team. He said, no, just him and one dog. This was unusual and I asked him why.

"Cynthia, I intend to catch you and only you. I used to be a successful hunter and I never had a team. That was a change in the rules after I stopped active hunting and just managed the club."

"Master, why did you stop?"

"I was too successful. I always caught my prey and it stopped being sporting. I didn't need to catch a girl in the hunt for sex. They were available to me whenever and however I wanted."

"OK Master, but why are you starting hunting again?"

"Because you made the sport harder, Cynthia. Your techniques will make the girls more elusive. I like a challenge."

I smiled at him, "Is that the only reason, Master?"

"You know me too well, Cynthia. Of course not. You are the clever, beautiful prey I want. And I don't do 'Catch and release.'"

"Master, this prey doesn't want to be released."

"Cynthia, I'm counting on you not to be caught by anyone else. I want you to be so good that only I am good enough to find you. If I have to let another team have you for the night I will be devastated and I'll light up your bottom so hot my pilots can use it for a landing light."

I think he means it. I made a mental note to spend extra time with my pack and set up a good evasion plan for me. "Yes, Master. I will try to be extra evasive at the hunt."

I gathered the girls and we brainstormed ideas to make us harder to find. Once found they would catch us easily.

One great idea was to find places where the would be stopped by heavy brush and close set trees they would have to circle around. If we could have some time in the woods, we could move brush and branches around to improve some of these places.

I arranged for a scouting party armed with a map to be on forestry duty the next day. I had six girls with work boots, leggings and work gloves assigned to collect loose branches and put them in piles for collection after the hunt. They were also to map the places where the woods were dense enough to be impenetrable for a horse and rider. Of course they were to place their piles to increase the width and density of these places.

Another tactic was to have the girls run in teams. Where a group of dogs could bring down a single running girl easily and pile on to hold her down. Their work became harder if there were two girls. If they tackled one girl but another kept going, all the dogs would release the downed girl to continue the chase. The dogs were fairly small and it would take three or four to hold a fit girl. Since six dogs were the norm for a pack, three girls acting as a team could keep the chase going indefinitely, or at least until a hunter on horseback caught one or two.

I added another twist. We had three gazelles, ten deer, and seven rabbits. So I formed them into teams. Three teams of three deer each to be to protect the gazelle by acting as a rear guard. The three gazelles would walk fast downwind in a group with their guards. All three of the guards would get the gazelle's scent on their fingers and rub it all over their bodies. If a dog team got too close they would separate from the gazelle and distract the dogs. By acting as a team and looking out for each other they should be able to draw the dogs into a game of leapfrog with the dogs unable to mass enough dogs to hold all three girls.

The remaining eight girls I formed into three teams of three, three, and two. They were the slowest girls and I had them each exchange scents with the both the other teams, so they could confuse the scent trails.. They were to run hard and sweat to spread their scent and go through the prepared thickets so the horses would be halted and have to circle around. The thickets were close enough that if the hunters didn't immediately run around the thicket, the girls could probably reach the next thicket before being caught.

The night before the hunt I had to sleep in the kennel with the other girls. The routine was unchanged. I had given each girl a tampon and now everyone was a part of the plan. We had enough body paint to completely cover all the girls. We were lined up for the dogs to sniff us and as always the girls were jittery and excited. The thrill of the chase was upon them. Then Brian, acting as pack master ordered, "Girls go," and the waiting was over. We jogged to the woods and after we were out of sight of the hunters, the team leaders marshaled their teams.

We checked the wind and selected Plan Beta. I gave my tampon to Sylvia. We all started on our planned routes. All the "Gazelle" groups headed downwind. I had three "Deer with me and first thing I did was let all three of them get my scent and rub it on their bodies. When they were all liberally anointed we started at a fast walk toward our hide zone. We were almost to our thicket when we heard the dogs start the chase. We entered the thicket and found my spot. The survey team had found a fallen sapling with a few sturdy branches. I was going to use it as a natural ladder. They stood it up onto a large evergreen with no branches lower than ten feet. I climbed up the ladder to the lower branches and then climbed up out of sight. The team removed the sapling and took it fifty feet away.

Then they commenced their evasion drill forcing the hunters to detour back and forth around the thicket while they ran back and forth through it. The dogs easily caught them, but couldn't hold with three girls to chase. Once the dogs led the hunters to the thicket there was a continuous baying as the hounds found the girls and chased them. The hunters were crashing through the bush trying to get on the same side of the thicket as their dogs. It was big enough they couldn't do this. I heard frustrated shouts and curses as the hunters were repeatedly frustrated. Finally the hunters understood what was happening. One team waited on one side of the thicket while another rode around to the other side. Both teams dismounted and finally caught one of the girls by hand. Then the dogs were able to bring down the other two for the hunters.

One capture was right under my tree and I herd the hunters taking their first use of the girl. She was certainly enjoying her taking. I wondered who it was. The hunters were appreciative of the clever girls and the great sport they had. They remounted and took their prey back to the manor.

It was quiet for a long time and I was considering climbing down when I heard footsteps in the brush below me. I heard a dog scampering around and yipping. It was Master and Jeb. Would he find me. I heard him walking slow close below me and wondered if I had left some clue. I heard him say, softly. "I know you're up in this tree Cynthia. Climb down now."

I had a command. I carefully climbed down until I hung from the lowest branch. He said, "Drop. I'll catch you."

I let go and landed in his arms. He caught me easily and kissed me. "Clever girl. Some hunters caught another girl bright under you and missed you."

"Thank you, Master. I heard them. Whoever they caught was very appreciative of their attentions after. Are you going to also claim your reward now?"

He handed me a bottle of water. I sucked it down in a very unladylike manner. 'Course I wasn't a lady.

He locked my hands behind me and lay me on my back. I spread my legs and smiled, happy my Master had been the one to capture me." His magic fingers enflamed every one of my erogenous zones. I came twice, quite noisily, before he mounted me. Then I came twice more. He was the best lover. We walked back to the manor him leading me on a leash and Jeb walking beside us. We weren't the last ones in. The hunters and prey were gathered on the big patio exchanging tales of the chase. Most of the girls were sitting in a hunter's lap being fed morsels from veggie platters and sipping water through straws their captors held for them. It was tradition that no prey had their hands freed until their paint was cleaned off. Master joined them and pulled me into his lap.

Both the other Gazelles had evaded capture. I would have too if Master hadn't been the one looking for me. I asked him afterwards how he found me. He said he had learned to track animals when he was a boy. He's sharpened his people skills in Force Recon and Jeb had followed my scent to the thicket. He'd watched the other teams chase my decoys. After they left without me, Jeb had brought him to the area of the tree. They'd searched and Jeb found my scent on the sapling. He followed the drag marks back to my tree and he'd found where the sapling made a hole in the soft ground. He knew then where I was hiding.

The hunters agreed that Master Robert's pack was the most elusive of all. They were fortunate that the girls enjoyed the after capture play. All of the girls who successfully evaded capture volunteered to play with the unlucky teams, so no one would sleep alone tonight.

Before we went to the pub, Master took me to the kennel and had Ms. Johansen make up my face. When she finished he strapped a black ball gag in my mouth and clipped a leash to my nose ring. He led me to the Pub for more tales of the hunt. We stayed there for a couple of hours before the hunters started drifting out of the Pub with their prey for a night of fun and debauchery. Master took me to his rooms and put me on the special bicycle. I pumped myself into a couple of orgasms while Master played with my breasts. My bells chimed like a church as I pumped fast. He came in me at least once. He had amazing stamina. He took me off the bike and locked my hands behind me. We showered and he used the shower wand to get me both clean inside and very aroused.

I watched him lay an absorbent pad on the bed. He lay me on the pad and changed my bondage so each wrist was locked to an ankle. I could wave my knees back and forth, but that was about it. Of course I wanted them spread wide open. Fortunately, so did he. I said, "Master, I can't move, so would you scratch an itch for me?"

He smiled benignly and put a hand on each breast and flicked the bells. My belly spasmed and I was instantly aroused.

"Like this," he asked?

"Master, that was great, but a little lower would be good too."

He took a bell in each hand and tugged on their chain, My nipples swelled before my eyes and turned into rock hard nubs. I watched as they grew larger and crept around my rings. I had never seen that before. It was extremely erotic to watch my body embrace its bondage. My arousal grew more intense. My body was on fire. I gasped, "Master, lower please."

He released my bells and slid his hands lower and stroked my belly with his fingers. He was driving me crazy. I was aflame and helpless. I whimpered in my need. He murmured, " You're on fire, Cynthia."

I moaned, "Yes, Master. Please take me. I need you. Please...."

I spread my knees as wide as I could. I felt his fingers stroke my lips and push me higher. Then they dipped into my overheated belly and I exploded into a wonderful orgasm. I felt my love juices run down my crack and onto the pad. When I came down he was stroking my pussy again. Or still, I didn't know. His fingers entered me again, then his hand followed and kicked my arousal up still higher. He used his hand to fuck me senseless and I fell into another orgasm. I felt his body weight press me into the damp pad and his cock thrust into my love canal. It was better than his hand. It fit me perfectly and I swooned at my next orgasm. He kept going and I felt him swell and flood me with his hot spend. Whoops, another orgasm for me and I went someplace nice.

When I was aware of things again I felt him roll me on my side and pull the damp pad out from under me. He locked my hands behind me and put my ankle chain back in lace. He put the sleeping chain on my collar and we settled down for the night. He said, "Tomorrow you're getting the rest of your rings. Its a reward for being here tonight."

My heart did a flip flop and I nearly swooned. "The full set, I asked?"

"Yes."

Finally I would be complete. I was in. Tears welled up in my eyes. Damn, I couldn't wipe them. I rolled over to face Master. "Oh, Thank you, Master. Thank you so much." I raised my lips to his. He pulled me to him and kissed back. We stayed like that a long time. I had difficulty going to sleep. Images of me and my rings flitted across my mind.

I was so excited next morning, Master took me to see Suzanne before breakfast. She was careful with infection as always and soon I had two beautiful gold rings in both of my labia lips. Master had had her put small bells on two inch chains on each ring. They chimed at a higher pitch than my others and they chimed at every step as they bounced off my legs and each other. I loved them. I loved their sound and the way they looked. I loved that every step

I took made me a symphony of emotion and lust. I loved the way Master smiled when he saw them.

I doubt I'd ever be good in a hunt again, but pleasing my Master was much higher priority. I couldn't think of a single thing I wanted now. I had love, a job that filled me with excitement, and a wonderful Master to care for me and love me. I thought, "Things had worked out fine.

Chapter 18

Home

Ruth had "Bit the Bullet" three months ago and begged Master to accept her as his slave too. He had accepted on the conditions that she undergo the slave training program at the estate and that Master Robert agree.

She had been accepted and I had only seen her occasionally. I last saw her two weeks ago. She had the same hardware as me, including the nose ring and leash. She was wearing a bit and was coming back from the pony girl stables, so she couldn't talk. Julie was leading her by her nose leash and paused a moment so we could communicate. Ruth was sweaty and nodded her head when I asked if she was happy.

The big day was here, Master was taking Ruth and me home. At last. I hadn't seen it for a year. He told me he had a house cleaning service and a gardening service taking care of it. He also told me he had made modifications for keeping two slave girls happy and obedient. I can only imagine what he has in store for us.

Master had Ruth and I pack up his things. We had finished and he knelt us by the door and locked both our leashes to the same ring. He left us there as he went to say his goodbyes. He came back and led us both to his SUV and opened the rear hatch. He said, "I had this made for you. I think its appropriate, don't you?"

I looked inside and saw a large cage made of welded steel, painted black. I gulped and said, "Yes, Master."

He set a stepstool on the ground and motioned me to get in. I climbed in awkwardly. He hadn't unlocked my hands or taken off my hobble. He held my arm in one hand and my nose leash in the other. The cage was just big enough for me to hunch over and crawl into on my knees. I squatted and he helped Ruth get in beside me. The cage was roomy, big enough for another girl. I wonder? He closed and locked the cage door and shut the rear hatch. I saw the windows were heavily tented and there was a plate over the rear seat, hiding us from view. Master had a briefcase with all our papers in it. . I had signed an agreement when I was first enslaved giving up all rights to our marital estate. Of course Ruth had no rights at all. Allen had his will redrawn giving everything to me and Ruth, equally. I was as secure as I could be. Now all I had to worry about was being a public slave. Ruth too.

Master started the engine and drove us home. It was only an hour and I watched as he pulled into the garage and lowered the garage door. He opened the rear hatch and then the cage. He put the stool in place and helped us out. I didn't recognize the garage. It was clean and all the junk was gone. My car was gone. I guess he sold it. He had told me I wasn't allowed to drive anymore. Ruth too, I imagine.

He led us to the garage door and inside. I saw my first new thing. There was a tall cabinet next to the garage door. There was a track on the ceiling. Four chains led then the track into the top of the cabinet. He opened the full height cabinet door and drew out a chain. It slid in the track and there was a padlock at its end, which was four inches off the floor. He fastened the end of the chain to my collar. He fastened another chain to Ruth's collar. He unlocked

376

our hands. He said, "This track runs into every room in the house but not outside. Follow me and I'll show you around."

He walked into the kitchen. I followed, gingerly and the track chain followed me easily, smoothly, quietly. I was much louder as my bells chimed and my hobble clinked. Ruth followed me and she was just as noisy. Most of the house looked as I remembered it. There was a new sofa and coffee table in the living room and Master had installed web cameras in every room of the house. The third bedroom had been converted to a "Games" room with bondage gear hanging on the walls and two pillories and two spanking benches. There were chains dangling from the ceiling. The master bedroom had a four poster bed a low cage, big enough for both of us. The most unusual new thing was the dining table. It was hinged with two holes in the middle for our necks. When we were in place only our heads would be visible. And there were rings for attaching us on every wall and floor space we saw. Master had made the whole place into a dungeon for us. A light, airy, inescapable dungeon.

After we saw every room he led us back to the dining room. He opened the table and knelt us with out necks in the cutout. He laid our track chains on the table behind us and closed the table. When we were sealed in he lay our leashes in front of him and sat down.

"Slaves, I have a work plan for you. Each day one of you will be the puppy and the other one the keeper. The keeper will do all the chores which are cleaning and food preparation. There is a precise schedule and I will check the recordings from the cameras regularly. If the schedule is not kept, the keeper will be punished. I have dismissed my cleaning and gardening services. I will take you outside for gardening detail when I'm home, weather permitting. When I'm having guests you will prepare and serve the food and there will be no puppy duty that day. Any questions?"

I said, "Master, may we use the furniture and toilet?"

"No, Rachel. There is a litter box in the laundry room."

"Thank you, Master."

Ruth said, "Master, will we eat as we are now?"

"Sometimes, Ruth. It will be either here and I will feed you or you will eat from your bowls."

"Thank you, Master."

"Master, you have locked us both in chastity belts. Will we war these often?"

"Rachel, I want both of you to appreciate your orgasms when I let you have them. I will unlock one of you at a time. When I think you have earned release. You will wear them most of the time."

Thank, you, Master."

I will take you in public as often as I can. I'm going to take one of you to the store with me now. Since I don't have any behavior to judge you on, I'll use my random number generator to choose." He took a coin from his pocket and said, Rachel, heads or tails?"

"Tails Master." He flipped the coin, caught it, and slapped it down on the table. It was tails. He said, "Tails it is. Rachel do you choose to stay here and clean and cook when we get back or go with me and show off your perfect body to the supermarket patrons?"

"Now what? I was embarrassed to be seen in public like this, but I didn't want him taking Ruth to show her off. "I choose the market, Master."

"Good choice. He opened the table and took me back to the garage door. He took the chain off my collar and put it away. He put me back in the cage in the back of the SUV and off we went. I steeled myself for my unveiling. He took me out and got a cart. He locked my leash to the cart handle and pushed it toward the store. I was careful to smile broadly. People walking to the store saw me first and did a double take. I watched a woman grab her man's arm and say something. They both stopped and watched me follow my leash into the store. We passed several people coming out with carts or bags and every one stopped and looked at me. I gave them my most dazzling smile. Master said hello to several of them, but of course I wasn't allowed to speak.

Master was nonchalant as he led my naked body through the store. I walked beside and behind him. He went through produce then meat, up and down every row. Several small girls asked me why my feet were chained as we passed them. Master said, "Answer them."

"Because I'm a slave girl," I said.

Every eye was making tracks all over me as I walked. It was kind of nice being the focus of attention. I saw several young men taking videos of me on their cell phones. "I'm going to be on the evening news and Facebook and every other social media site in ten minutes," I thought.

Master checked out and the cashier wanted to talk. "You lose a bet, ma'am," she asked?"

Master said, "Answer her, Rachel."

I said, "No, Mistress. I'm a slave girl and Master wants everyone to see me."

"You OK with that," she asked?"

"Yes, Mistress. I volunteered and I like being Master's slave."

There really wasn't anything hard about being naked and chained in public. I just told the truth and everyone accepted me. I expected the police to arrest both of us, but nothing happened. I guess consensual slavery is legal and easily accepted. Live and let live. I'm sure some do-gooder will try and mess things up, but they aren't here yet.

I rode home in my cage, sort of shocked at how easy it had been, considering my year-long fears. I helped carry in the food and he put my tether back on me. Ruth and I cooked a simple meal: ham slices, rice, and a green salad. We kept getting our tethers twisted together and giggling. Master put us back into the table and fed us our dinners. It worked out well. Two people could talk while one chewed. He had a glass of red wine with dinner and gave us each sips. It was the first wine I'd had in a year.

Master had left our hands free under the table. We couldn't reach much there. I was surprised to feel Ruth's hand take hold of my nipple bell and tug on it. I was sill wearing the nipple shields so she couldn't reach my nipple. I reached over and grabbed hers, too. It turned out we could get each other pretty aroused, even with our loins locked up. It made dinner more interesting. After the meal, Master said, "Rachel, you were excellent in the store. I have a reward for you.

He took me to the garage and cut the leash off my nose ring. He discarded the cut link and showed me what looked like another separate link. He used what looked like a tiny handcuff key and turned it in the end of the link. The top half of the link pivoted up and he slid it down through the last link on the leash ring until it cleared. The link then snapped shut and locked from the snap it made. He said, this is a lockable link. If I want to put the leash back on you, I just have to open the link and close it around your nose ring. I don't imagine you would like to wear it again, so be good."

Thank you, Master. It feels good to get rid of the weight and I'll try never to make you feel I need it again."

He took me back in the house and locked my tether to my collar.

I rushed over to Ruth, hugged her, and showed her my naked nose ring. I said, If you're good in public, Master may take yours off too."

Ruth squealed with joy, "You look so elegant now, sleek and happy."

"I am happy, sis."

Master smiled at us and said, "I saw how you behaved at dinner. I guess I'll have to lock your hands up before closing the table." Rats.

Ruth and I looked at each other and smiled ruefully. We both knew we wouldn't be able to fool Master and we'd have to learn to please him if we were going to get release.

Ruth said, with a voice that wouldn't melt butter, "Why, Master, I'm sure I don't know what you mean. We were both very good at dinner."

I thought, "We can do this. Things had worked out fine."

THE END

Other Kindle Titles by Alan Horn

Total Control:
        Total Control 1
        Total Control 2
        Total Control 3
Wage Slaves:
        Submissives
        Wage Slaves 2
Gods of Olympus:
        Pony Girl Sentence
        Consequences
        Julie
Coffle:
        The Coffle
        Coffled Future
        Coffle Cure
Pony Girl Dreams
Ensnared
The Love Ring
A Natural Slave
Humiliation

Printed in Great Britain
by Amazon

43259631R00219